<u>Other Titles by TW Brown</u>

The DEAD Series:

DEAD: The Ugly Beginning

DEAD: Revelations

DEAD: Fortunes & Failures

DEAD: Winter

DEAD: Siege & Survival

DEAD: Confrontation

DEAD: Reborn

DEAD: Darkness Before Dawn

DEAD: Spring

DEAD: The Reclamation

DEAD: End

The New DEAD series

DEAD: Onset (Book 1 of the New DEAD series)

DEAD: Alone (Book 2 of the New DEAD series)

Zomblog

That Ghoul Ava

The World of the *DEAD* expands with:

Snapshot — **Estacada, Oregon**

(Coming 2018)

To see your town die in the *DEAD* world, email TW

Brown at: <u>twbrown.maydecpub@gmail.com</u>

ISBN 978-1-940734-62-0

A moment with the author...

Well, you waited, and it is finally here. Book 3 of the *New DEAD* series. So many of you hit me up the past several months asking if I was done writing? I guess I just needed to take a break and recharge.

I know that my personal life is an open book to those who choose to follow, so many undoubtedly are aware of the depression issue I struggle with, and to be honest, it got the upper hand for a bit. Add in my big fall during the 2017 Seattle Spartan Beast (which you can watch on YouTube if you Google 'Spartan Beast 2017 Ladder Fall in 360') and a dose of pneumonia...yeah, I hit a wall.

2018 is going to be a return to what I do best. Disturb you with horrific tales of zombies, zombie children, and humans taking advantage of the chaos. I have one Snapshot to write since it was bid on at a charity event last spring, but then the rest of the year is SOLELY dedicated to the *New DEAD* series.

If all goes mostly well, then you should expect at least three more offerings this year. By the end of that time, perhaps Evan will meet up with the cast of *DEAD: Snapshot — Las Vegas, Nevada*. If you haven't read it, you might want to…if you are okay with seeing the world through the eyes of the man who will be my next "Big Bad".

Anyway, you've waited long enough, so let me just thank my amazing Beta Team for helping me clean up the edges, my wife (as always) for continuing to let me do what I love, and to you…the person reading this. I know my absence cost me a lot of you, and hopefully those that stuck around will spread the word that I'm back. (That is my subtle way of begging for reviews.)

Thanks for picking this book.

Aroo! Aroo! Aroo!

TW Brown

January 2018

To My Amazing Readers

Thank you for sticking with me:

Malik Wyrick, Nigel Ward, Debra Allen, Caroline Harmon, Will Barnes, Sherri Barnes, Terri Deese, Stephen Deese, Amanda Riddle, Roy Husebø, Maggie Serna, Wanda Beers, Christina Burns, Kevin Wright, Michele Kiltz, Richard Kiltz, Leslie Brussel, Janet Brown, Sian Coburn-Nicol, Cathryn Kiana, Steve Delien, Ashley Pinkham, Edward Taylor, Lysa Chetney, Bill Stokes, Rick Stokes, Paul Stokes…and you.

Contents

1

Chewie

I felt my stomach clench as the wave of nausea hit me hard. The smells of the dead and undead hardly registered as I knelt beside the dark mass of fur that lie sprawled in the weeds and shrubs. My hands plunged into the fur and came away bloody.

"No," I managed around a throat that was closing to a pinhole.

My vision blurred as the tears built up and then spilled over from my eyes to carve tracks down the dirt, dust, and grime of the past few days that covered my face — and everything else for that matter. With a huff, my beloved Newfoundland tried to roll her head up and look at me.

"Easy, girl," I crooned as I leaned my face down and nuzzled Chewie. I didn't care if I came away covered in

1

blood. At this exact moment in time, all I wanted to do was let my dog know I was there with her.

"Here, Evan," a voice whispered from behind me.

I glanced back to see Marshawn standing with a shallow bowl in his hands. "Maybe some water will help."

I accepted the dish with thanks and then brought it to Chewie's muzzle. The dog's large tongue came out to lap at the offered water. As she drank, her head rose higher. It was almost like watching a flower open to the sun as she appeared to visibly strengthen.

Eventually, I had to pull the dish away for fear that she would drink too much too fast. Setting it aside, I ran my hands over the Newfoundland's body as I sought out the injuries responsible for so much blood. I found one nasty slash down her right side that ran about four inches. Careful probing revealed that, other than needing stitches, it did not appear to penetrate any vital organs.

Her right ear was also very ragged. I couldn't tell what had caused the injury, but I was willing to bet it had been chewed on. She also had another deep cut on her left shoulder. This one was full of dirt and had almost stopped bleeding. Additionally, she had a few areas where the fur looked to have been yanked out by the roots. I hugged her

2

again, vowing silently to care for her and get her back to being healthy.

All around me, I heard occasional thuds and meaty smacks. It took a concentrated effort for me to tear my eyes away from Chewie to realize that, despite things being mostly disposed of, there were still a few of the undead able to move. One had been in the act of dragging itself towards Chewie and me and was perhaps a dozen feet away. Marshawn stood over it, yanking his machete free from the back of its head.

"We need to secure this area, Evan," the man said simply before heading towards the next zombie still able to move.

"It's gonna be okay, girl," I whispered, giving Chewie a gentle pat on the side of her neck.

Getting to my feet, I edged the bowl of water closer to her and then joined in on the elimination of the zombies still wandering the grounds. As soon as that was under control, we all set about the task of plugging the gaping holes in the wall that circled the place.

By the time we finished and I returned to my dog's side, the big Newfoundland was snoring softly in the shade. Somebody had even cleaned and dressed her wounds. Her fur was still matted and filthy, but she appeared to be sleeping comfortably.

"Evan?" a voice called from somewhere inside the house.

"Coming," I shouted back. The sun was starting to set, and shadows had stretched out to soak the entire ground in their cool darkness.

I walked into the house for the first time and was hit by the stench of death. There was blood splattered on the wall of one staircase where it looked like somebody had been gunned down. A few zombies had been dropped in here, but from the looks of it, that had been a few days ago.

Marshawn appeared at the top of the stairs. "Up here," he called.

I trudged up the stairs and did my best not to look at the chunks of meat that still decorated the wooden staircase that had once been a person. I reached the top and felt my stomach try to fold in on itself and expel everything it might contain...which, now that I thought about it, wasn't much.

I hadn't been on very good terms with Betty Sims, but she deserved better than what fate had dealt. I flashed to the bits and pieces of human body that I'd just passed. Somebody had taken the time to mount her head on what had probably been a very expensive mahogany table. Her eyes were filmed over and shot with black tracers and they followed me as I approached. Her mouth opened and closed, but no sound came except for that of her teeth clicking together when she snapped them at me as I drew near. Her gray tongue swished around and darted from her mouth in between the chomping snaps in a hideous display.

"Jesus," I gasped as I took a few unsteady steps closer. The eyes followed me, and maybe it was just my imagination, but I thought I saw hatred glaring at me from those tracer-riddled, milky orbs.

Condemnation.

I drew a blade from my hip and stood before the accusatory glare of Betty's undead gaze. Grabbing the top of her head, I plunged the point of the knife into her eye socket and stepped back.

"I take it you knew her," Marshawn whispered as he put a big hand on my shoulder and gave me a squeeze.

"She was part of my original group." I pulled the knife free and wiped it off before sliding it back into its sheath.

My mind whirled through the brief span of time that I'd actually known Betty, starting from our first encounter when I'd pulled into work for the first and last day of my new job as a music teacher.

That moment in time felt like forever ago, but in reality, it had only been a couple of months. My God...all of this in such a short span. Was there any hope of humanity surviving this? Had lawlessness risen to such proportions so quickly? Were we really that flawed as a species?

"We can stay tonight, but I think it would be better for us if we bail out of here first thing tomorrow." Marshawn's voice brought me back and I nodded. "You should get some rest."

I don't know why, but for some reason, I stumbled to what had been my room until I'd left with the thought that I was sparing my friends the issue of having to put me down. Now that I knew I was immune, I almost wished that I'd never undergone that journey. Why does hindsight have to be so damned perfect?

My room was nothing like I'd left it. It had been ransacked. The closet had been gone through, much of its contents tossed out into the bedroom in heaps that had been stomped on and kicked about. The bed was a horrid mess and I shuddered to think what might've happened on it. I could not bring myself to lie down until I flipped the mattress over. Even then, sleep took much longer than I expected considering how exhausted I knew myself to be.

***

"Rise and shine," a deep voice rumbled almost right next to my ear, causing me to awake with a start, my hands going for a weapon. "Easy, cowboy."

I opened my eyes to see Marshawn leaning over me with a smile. A strange growl caused me to scramble away as sleep refused to relinquish its hold on my brain. I landed on the floor with a painful thud that reminded me how much of a beating my body had taken over the past several days.

"That looked like it hurt," a deep laughing voice chortled from above me. It was followed by a snuffling sound and Marshawn leaned over me and seemed to be grabbing something on my bed.

I sat up, rubbing the sore spot where my shoulder had taken the brunt of the impact. I wasn't even fully upright when a dark shape filled my face and a huge, warm, wet tongue swabbed at it with gusto.

"Chewie," I gasped, getting to my knees and burying my face in the thick fur of her neck.

I leaned back when it struck me. "What...when...?"

"She got a bit of a bath last night. Seems she has won the hearts of pretty much everybody in short order." Marshawn plopped down in the bed beside my Newfoundland and scratched behind one of her ears before turning his attention back to me. "Did you know this place has a pool?"

I nodded. "It wasn't all gross and scummy?"

"I wouldn't swim in it," Marshawn made a face. "But I would bet it is cleaner than most of the rivers in the area...or it was." He ruffled Chewie's thick mane and stood up. "They decided that it was useless to us, but that it would at least get the worst of the filth from your dog."

The big, black dog did a combination of sliding and dragging herself off the bed and laid her head on my lap. I reached for her and she immediately rolled herself over so that I could scratch her belly.

"I doubt that you came in here to wake me and tell me that my dog was bathed." I looked up at Marshawn who had drifted to the window and was staring outside at a darkly overcast spring day. The sounds and smells of rain drifted in and I wanted desperately to allow myself to enjoy those sensations. Unfortunately, I had a feeling my day was going to start with unwelcome news.

"I sent patrols out last night just to get an idea of the area. I didn't want us to get any nasty surprises in the middle of the night," Marshawn explained. "They found that kid, Nickie."

I tried to make that name mean something, but it wasn't ringing any bells. I looked up as Marshawn turned back to face me and gave a shrug and gestured for him to explain.

"The kid that went with Miranda."

It all came back to me. When I'd given everybody one last chance to back out of what I'd hoped to be the last confrontation with Don Evans, he'd been the one who had opted out and agreed to join Miranda in bringing the car that she and I had loaded with supplies back here to what I'd hoped was a safe and firmly entrenched Carl and the others.

I had a wash of guilt hit me when I realized that, after seeing the supplies had been delivered (but also torched, presumably by Don's people), I had all but forgotten about Miranda. Much less given even the slightest thought to the young man who'd joined her.

"I take it that, by *found* him, you mean..." I let that statement hang for Marshawn to finish.

"Nailed to the side of a house down the hill." Marshawn's voice was flat and almost void of any emotion.

"Why?" I blurted.

I was really having a tough time believing that things had gone so bad so fast when it came to people. I'd been one of those people who rolled his eyes when all the zombie stories seemed to just spawn this parade of bad guys. It was almost laughable.

Or at least I'd thought so.

Yet, here I was...facing my own version of a super-villain. Don Evans was proving to be the epitome of ultimate evil. I knew in that moment that I would have no choice but to go after this guy and kill him. If not for myself, or for those I'd know personally that he'd murdered, then for the poor souls that might cross his path in the future.

"Evan!" Marshawn snapped his fingers in front of my face and I looked up at him. "There's more bad news, I'm afraid."

'You realize I haven't even had a cup of coffee yet?" I sulked as I gave Chewie one more good belly scratch before standing. She made one of her annoyed Wookie noises in protest of me slipping out from beneath her.

"There is a herd numbering in the thousands...and they are headed this direction. Best guess, we have about three hours to gather anything useful left behind here and move out."

I shuddered at the thought of this place being surrounded by a massive mob of the walking dead. With the walls already breached in a number of locations, there would be no way we could shore them up to withstand anything as large as Marshawn described. We had no choice but to vacate.

"So much for coffee," I groused.

Ten minutes later I was outside looking at the meager amount of supplies that we'd been able to scrounge from this place. Don and his crew had done a thorough job of either taking what they wanted or destroying what they didn't. My hatred for him was growing exponentially by the day.

"Is this everybody?" I asked the man I'd nicknamed

Superfly in my head.

"A few of the folks vanished in the night." The big man pushed a wheeled cart to the location where all the supplies were being stacked.

We were going to have to figure out what was the most vital—despite the fact that a lot of the stuff here had been looted—we would still be leaving things behind since we could only carry so much. My eyes scanned the people scurrying around like ants who'd had their hill kicked.

"Figures," I muttered as my eyes found Neil Pearson exiting the house with a pair of hiking packs in his hands. "Why couldn't that prick be one of the individuals that had skipped out in the night?"

Neil and I were not on good terms. He was just that kind of person who instantly grated on my nerves from the first time we'd met.

"What's that?" Superfly said with a cocked eyebrow that would've made the Rock proud.

"Sorry, just bitching out loud," I said with a wave of my hand.

"Yeah, I was a bit annoyed to see that Neil was still here myself." The big man frowned and then glanced over his shoulder at Neil before turning back to me.

"Hey…forgot to tell you that I was glad to see your dog is doing better."

"Celebrate the small victories, right?"

"Amen, bruddah." That was the first time his voice carried any sort of accent.

"Name's Evan Berry, by the way." I extended a hand to the man. "I don't think we've ever actually been introduced."

"Rickey Lepinski." He accepted my handshake, and the first thing I noticed was how massively thick his fingers were. "Introductions are sorta falling by the wayside lately."

I saw what I thought might be sadness filter into Rickey's eyes. Now that we were standing face-to-face, I could actually get a better look at him. He was about six inches taller than me, but his chest was much broader. His arms were just as impressive with corded muscles flexing with even the slightest movement. His hair was long and jet black. Currently it was pulled back in a ponytail. His legs were tree trunks holding the man and I had to imagine he could've been a pro wrestler if he'd chosen that path.

I gave the man a nod and then joined in with going over the place as fast as possible and bringing anything and everything that might be useful down to where it was all being piled. As I did, I had mixed feelings. I understood why it was important to have everything in one location so we could grab the best and most useful stuff possible. My problem was that, if this zombie herd swept through here, everything we didn't take would likely be destroyed.

At last it seemed as if we had everything scrounged up. There was very little rhyme or reason as people moved in and began plucking things they deemed important. I realized, after giving the stuff I'd grabbed a good once over, that we'd all basically equipped ourselves as if we'd be alone. I also discovered that this crap was heavy, and any lengthy trip would sap what little strength I'd managed to regain.

Marshawn leaned over to me and whispered, "Where do you think we should go?"

My mind went blank for a moment. Then a bulb flickered and sputtered to life. "There was a nice house with a wall and even an iron gate."

Of course, there was also a dead Hispanic family inside the house as well as a group of zombies gathered out front. Hopefully they would've moved on by now. If not, and the numbers hadn't swollen too big, the group I was with should be able to handle it.

I shoved all the memories of that family and their fate from my head as I informed the group of what I figured to be the best possible location for us to retreat, catch our breath, and figure out what to do next.

"Evan!" a female voice said from beside me.

There was something in her quiet tone that instantly grabbed my attention. She hadn't screamed or sounded hysterical, but there had been something in her voice that sank into me like a fishing hook.

I glanced over at her and saw that she was staring back at the house. Specifically, her eyes were glued on the main entrance to the place.

Standing in the doorway was a small child. He or she—the degree of filth the child was covered in made it impossible to be certain of the gender—was simply standing there regarding us. His head cocked first to one side, then the other. I felt my stomach clench. How had a zombie child escaped our notice all this time? Unless, of course, there was a breach in the defenses that this child had recently walked through. I quickly dismissed that possibility since it was obvious that the child was coming from *inside* the house. That brought on another new chill as I realized that some, if not all, of us had slept in there last night.

All of those thoughts zipped through my mind in the blink of an eye. Which was also how long it took for the child to lift an arm and point in my direction.

"Chewie, come!" the tiny figure rasped from a throat that was in obvious need of water.

Before I could react, my dog rose up and padded over to the child. The child raised a single finger and the dog sat obediently. She was rewarded for her efforts by something the child produced from pants pockets that were so covered in filth that I swear I heard them make a ripping sound as a grubby hand plunged inside and produced something that my dog happily and amazingly gently accepted.

"Michael?" I said quietly.

The filthy face looked up from Chewie to me. "You didn't commit murder to all the bad people," he said with simple innocence. "They came and did bad things."

Without thought, I rushed to the boy and knelt before him. "Michael, how...I don't..." Just that quick, I was tongue-tied. A million questions tried to reach my lips all at once, but none of them would give way to the other, so I just stuttered and stammered.

"They did bad things to Chewie." Michael looked down at the dog and a single tear crested his lower eyelid and rolled down his face. The grime was too thick and too dry to be cut through by one single tear and so it ran down his cheek quickly and plopped onto the ground.

"You know this kid?" a voice said from behind me, causing me to start.

"Yes, his name is Michael Killian." I looked over my shoulder and up at Marshawn. When his eyes met mine, I mouthed the words, '*I think he is autistic.*'

"Hey, Michael, my name is Marshawn." The man knelt beside me to put himself at Michael's level. "Have you been here this whole time?"

The boy's gaze drifted past the two of us, but never stopped until he was looking away and sort of down at the ground. His hands ran over Chewie's head and took an ear in each as he began to massage them.

"You have very dark skin, that bad man would not like you." His words were simple, but they left no doubt as to what "bad man" he was referring to.

"Why would you say that, Michael?" I asked, bringing my hands up to join his in Chewie's fur.

"He kept saying the bad word to the three ladies who had skin like that. He made them cry." Michael paused. He sighed heavily like the weight of the world was resting squarely on his shoulders. "That is when Betty got angry and slapped him. He did bad things to her and let one of the monster people bite her arm."

I didn't want to know what bad things he could've done that were worse than having her intentionally bitten. However, now that he was talking, I was hoping that Michael might shed some light on what had happened to the others.

"What about Carl and Selina?" I asked.

The boy just continued to run his hands through the thick fur of Chewie's neck for several seconds. I wished I knew more about the young boy's condition. Honestly, all I knew about autism was that it had a funny-colored puzzle piece as part of the logo.

"Are we gonna sit here and wait for the zombie herd to arrive?" Neil's voice called out.

I bit back my initial replay which might've been something along the lines of how much I would like for him to do exactly that. Instead, I stood, turned to the people gathered, and let my eyes take in what now consisted of my new group.

There was me, Marshawn, Rickey, Tracy Gibbons, Neil (of course), Darya Kennedy (formerly Darya Petrov, sister to Don Evans' righthand woman) and her son, a little boy not much older than Michael. Why had I thought there were more of us?

"Why don't we try to distract them...send them in a different direction?" Darya asked.

We all looked at each other and then back to her. She seemed to wilt under the sudden attention of everybody now studying at her. I gave her a nod to continue.

"That's how we kept the larger groups away from our last place. We sent out people with noisemakers and acti- vated them to divert the zombies in a new direction," she explained.

We all looked at each other with varying expressions of curiosity. Could we do this and not have to venture out into the unknown again? Of course, I already knew that I would have no choice but to leave again. The only differ- ence being that I would prefer to do so after I'd had some recovery time. I hated to admit it, but my body was beat to hell and back. As much as I wanted to get out there and not only hunt down Don Evans and his crew, I also wanted to find out if any of my people managed to survive.

"He took some of them," Michael said as he nuzzled Chewie, burying his face in her fur and hugging her.

I felt my heart jump up to my throat. If he took some of the people from here, then there was a chance they might still be alive. That meant that, if I could find where Don Evans and his people went, then I might be able to save some of them. What I couldn't say to these people who had fallen in with me was that this was basically my fault. I'd given up this location when I'd been being held prisoner. I could try to color it any way I wanted, but that was the cold, hard truth.

"Did he take Selina? Carl?" I repeated, doing my best to be as gentle as I could and not spook the boy.

I caught movement out of the corner of my eye and saw Neil stomp off throwing his hands up in the air. I didn't know how much longer I would last before I beat the living daylights out of the guy.

"He made Carl walk," Michael whispered.

I had no idea what that meant. All I could try to take from it was that perhaps the man was still alive.

"Amanda would not go on the bus unless the bad man promised to not hurt Selina." Michael glanced up at me so fast and so briefly that I might've imagined it.

It took me a moment to recall who Amanda was. I finally remembered that she'd been the one we rescued during all the madness with Brandon Cook.

"So, are we going to try this noisemaker thing?" Marshawn whispered. "If it works, great. But if not…we are probably screwed seven ways to Sunday."

I stood and looked around at my tiny group. Once more I could not help but flash back to so many of the zombie movies and shows where everybody looked so good. Maybe there would be an obligatory smudge of dirt on the cheek or something, but that was about it.

These people were exhausted. Clothing was hanging from a few, indicating the lack of food they'd consumed the past several days while still having to run for their lives. Looking down at Chewie, she was in no condition to make a long trip.

On a good day, she was not up for much past a couple of miles of straight walking. Her thick, black coat sucked in every bit of heat which meant I had to keep her hydrated. That would be a challenge on a trip that I wasn't entirely sure of when it came to distance. Sure, I could deny myself water and carry enough for her, but how long would I last?

"Who wants to try to hold up here a bit longer and give this noisemaker thing a shot?" I asked the group.

Darya's hand shot up before I'd even finished asking the question. Her little boy looked up at her and copied his mom. The next hand to go up was the other lady in our group, Tracy Gibbons. Having seen her fight, I knew it wasn't because she was a coward.

Marshawn gave a shrug and his hand went up, followed by Rickey's. That left Neil Pearson. Personally, I didn't care which way he voted, the majority had already taken it. We were staying put and trying the noisemaker trick, but I still wanted to see what he would do. I was a little surprised when he raised his hand to make it unanimous.

"All we need to do now is find something to make plenty of noise with," I said, clapping my hands together.

"I think I have just the thing."

If it would've been physiologically possible, I would've bruised my chin when my jaw bounced off the ground. Of all the people to have an idea, the last person I figured would be Neil.

He seemed to realize that all eyes had tracked to him.

He glared back with a look of what could only be defiance. Almost as if he dared any of us to challenge him now that he'd told us he had an idea.

"There were a few abandoned police cars down the hill at that medical center," he said.

I could not help but laugh out loud. Considering our relationship, that was probably not the best reaction, but I was laughing at myself. How had I forgotten about them? And why hadn't the idea occurred to me?

"If you have—" Neil started, his face turning red and his fists clenching at his sides.

"No, you are absolutely right." I raised my hands, gesturing for him to relax. "I can't believe I forgot about them." Then a thought hit me. "When were you down there?"

Now the red in his face was from embarrassment rather than anger if his expression was any indication. He mumbled something that I couldn't hear.

"I didn't get that." I made it a point to keep my tone even.

"A couple of the people that took off last night made it a point to take some of our stuff. I didn't see how they deserved it seeing as how they were bailing." He ran his hands through his greasy, brown hair. "I went after them."

I didn't see the big deal; apparently Marshawn did. He leaned over to me and whispered, "Drop it, I'll tell you later."

"So, who is going to make this little run?" Rickey asked in his deep voice.

"I'll go," I said.

"I'm game," Marshawn offered.

"I'm in."

Every head turned and I was glad to see that I wasn't the only person surprised at Neil's statement. He didn't seem all that stunned by the reaction. Maybe he was one of those rare sorts that knows he's a dick.

"Then we need to grab some gear and go." I motioned toward the pile of supplies we'd piled up. "Everybody else gear up just in case this doesn't work. It would be appreciated if packs were put together for the three of us."

"I will watch Chewie," Michael said, sitting down on the ground beside my dog.

I might've been the only person to hear him. I was certainly the only one to react. I knelt down by the pair. Chewie immediately rolled onto her back, offering up her belly to be scratched. It was nice to see her snapping back to normal so fast.

"Could you see if any of her food is still okay?" I hiked a thumb at the burnt pile of sacks of dog food.

"The bad man said dogs are a waste of sources." Michael ran his hands over my dog's belly, careful to avoid any of the injuries.

Neil muttered something, but I couldn't make it out; which was probably for the best. I was about to venture outside the relative safety of the camp. There would not be any witnesses soon, but right now I needed to put all that behind me and operate as a cohesive unit.

I got to my feet and joined the two men in putting together the necessities for our little adventure. I grabbed a pair of canteens and checked that they were full. I selected a .22 caliber six-shooter and pocketed three boxes that held fifty bullets each. I added a pair of Buck knives, a machete, and a baseball bat. That last item I would simply carry.

It wasn't the most effective weapon despite what pop-fiction had led folks to believe. It would take several swings—in most cases—to crush the skull and end a zombie versus one with a machete. On the other hand, nothing beat it for knocking something away if it popped out and surprised you.

I watched Marshawn gear up and was surprised when all he grabbed was a non-descript .45 caliber pistol and a pair of brutal looking machetes. As for Neil, you would've thought he was a soldier in the Middle East heading into a full-on war zone. He had two rifles — one slung over each shoulder — a large machete, a hand axe, an assortment of knives dangling from his webbed belt, some sort of filled pack where I guess he stowed his ammo, a shoulder-harnessed pistol that would've made Dirty Harry say, "Damn!", and he was carrying a shotgun in his hands.

The three of us headed for one of the breaches in the wall and exited the grounds. Just before I stepped through the gap in the wall, I turned back to the group who stood watching us leave.

"Shore up all these spots where the wall was busted down," I said. "And everybody be ready to do a grab-and-go if we come back with bad news."

I waded through the tall grass and caught up with Marshawn and Neil who were making their way down to Johnson Creek Boulevard. This massive mob was supposedly on the other side of Interstate 205.

"Who found this herd?" I asked as I caught up.

"Me," Neil muttered.

I could tell there was something he wasn't saying. He wasn't giving me the stare down of defiance. I really wanted to ask, but I figured if I pressed, we'd end up fighting, and right now, like it or not, I needed him.

"I was gonna split," he finally admitted. "I know I'm not wanted or welcome. And after my throw-down with the deserters, I just wanted to bail."

The funny thing was, I could understand his point. In the simplest terms, he was embarrassed. I really didn't know what to say. He and I had been at odds since meeting. Setting that aside wasn't easy. I heard Stephanie's voice in my head telling me to get over myself.

"If you hadn't gone for a...walk..." I gave a shrug, hoping it came across as me being accepting, "...then we would've been sitting around with our thumbs up our collective butts when this herd you spotted came rolling up to our door."

Neil didn't say anything, but that was sorta good. He hadn't said anything that made me want to kill him. Of course, the reason he was quiet could've been what was just now reaching the interstate overpass.

2

Diversion

No movie could do this mob the justice it deserved. We had just reached the driveway entrance to the medical center, but we could see very clearly the far side of Interstate 205. They had already crested the ridge and were now coming our direction.

I wouldn't have been so worried if there had only been a few hundred...or even just a couple of thousand. But this was a sea of mobile undeath. I have no idea how, but up until this moment, I hadn't heard them.

I heard them now. It was a steady stream of moans that melded into a seemingly infinite one...interspersed with cries. And for me to be able to pick that particular sound out...there had to be a lot of those crybaby zombies in the mix.

My best guess? The wall of the undead had to be a half mile wide at least. They were destroying everything in their path like a plague of locusts. I could only imagine what they were leaving in their wake.

"This way," Neil hissed like they might be able to hear us.

Returning to this parking lot brought back a wave of memories. This was where Carl and I had killed Brandon and his cohort. We'd also loaded what we could in the back of a military truck and brought back some decent firepower. All of it gone now, thanks to Don Evans.

There were a couple of local and county police cars in the lot. Neil beelined for one in particular and I had to bite my tongue when he fished a set of keys out of his pocket. He didn't make eye contact with me or Marshawn, which was probably for the best since Marshawn and I shared a look that spoke volumes of what we were both thinking of Neil at the moment.

"Couple more weeks, and lots of cars won't be turning over," Marshawn said instead. "The batteries will lose their charge first. After that...the gas will go bad. Always loved those zombie flicks where people drive all over, swap into some random vehicle they find just in time. Not to mention the newer cars are harder to hotwire unless you really know your shit."

Neil turned the key and the car gave a sputter and cough, but it started. He slapped the steering wheel in a little victory celebration.

"Shotgun!" I barked.

"Oh...so the brother has to ride in the back," Marshawn quipped.

I felt my face flush. Honestly, it hadn't even occurred to me. "Hey, if you're not comfortable riding in back..."

Marshawn glared at me and opened the front seat after opening the back door on the passenger side so I could climb in. He shut the door and then hopped in front. As soon as he shut the door, he turned back to face me through the Plexiglas divider. "You white folks gotta stop being so damned sensitive...but thanks for swapping." His serious demeanor broke into a huge grin.

He turned back, facing front. I thought I heard him chuckle something about 'gullible white boys' as Neil shifted into drive and headed out of the parking lot.

"Where should I go?" he asked, snapping me back to more serious matters.

"I'd take the interstate and head south," I offered.

"Why?" Neil came to a stop on the middle of the street.

"Population thins out that way. Maybe fewer zombies," I answered, explaining what I thought should be obvious.

"Huh...would've never made that connection." Neil allowed the car to start rolling and then slammed on the brakes. "The southbound onramp is on the far side of the overpass. The zombies are already to it. We won't make it."

"You don't have to take the southbound exit," Marshawn said with a degree of patience that I wouldn't have come close to pulling off convincingly.

"Oh...yeah," Neil said sheepishly. He cut the steering wheel over hard to the left and hit all the toggles and switches that activated the lights and siren.

As we started down to the interstate, Neil stomped on the gas. The police car roared to life, pressing me into the seat just a bit.

"What are you doing?" Marshawn yelped as we skirted past an abandoned vehicle with inches to spare.

"I always heard these things have some killer engines." Neil let out a hoot that belonged in a cowboy bar more than it did in this vehicle at the moment.

"Yeah, well, we need to make sure the zombies follow us." Marshawn craned his neck to look back at the overpass where the undead were now halfway across.

"Oh…yeah."

Neil took his foot off the gas and we slowed. I got up on my knees and looked out the back window. Not all the zombies had been able to fit into the bottleneck that was the overpass. A lot of them were stumbling and making their way down the embankment, but there were so many already on it that they were going to cross no matter what we did.

"Stop the car," Marshawn barked.

Neil did as he was told, and Marshawn jumped out of the car. I was a bit curious and more than a little concerned. Then I realized what he was doing. I watched as he started jogging toward an ambulance abandoned in the southbound lane. He would have to cross a huge grass median to reach it; there were a few zombies that had already spotted him and were converging.

"He's crazy," Neil gasped as he watched Marshawn sidestep a pair of zombies that were lunging for him.

I felt a tight feeling in my chest and took a breath once I realized I'd been holding it. I could not just sit here and do nothing. If something went bad all of a sudden for Marshawn, I needed to be able to at least make an attempt to help him. I tried to open my door and...nothing. There were handles, but they did not engage anything that would open the door for me. I tried again, this time a bit more frantically as I watched Marshawn yank open the driver's side door of the ambulance. A body tumbled out, but, at least so far, it wasn't trying to get up off the pavement.

"Neil," I hissed when the realization struck me, "I need you to open my door. The safety locks are engaged, and I can't get out."

He never even looked back as he replied, "Why do you need to get out?"

"Dude, just open the door!" I tried not to snap, but now I could see four more of the undead stumbling around the back of the derelict ambulance and heading toward Marshawn.

"Jesus, cool your jets," Neil sighed. He looked back over his shoulder at me, and something in his expression told me that he really liked my being so helpless and at his mercy.

I felt the giant exhale of relief when he climbed out and came to my door. He opened it and I might've tossed a quick thanks to him as I sprinted towards where Marshawn still had his upper body jammed in under the steering column of the ambulance.

I pulled out a pistol and checked to ensure the safety was off as I crossed the median. Pulling up, I raised my arm and squinted at my target. The pull of the trigger on a .22 caliber weapon is not that impressive. This was no exception as the 'pop' sound accompanied the puff of smoke that wafted from the barrel.

I have no idea where the bullet hit. Maybe it struck a zombie, but more than likely it just whistled off into the grassy hilled embankment beyond. I adjusted my aim and fired again just as Marshawn's head came out and he looked around before realizing it was me doing the shooting.

"What the...?" he started, but then had to shove away the zombie that had closed on him.

I could feel my pulse in my temples, and the steady whoosh of blood rushing that echoed in my ears almost drowned out my next shot. I thought I heard a metallic 'ting' as the round likely hit somewhere on the side of the ambulance.

Realizing that I wasn't close enough for my aim to be worth a damn, I rushed forward to close the gap. As I approached, my stomach churned not only at the smell, but at the violence these poor souls had endured at the mouths of the undead.

The woman I'd been taking shots at looked to have been in her early thirties. If I'd passed her on the street, I probably would've at least taken a glance. Her body was well-toned despite undeath causing her muscles to go slack. Her dark brown hair was still partially pulled back in a ponytail, but it was almost a solid spike due to the dried blood and God knows what else. Her face was where it became difficult. Her attacker or attackers had chewed off most of the right side of her face. That eye was gone, and the socket was so crusted over that it looked like the grime had formed a shell over where the orb had once been.

I adjusted my arm a little and pulled the trigger. The soft pop of the .22 was almost a whisper against the moans of the undead that had now all discovered the new source of available food standing just a few feet away…me!

"Crap," I snarled as I backed up a few steps and fired again.

This time it was a man who appeared to have wandered out of his job as a bank teller and had one arm torn away for his troubles. There was something horribly disturbing about how his left arm was gone. The dried flesh at the shoulder looked like it had been twirled by a giant pasta fork. That entire side of his body was a massive stain of dried blood that made everything stiff, and I swear I could hear it crunching.

I fired another shot and the crunchy, one-armed man toppled. There were still a couple more, and Marshawn was quick to stick the one closest to him.

That left one. I couldn't see any other zombies near, but I couldn't shake the certainty that I'd seen more movement. "Hurry up, Marshawn," I urged.

"The damn key was busted off in the ignition," he said as he stuck his head back into the ambulance driver's side.

"Then what are you doing, let's just go." I looked around, feeling the hairs on my neck stand up. I was certain that something was stalking me.

Almost like he'd been cued, Neil flicked on all the sirens. I spun to where he was still parked in the police cruiser, the lights flashing, but not really standing out in the bright, sunlit day. He seemed to be waving his arms wildly. That was definitely not good.

I turned a full circle, doing my best to look everywhere at once. As I stepped back from the ambulance so that I could get a look on the other side, I discovered what I was pretty certain had Neil in such a panic.

"Damn," was all I managed to be able to say, and I wasn't sure I'd said it out loud until Marshawn popped his head out of the ambulance once again.

"What's up?"

Marshawn walked over to where I stood staring at the embankment. Lining the ridge were at least fifty tiny figures. They were in the shadows of some large building, but I knew what I was seeing.

"Are all of those..." Marshawn's voice faded as he realized what he was seeing.

"Children."

That one word fell from my lips, but I was so entranced that I barely heard my own statement. I took a few steps forward and felt a hand on my arm that stopped me from going any closer.

"We need to go."

I heard the words. I could also hear the siren blaring from the police car being joined by the car's horn. All of that competed against the rush of my heart pumping blood through my body that echoed in my ears. The dryness that emptied my mouth of all moisture. The feel of my skin pebbling up.

I knew somewhere down deep that this was important. The child versions of the undead were different. I was certain of it now after so many odd encounters.

They came flooding to me. The church. The school. That ambush created by a single child banging metal on metal to bring the adults. The way they seemed to hesitate and regard me when we'd come face-to-face.

"Evan!" Marshawn's voice cut through the haze and snapped me out of my trance.

"Did you find a way to start the ambulance?" I asked as I took a few unsteady steps backwards, my eyes not leaving the line of zombie children gathered at the top of the ridge.

"It's beyond me. There is dried blood everywhere inside the cab. Somehow, the key got snapped off and I can't even find the rest of it to try and force it together...not that I'm sure that would've even worked," Marshawn explained.

"Are you guys trying to get yourselves killed?" Neil shouted from where he stood leaning over the hood of the police car.

I had to admit...he had a point. This whole endeavor had been for nothing. Glancing back towards the massive swarm of zombies we'd been sent to try and divert, I adjusted my assessment.

They were coming for us!

Normally that would not be something I would be glad about, but this looked like it was actually going to work. Even the ones that had crossed the overpass were now coming down the embankment and making their way to the interstate.

I hurried to the car and climbed into the back seat again as Marshawn hopped into the front with Neil. As we pulled away, I glanced back to get another glimpse of that group of zombie children.

"What the..." I was really making it a habit of not being able to finish my sentences.

The ridge was empty. It was as if they'd never been there. I searched all along that area as we pulled away slowly, but there was no sign of them. Craning around and looking directly behind us, that herd was a different story.

"Umm...we gotta figure something out," Neil said, bringing mine and Marshawn's attention back around to what was ahead.

"No way," managed to slip from my mouth.

If the horde behind us was a lake...this was the ocean. We were just rounding a large bend that had some undulating hills, so it had made seeing them impossible, but now...

"This is so bad," Marshawn muttered.

The cruiser came to a stop as Neil's foot came off the gas. On either side of the interstate were very tall, very solid concrete walls. Still, there was no way we could just sit here. Whether or not those things could eventually exert enough force to break this vehicle open like an egg was not even a doubt in my mind. I'd seen the group behind us folding back the guard rails along the edge of the interstate and the overpass like they were nothing. It was a matter of physics. There would be enough pressure eventually from so many bodies pressed against the car that it would pop like a giant zit.

The way I saw it, we only had one chance.

"Neil?" Nothing. "Neil! Take us over to the wall," I said, leaning forward and almost yelling in Neil's ear to snap him out of the trance he'd fallen into.

He turned us hard to the left and drove us up the steep, grassy incline until the nose of the police car actually bounced off the concrete wall causing me to smack my face into the divider that separated me from the pair up front.

Marshawn obviously knew what I was thinking and hopped out of the car, quickly opening my door so I could get out. I climbed onto the hood and was about to reach up and grab the lip of the concrete barrier when I realized that Neil hadn't moved. He was still sitting in the car with his hands on the wheel.

"C'mon, Neil, we gotta go," I called down to him as Marshawn climbed up onto the lip of the concrete barrier and started to make his way up the chain link fence that unfortunately had to be topped with barbed wire.

The man didn't budge. In fact, he didn't even glance my direction. I shot a look over to the mob we'd been driving into. It was the stuff of nightmares. The undead were packed in shoulder to shoulder all the way across the north- and southbound lanes. Many were starting to cause a bubble towards the middle as we were now obviously spotted or sensed or whatever.

"Neil, buddy, we gotta go," I urged. He continued to just sit there. His mouth was moving, but I couldn't hear anything between him being inside the vehicle and the growing roar coming from the zombies that were now perhaps a quarter of a mile away.

That used to seem like a long way, but when that is the span of distance that determines your fate, it is really not that far at all. I took a step towards him, but the voice in my head telling me to get my ass up and over that fence was making it very difficult.

I forced the voice away and rushed to the driver's side front door and yanked it open. Neil was still staring straight ahead like he didn't even see me.

"...no use...we can't survive this...it's just no use...we can't survive this..."

He kept repeating that almost like a mantra. I looked at his hands and realized he was white-knuckling the steering wheel. I grabbed his shoulder and shook him, but he didn't make any indication he knew I was even there.

"Neil!" I shouted.

Very slowly, he rotated his head to me. His eyes were glassy and unfocused, so I wasn't sure he was even seeing me.

"Evan." He scowled. "You hate me. I don't much like you either. Guess that makes us even."

"Umm...yeah, okay." I glanced up at Marshawn who was looking over his shoulder at me with a curious expression.

"What the hell is he doing?" Marshawn barked. "Tell him to move his ass."

"Yeah, I think Neil's checked out."

"Say what?"

"Yeah, he won't let go of the steering wheel. He keeps saying something about it being no use or something."

After another glance over at the closer of the two approaching herds, Marshawn jumped back down and stomped over to the car.

"Hey! Neil, we gotta get going, man." Marshawn snapped his fingers in front of the man's eyes, but the guy didn't even seem to blink.

"Maybe pry his hands off the wheel?" I suggested.

Marshawn reached in and had to really strain to get the first hand free. Only, when he reached over to pull his finger up on the other hand, Neil simply grabbed hold again with the hand Marshawn had just freed.

"I hate to say it, but we don't have time for this." Marshawn stepped back.

"We can't just leave him here." I looked past the car to the approaching horde, then glanced over my shoulder at the other one. Things were dire at best. "He won't stand a chance."

"And we can't stay here with him or we die."

It really was that simple. I had one thought. It was sorta strange, and wasn't likely to help, but it was a last-ditch effort. At least maybe I would be able to let this one slide off my conscience.

I took a deep breath, clenched my fist, and punched Neil right in the side of the face. His head snapped, and he fell over, slumping over the island in the middle where the guns had once been locked into place.

"Damn, Evan!" Marshawn gasped. "You really think now is the best time to score your get-back on the guy?"

"Owww," Neil moaned. He sat up and looked over at me with a look of confusion on his face. "What the hell is your problem, Evan?"

"Dude, you were just sitting there…frozen to the steering wheel. I wasn't going to just leave you here to be washed over by that wave of zombies headed this way." I gave a nod of my head toward the closest for emphasis.

Neil glanced over at the oncoming horde and then looked back at me with a dubious expression. He rubbed his cheek where I'd socked him and frowned.

"Can we do this later?" Marshawn growled.

I agreed. And now that I'd done my part and could walk away with a clear conscience, it was time to move. I ran to the concrete wall and jumped to grab the lip at the top. This was another problem with fiction. This stuff looked easy in the movies. I strained a bit and finally threw my leg up so that I could pull myself onto the small ledge on this side of the fence.

In a flash, Marshawn was up beside me. Neil was busy shutting the doors on the car when I turned to see where he was and why he had still not joined us.

"What the hell?" Marshawn called to the man who was acting like he had all the time in the world despite the fact that the leading edge of the zombie mob was now maybe sixty or so yards away.

"I had to close the doors. You guys left everything open," he shouted back.

"Who cares about if the doors are open or closed?" I snapped, starting to regret my efforts to break him out of his daze.

"That's all good until a zombie gets inside the car and ends up hitting the switches that shut off the siren. We came out here with a purpose, remember?" Neil glanced over at the oncoming zombies and slammed his door before jogging to the wall.

He started to struggle as he tried to get himself up, and both Marshawn and I leaned down, grabbing him under the arms and hauling him up to us. He gave a nod and mumbled something that might've been thanks.

47

"How we gonna get over that barbed wire without cutting ourselves to crap?" he asked now that he was between Marshawn and me.

Marshawn stripped off his jacket and threw it up and over the three strands of rusty barbed wire and started climbing the fence. I followed suit and scrambled up. I still felt the barbs poking me through the material, but it was better than ripping myself open on it and coming down with some sort of infection. It would really suck if that ended up killing me considering we didn't have any kind of antibiotics or any other sort of medication for that matter. That thought made me make a note to address that once we got back to the group.

Now that we were up and over, I took a look around. We were on a street that ran parallel to the interstate. It was running along the backside of what looked to be just another neighborhood.

"We need to get out of sight first," Marshawn yelled as Neil just decided he was going to start jogging along this road back towards the compound.

He pulled up and turned back, a sheepish expression on his face. I wasn't sure what it was, but there was some-

48

thing very...*off* about Neil. It was as if he'd just turned into the world's biggest idiot.

I started for the thick growth that had once probably acted as a noise barrier for the people living so close to the interstate. I pushed through to the other side and stopped so suddenly that Marshawn bumped into me.

"What the hell?" he snarled, and then shut his mouth so quick that I heard his teeth click.

"We aren't catching any breaks," I whispered.

What I'd mistook for a neighborhood was actually a sprawling apartment complex. The undead were all over the place. In singles and small groups they wandered about, doing whatever it is that zombies do when they aren't massing up into armies or ripping people apart.

In the mix were a handful of dogs varying from those annoying little balls of fur that yip at everything that moves to a German Shepherd that had its face buried in something furry. It could've been another dog or perhaps a cat, but its body was doing me the favor of blocking the view.

"*Yo quiero* braaiiins," Marshawn hissed in my ear as he pointed to a Chihuahua that was dragging most of its insides along behind it from the nasty rip in its belly.

I turned and saw a big, stupid grin on his face. For whatever reason…maybe it was all the piled-on stress, or perhaps I was about to join Neil in the mental checkout lane. Whatever the reason, I had to cover my mouth with my hands as a snorting laugh burst from me.

I turned back to the apartment complex so fast I felt something pop in my neck. Sure enough, a lone zombie that had been trudging along towards who-knows-where had stopped and was now turning slowly to orient on our general direction.

"It isn't like we have a lot of choices," I said with a shrug as I pulled my machete free.

"With them spread out like this, I think we can get to the other side of this place." Marshawn drew a blade as well.

Neil didn't say anything. He just stood there looking at the two of us like we'd both sprouted a second head. I was done babysitting him. Whatever was going on in his mind was officially his problem. I'd done all I could…or would.

I pushed through the hedge and came at the zombie with a sidearm swing. My blade dug into the temple and made it about a quarter of the way through the skull. I

50

might've been able to actually cleave all the way through if I was using my good arm, but I'd done enough, and the zombie dropped to the ground as I yanked back to pull my weapon free.

Looking around, there didn't seem to be any of the other zombies taking notice. I scurried to the first of the several vehicles still occupying parking spots in a long, covered section of the parking lot. We'd actually come out in almost the perfect location by the looks of things. We were on the edge of the complex and had a straight shot to a street at the end of this long drive.

I started towards the next car, doing my best to be quiet as possible. When I reached it, I glanced back to see Marshawn right on my heels. What I didn't see was Neil. I pushed that out of my mind and returned to concentrating on what was important: getting the hell out of here.

I was finally at the end of the first bank of apartments. From the looks of the scene, there were at least two more buildings before we would be free of this place. I could see movement in the windows and on some of the balconies, but nothing to indicate there were any survivors here.

I was halfway between an old beater of a car and what I always considered a penile-compensation truck. The wheels on the thing were just a shade smaller than what you would find on a monster truck and it had fairly impressive lift kit installed. There was no way a person got into that beast without a stepladder.

The sound of a baby's cry froze me in my tracks. It wasn't the sound as much as it was the proximity. It was coming from the general area of the pickup truck.

A moment later, what was left of a woman crawled out from under the white truck. Her face was smeared with fresh blood that dripped from her chin in thick, red droplets that I swear I could hear hitting the pavement. She was wearing the remnants of a blue tank top, the tattered meat of her left breast clearly visible. Her jeans had numerous rips and tears, most of them highlighted by the dark stains of dried blood. She had long, dark hair that hung down to mask much of her face, but some of it was clumped to her cheeks from the blood of what had to be a recent kill.

She opened her mouth as her eyes locked on me and I cringed as that awful sound carved its way into my ears. I was just about to commit to hurrying over and finishing it before it could get to its feet, or, God forbid, make that sound again.

I had come up from a full crouch to just slightly bent at the waist and broke into a fast jog when another head popped out from behind the rear driver's side wheel. What I saw caused me to trip, fall, and land hard on my stomach. That fall also caused me to lose my grip of my machete which went clattering away...and right under the truck where it came to a stop.

It looked like one of those cute little Australian Shepherds. The only problem with this cute little pup was that it had been bitten into. One of its little ears was literally dangling on the ground by a strip of gore-soaked flesh and fur. Its lips were curled back as it regarded me with glazed over eyes shot full of those giveaway dark tracers.

I wasn't sure what I'd eaten last, but I felt it rise up to the back of my throat. The slightest bit of the bile-laced mixture coated my esophagus with its molten slurry and I forced the rest down before I spewed all over myself.

A dark figure shot past me and there was a solid 'THUNK' as a heavy blade cleaved the woman's skull almost into two perfect halves. The figure made a slight adjustment and then stabbed the point of the blade into the open mouth of the little pup that was just starting to make a horridly low moan that was very out of place for such a tiny thing.

"C'mon, Evan, we gotta move."

I looked up, my brain still expecting Marshawn. Only, it was Neil who stared down at me with wide eyes. I got up just as Marshawn reached me and saw that a handful of the undead had obviously taken notice of our presence.

We jogged now, no longer trying to go for stealth. Once we reached the street, we paused to take a breath and look around. I knew the general direction we needed to go, and there didn't seem to be anything stumbling around in that area.

"You okay, Neil?" Marshawn asked, sounding more than a tad bit skeptical.

"Nope. Not at all," he said. And with that very simple and to-the-point answer, he started up the street.

I looked at Marshawn and he looked at me with a raised eyebrow that once again reminded me of The Rock. After a few seconds, we both shrugged and jogged to catch up.

I didn't know about Marshawn, but I just couldn't let that answer go without some sort of follow-up question. "Are you going to trip offline on us again?"

"I don't know," Neil answered with a shrug as he continued walking without glancing at either of us as we came up on both sides of him.

"What made you move your butt the last time?" I pressed.

"Don't know."

Our pace was actually pretty quick as we made like Olympic speed-walkers down the middle of an empty street that the sign we passed proclaimed as Southeast Stevens Road. We reached the first intersection and I skidded to a halt. Marshawn glanced back at me, then followed my gaze.

Mt. Scott Elementary School sat just across the intersection and to our left. From the looks, a group of people had obviously tried to seek refuge here. There were a cluster of cars in the parking lot; none of them parked as much as simply abandoned.

The windows I could see had all been busted and there were dark smears on the exterior brick walls all around the busted windows. While this place might be an elementary school, that didn't necessarily mean that there would be children here. Right?

Neil had not slowed down one iota, and was already across the intersection and still moving fast along Stevens Road. Nothing came pouring out of the school, and so Marshawn and I broke into a jog to catch up.

As we hurried along, I actually saw more movement in a few of the houses on our right than I did from the school which, as we passed by, had obviously been the scene of something horrific. The main entrance looked to have been absolutely destroyed. There was not a single door or pane of glass still intact, and even in the shadows of the awning, I could see dark stains everywhere.

One of the houses to our right had caught fire and most of it was now just blackened ruins, but there was one window that looked completely untouched by the fire. The outer façade around it was free of any of the dark smudges of the fire. Standing in that one window was what looked like an elderly woman.

As that block faded behind us, I had to convince myself that the woman had to have been a zombie. I didn't know why she was just standing there, but I didn't have the mental energy to give her much more thought.

We were now plunging into the heart of a residential neighborhood. I didn't like it, but as we walk/jogged through the next intersection, I could see that we were a little above the interstate in elevation. I wanted to cry at what I saw. From all indications, it looked like our plan had worked. From what I could see, the zombies were still moving away from our people and the little oasis we were currently calling home. It hadn't all been for nothing.

On the bad side, I could still hear the low thrum of a multitude of moans even from a few blocks away. It chilled me to the core. So many zombies; that could only mean that many people had perished.

"How far?" Marshawn asked as we plunged into a residential area that seemed to be plucked from the very bowels of hell.

"We got a ways to go," I huffed.

Suddenly, Neil stopped. He was about a half a block in front of us and just about to vanish around the bend in the road. At this point I could not even hazard a guess as to why he'd stopped. For all I knew, his brain simply shut down again and he'd stopped moving like a car that ran out of gas.

I reached him just ahead of Marshawn and instantly knew why he'd stopped.

"Fuck me," Marshawn whispered.

3

Liar

Neil continued to keep walking. Marshawn and I both had the same idea, but chose different routes. Basically, I broke right, and he went left. I dove into the hedges that lined the front of an average looking home and stayed as low as I could as I made a beeline for the far side of the house.

There was a tall wooden fence separating the front and back yards. I was really hoping there were no nasty surprises waiting on the other side, but I would take zombies—dog or human versions—versus a school bus with a machine gun mounted on top.

That meant that Don Evans was close, if not on that very bus that prowled down the street up ahead and coming our way. I'd hoped that Don and his people had gone

59

farther away. To be honest, I hadn't thought for a moment that I had the chance of running into him on this little foray.

As I lifted the latch and slipped through the gate, I realized that Neil had not made any attempt to hide. He hadn't gone left or right. He'd kept walking straight into the jaws of the lion. I hunched in on myself and waited for the chatter of the machine gun that would signal him being ripped to shreds.

"Jesus…took you long enough!" a familiar voice shouted. "You were supposed to show up as soon as I activated the siren. I thought we had that all worked out."

I felt my stomach turn, and it had nothing to do with the stench of the undead—which, fortunately, this yard was blessedly clear of. I could not be hearing what I thought I was hearing. There was no way.

"Yeah, well you were supposed to take them north," the haunting baritone of Don Evans shouted back. "You cut us off and I had to circle way the fuck around. As it was, there was no way to get to you. Did you see the size of that other herd?"

"Did my flare help at all?" Neil called back.

"I found you, didn't I?" Don snorted.

"Yeah, well I had both of them following me, but they obviously saw you. I thought you were going to park someplace and wait for us to pass by."

"I was just about to do that. I didn't realize you were so close."

"Yeah, well the nigger took off to the right. That piece of shit Evan went left...so they are both on their own."

I heard the sound of squealing brakes from way too close. I'd been sitting here listening the whole time when I should've been running for my life. It was time to remedy that. I just had to hope that Marshawn was already moving.

So much for us being able to stay at that house. Once again, it wasn't zombies that proved to be the problem. It was the living.

Part of me was really mad at myself for not having seen this guy for what he was. Another part of me was laughing at the stereotypical "zombie fiction bad guy" that had been waving a flag in front of me these past few days.

"I'll go after Evan," Neil snorted. "I know how bad you want to deal with that other guy."

"You said he went to the right?" Don shouted over the sound of the bus revving up.

I heard a big commotion and had to imagine that he was probably driving through somebody's yard. It hadn't been long enough, and spring was not yet in full swing, so most of the yards were just reaching that point where everybody would be waiting for that first sunny weekend to go out and mow, plant those first flowers in their yard, and spruce things up outside.

This was one of those neighborhoods that I imagined had dutiful husbands pushing their mowers and waving to each other as the wives were using tiny hand shovels to dig holes where the fresh flowers would go, and everybody had a compost tumbler. Kids probably rode bikes up and down the street and played basketball in the driveway.

I knew I had to get moving, but part of me just wanted to quit running. It seemed that I was falling from one dire situation to the next. I was tired. Tired of running. Tired of seeing the dregs of humanity run roughshod over the clinging remnants of civilization. Just plain tired.

But I was not about to go out this way at the hands of some piece of crap like Neil Pearson. I forced myself to trudge across the yard and was almost to the fence that separated this yard from the one behind it when I heard the meaty slap of a hand on glass.

I already knew what I would see before my head instinctively craned around to see the zombie I'd been certain would be standing at the sliding glass back door of this house. I was only partially correct.

Staring out at me were three zombie children that I guessed had to be between the ages of maybe three and twelve. There were two boys and a little girl.

That one glimpse practically seared itself into my head. Once again, I found myself struck weak at the horror of what might've played out here.

The little girl, and youngest of the trio, had my heart ripping in half as that single glimpse of her made itself the new star of my nightmares. She was a teeny little blonde-haired thing. Both of her arms were gone as if maybe she'd been part of some hellish tug-o-war. Her sides were both blackened from all the blood I am sure gushed from where her tiny arms had been literally ripped from the sockets. My only hope was that it had happened in death, because the alternative would be too horrific to consider.

The two boys, both older, had dark stains around their mouths. That was the other detail that stood out. Only the little girl's face was free of any signs that she'd fed. One of the boys, the oldest of the pair based on just looking at them, had his belly torn open and large spools of his insides dangling. They had dried somewhat over time and now looked more like black cords than anything else.

The smaller of the two boys had most of his throat ripped out. I was wondering where the parents might be and if perhaps they'd been the ones to attack their children and turn them.

All of that raced through my head in a matter of just a couple of seconds as I reached the back fence. There was a swing set close enough that I was able to climb up on it and make it over the top of the wooden fence. My feet touched down in the neighboring yard when I heard a soft moan just to my left.

A teenaged boy was standing amidst a cluster of bamboo, his eyes regarding me as his teeth clicked together seemingly in anticipation of getting a bite of my warm flesh. I felt my heart leap to my throat, but almost just as quickly settle back down to a more reasonable rate.

He tried to lunge for me, but somehow, he'd gotten his clothing so tangled and snagged on a few of the broken stalks of bamboo that he was trapped and unable to get free to reach me. I could see up the side of this home and spotted the gate that would open to the front. Beyond that were dense woods. Thank God for the tree-loving folks of the Pacific Northwest that loved keeping decent sized wooded lots intact. That was my objective. Once in the woods, I could hopefully lose Neil and find my way back to the compound in time to warn everybody and haul ass before Don and that prick Neil returned to finish everybody off.

I took off as fast as I could run, and I'd just reached the gate when I heard a voice from behind me. "Evan!"

This wasn't some sort of "I have you now!" shout of triumph. It was a whispered hiss that sounded urgent and…scared?

I spun to see Neil with one leg tossed over the fence. All I had to do was pull a gun, aim, and end him here and now. And that was exactly what my body was already in the process of doing. Only…something was strange. Off.

Wrong.

"Evan, please," Neil pleaded in a whispered hiss. "Wait for me."

I now had a pistol out before me in a two-handed grip. I had his center mass lined up for an easy shot. After all, he wasn't that far away, I wasn't going to miss. The look in his eyes told me that he knew I had him.

Then why hadn't I pulled the trigger?

"We have to get out of here before that maniac figures things out and circles back to the compound." Neil hadn't so much as tried to throw his other leg over. He was sitting there in my sights. I could drop him easy. So why wasn't I?

He had no weapon in his hands. Was it because I couldn't shoot a defenseless person? No, that wasn't it. If I had the drop on Don Evans, I'd shoot him in the back or even in the face if he was where Neil was at this exact moment.

"I didn't have a choice, but I tried to set them up and lure them into a trap. Somehow they managed to either avoid it or get free." He glanced over his shoulder and then back at me. "Shoot me or let me come with you, but we don't have time to waste."

"You gave up Marshawn," I hissed.

"Because he got the jump on you. He will get away, I'd be willing to bet on it. You aren't able to move as fast. Your arm is still messed up. If Don came after you, chances are he would've caught you."

All of this seemed to make some kind of perverse

sense. Also, why would he go through all this to call me and risk that I would've shot first and asked questions later?

"I told Evan not to trust you," a familiar and gravelly voice barked from the other side of the fence and the yard I'd just exited.

Neil turned to look back over his shoulder. His hands rose and all I could think was that the bastard had been telling the truth. I have no idea what or how things had shaken down to where they were at the moment, but, as strange as it seemed, Neil had not been lying...at least not to me.

That thought only had a fraction of a second to gel in my head before a thunderous boom sounded. I saw something chunky explode from Neil's back where the round of from a high-caliber weapon blew a hole in him. He toppled backwards and landed hard in the yard I was in.

"We're coming to get you, Evan," Natasha Petrov growled from the other side of the fence.

That broke whatever spell had kept me from taking off the moment Neil had been shot. I reached the gate and flipped up the latch. Just as I ducked through, I heard another thunderous boom and a chunk of the fence evaporated in splinters that plunged into the back of my head and neck.

I stumbled forward, the stinging sensation just enough to motivate me to run faster. I looked around and saw that I was at the end of a cul-de-sac. Directly across the street were the woods that would hopefully allow me to evade Natasha.

As I ran, I tried to make sense of what had just happened. Nothing came to mind that could explain it away. And now Neil was dead, so the chances that I would get to the bottom of things seemed unlikely.

"Keep running, Evan...too bad that little girl you promised to protect didn't have the same chance," Natasha called after me as I ducked into the dark shadows of the grove of dense pines.

She was talking about Ariel Mannheim. Ariel and I had met while I was on the run. I'd rescued her only to have her pull a gun on me. We'd both been captured by Don Evans and he'd kept her as supposed insurance when he sent me out on a run with his goons. All I had to do was come back, and she would be fine. If I didn't, then he said he would give her to the zombies he kept in the basement of the church he was using at the time for a base. That was just one of my many sins starting to pile up. I doubted that I would ever have a night of sleep that was not haunted by either the ghosts of those whose deaths were my direct responsibility, or by visions of the things I'd seen, like those children back at that house.

Part of me really wanted to find a spot and hunker down. Maybe that bitch Natasha would pursue me and I could get a shot at her. Next to Don Evans, there was nobody I would rather kill.

That sentiment made me stumble. Or maybe it was just the root in the ground that I hadn't seen. Whatever the case, I was faced with a stark reality.

I was prepared to kill living human beings.

If I was being absolutely honest...I wanted to kill. Maybe I was devolving like the rest of society seemed to be doing. Perhaps I was simply adapting to the current ways of the world. Whatever the reason, there was still a small part of me that was uncomfortable as to where my conscience was drifting.

I went a good distance into the woods, but I didn't hear any sound of pursuit. That didn't mean there wasn't any. It only meant that I couldn't hear anything. I crouched down just behind some really thick sticker bushes and tried to see if anybody had come after me.

I could see the front of the house I'd cut through the yard of...the place where Neil lay dead, hanging head down from the top of the fence where he'd been shot. There was nothing. No movement at all.

After a few seconds that ticked by with terminal slowness, I got up and took off. Thankfully, the woods were basically zombie free. They were also much too small for my liking. I emerged on the backside of the continuation of this neighborhood.

It took all of my control to stay put for as long as I could stand — which was probably not nearly long enough — before I ventured out and started cutting through one back yard after another. Occasionally I heard something pound or slap on a window, but I didn't stop to look.

Finally, I came to the edge of the neighborhood that sat just behind the place I considered our base. I was at the neighborhood I called the race track. It was clear that every single one of these residences had been stripped. Probably by Carl and the individuals that had magically appeared and joined him on the same day that I'd left.

When I crossed the grassy field, I was ridiculously

happy to see the remnants of my noisemaker devices. Obviously Carl had thought the idea good enough to implement on what appeared to be a larger scale. I wish it'd helped him when it came to the living. One thing for certain, I would take that into account if we ever found someplace we could settle into. I would make precautions to deal with the zombies, sure. But there would be a helluva lot of prep to deal with people like Don Evans and Natasha.

I reached the wall and was halfway over when something struck me. Nobody was noticing. Not one person was visible. The pile of stuff was still where it had been when we'd left, and there was even a neat row of packs presumably belonging to the few folks we'd left behind.

"They are in the house," a voice whispered from behind me.

I turned to see Michael standing there with Chewie. From the looks of things, the two had been hiding inside one of the shot-up cars parked inside the walls.

"Why are you two outside and everybody else is inside?" I asked what I considered a logical question.

"They are drinking the icky stuff from those smelly bottles." He wrinkled his nose for emphasis and Chewie made a low woof that almost sounded like agreement.

Great. We go out and risk our butts and the rest of the group decides this is a good time to tie one on? We were going to have to bail on this place. And it wasn't zombies that I worried about.

I walked into the main entry hall and could hear a bunch of loud talking and laughter coming from the living room. What I saw when I walked in was enough to make me want to just turn around and walk back out.

Rickey was in the act of passing a bottle of Jack to Tracy. Darya was reclined in one of the over-stuffed chairs, a stupid grin on her face and eyes lidded, looking like she was on the bad side of inebriated. Her kid was curled up on the floor in a blanket and snoring softly, his mouth open just a little, and a line of drool trickling from one corner.

"This is going to seem like a stupid question," I said, doing my best to keep my voice even. "But what the hell are you guys doing?"

"We saw you lead that horde away. We were celebrating," Rickey huffed, no sign of a slur in his voice…yet.

"Well you got excited just a bit early," I snapped, failing at hiding the annoyance in my voice. "And did you get that kid drunk, too?" I hiked a thumb at Darya's sleeping son and realized I hadn't ever bothered to even learn the kid's name.

That seemed to be all it took to sober Darya Kennedy up as she bounded to her feet and stomped to me. "How dare you!" she hissed. "My son is exhausted. In case you haven't been paying attention, we have been on the go for over three days straight. He is just a child and was on the verge of collapse."

"Well I hate to be the bearer of bad news, but we need to bail from this location right freaking now." I leveled my glare at everybody.

"But we watched you draw the zombies away," Tracy insisted. "I thought we were going to stay here at least for the time being if you could lead them away."

"But we didn't count on Don Evans and his people being in the area. We—" I started, but was cut off.

"Grab your packs and let's go!"

I spun to see Marshawn standing in the doorway, his hands on his knees as he sucked in great lungsful of air. I was torn between being relieved that he'd made it, and horrified at the prospects in knowing we were safer out among the undead than we were here.

"How close behind you?" I asked, my voice barely able to go much beyond a whisper as all the moisture had suddenly evaporated from my mouth in the last few seconds.

"No idea, I was hauling ass and not bothering to stop and see," Marshawn gasped as he struggled to catch his breath. "But they were coming this way. They know we are here."

That seemed to sober everybody up. It didn't take long for us to grab what we deemed important and be ready to move.

"I know where we should go," I offered as I slung my pack over my shoulder and took Michael by the hand. "Right across the way there is a small community. The entire neighborhood has a wall around it. They might not think to look for us there."

I was grasping at straws, but I also knew that we were in no shape for a long run. We had two kids with us, three of our number had been drinking, and when I shot them a glance, I noticed both the ladies swaying a bit on their feet. Then there was my Chewie. She would push on if I made her, but I worried she might eventually collapse. She was still beat up pretty bad and I could see some darker spots on her where some of her wounds were seeping blood still. Is this what Neil had meant about how pointless our struggle might be? Would it perhaps be easier to just roll over and let the waves wash us away?

I shook my head and forced those thoughts away. As long as I could draw breath, I would fight. That was it. And in that moment, it was as if my resolve finally etched itself in my soul once and for all. I would not doubt, and I would not quit.

Everybody started for the wall and I paused. "Get over, I will catch up," I said.

I jogged back to all our supplies that we'd be leaving behind. There was still a good amount of stuff here, and sure, it was possible that we might be able to come back and scavenge a few things, but I was willing to bet that if Don Evans and his crew rolled back into this place, they would not leave any of it behind.

I tossed a few lids aside as I scrounged around. I knew what I wanted, and even made a little cry of victory when I found it. It only took a moment, but when I reached the wall and managed to haul myself up and take one last look back, I couldn't help but smile. It was a small victory...but a win is a win as my old high school coach used to preach. It didn't matter if it was by one point or a hundred. The pile of supplies that we hadn't been able to bring with us was quickly becoming a decent-sized bonfire.

I hadn't seen who helped Chewie over, but I wasn't surprised to see her padding along beside Michael. Marshawn was walking beside the pair, his head on a swivel as he tried to look in every direction at once. The good news was that not a single zombie stumbled along at the moment.

We crossed Johnson Creek Boulevard and started up the hill towards the walled-in community. I had picked up my pace so that I was in the lead. I knew exactly where I wanted us to enter.

It only took another moment, and I had reached the gate that was blocked with cars. I'd entered the place at this exact location just a few days ago when I'd thought that I was going to turn.

I watched as Rickey stopped, turned and then just began hoisting the ladies over the gate. Then, with a gentleness that surprised me, he knelt in front of Chewie, whispered something to her, and then picked her up as he used the bumper of a car for a stairstep. He climbed onto the hood and very carefully set my beloved Newfound-land down on the hood of the car on the other side. In the blink of an eye, he scooped up both the young boys and set them down on the other side.

With an agility that you would not believe possible for such a big, bulky guy, he hopped the gate and then got down on the ground, quickly transferring my dog from the hood of the car to the street.

When I climbed over last, I looked around and was surprised not to see any undead shambling our direction. We weren't out of the water yet...but it was a start. We headed into the neighborhood just as the teeth-jarring chatter of a machine gun started up back in the place we'd just vacated.

Now I had to hope and pray that they didn't decide to come over here and check this place out. I had a few places that I knew were cleared out, so I took them to the house I'd spent that first night in.

We made it inside the door just as a low moan sound-ed from someplace close. I wasn't sure if we'd been spotted by the zombies, but we could deal with that in a minute once everybody got inside.

Turned out that was about all the time we had before a

meaty hand slapped on the front door we'd just come through. I jerked my machete free and stalked to the door with the intention of ending the zombie quickly.

"Water..." a woman's voice rasped from behind a netted veil that draped around the front of her camo-colored bush hat.

She dropped to her knees and sprawled with her arms hardly breaking her fall as her face bounced off the concrete step-up entry to the house. There was something oddly familiar about her, but I couldn't figure out what it might be.

"Get her inside, quick," Rickey hissed.

I looked up to see a trio of zombies shambling past the house we were going to try and hide out in for a little bit while we figured out what to do next. I grabbed her under one arm and Rickey grabbed the other. We pulled her in as quietly as we could and eased the door shut once she was inside.

Now that she was inside, I gave her a quick once over. She was packing more firepower than any two of us combined. And while we had a few police weapons in the mix, she was carrying one rifle in particular that I was guessing had been very much on the illegal side of things a few months ago when that sort of thing mattered.

"You did hear the poor thing ask for water?" Tracy snapped as she shouldered past us and knelt down with a canteen that she brought to the young woman's lips.

In a flash, and way before any of us would've been able to react had we been watching out for something, the woman whipped her body around and was suddenly on her knees and crouched behind Tracy with a very ugly knife that was filthy with dark blood that was so fresh it still dripped from the blade.

"Who are you people, and what do you want?" the woman hissed through clenched teeth.

"Whoa there, sister," Rickey said calmly, stepping back and raising his hands to show he was unarmed. "We're just passing through. If this is your place, we apologize. We was just following our boy here. Thought he knew what was what in these parts." The nasty look he shot me was very obvious.

"You." The woman gestured to me. "I seen you in here before. Wasn't you with those poor bastards across the way?"

I processed that comment as having the possibility that maybe she'd seen something when Don Evans and his people rolled in and did what they did. And as much as I wanted details, I knew that would obviously have to come later.

"You set those bastards up and sic that crazy bunch of heathens on 'em?" the strange woman pressed.

Yeah…much later.

"No, I was actually trying to find them. I left when I thought that I was infected, but it turned out that I wasn't." I was talking way too fast…babbling even. I hiked my sleeve up to show my healed scratch.

She gave my arm a cursory glance and then cocked an eyebrow in wry amusement. "Am I supposed to see something?"

"Yeah…well…there was a scratch there. It's healed up since."

"And not left so much as a scar?" She snorted a laugh that was definitely "at" me and not "with" me.

"Look, it doesn't matter how big—" I started to protest.

"Says every single guy in the world."

That caused Tracy to force back a laugh despite the knife at her throat. Darya had the courtesy to at least look away. But she made very little attempt at holding back her own chuckle.

"Listen, we aren't wanting any trouble," I said, doing my best to claw back a shade of my pride that was becoming a bit of a casualty of this woman's quips. "We will roll out of here if you'll just let us ride things out for a while. The same people that hit my friends are back and hunting for us to finish us off."

"So you bring them to my place?"

She had a point, but in my defense, I had no idea she'd been here. She certainly hadn't been the last time —

"I think I've saved your ass once already." She removed her knife from Tracy's throat and took a step back.

That was when it had hit me. During that madness with Brandon Cook, I'd run into some zombie trouble. A complete stranger dressed from head to toe in hunter's camo had gunned down the closest threats. I hadn't ever seen the person up close, and they'd just gave a tip of their hat and ducked back into the woods after basically saving my ass.

"You...?" I let that hang in the air.

"And here we go," she grumbled.

The woman tore the hat from her head to allow long reddish-brown locks to fall in a cascade past her shoulders. And now, as things appeared to be settling down, I could get a better look at her. The thing is, I was having a tough time making it all fit. There was one part of me that was appraising a very female body that had all the right amount of curves offering a teasing glimpse of what was probably an extremely attractive figure under that open camo jacket and those loose-fitting camo pants. She was wearing some sort of skin tight black top with a logo I didn't recognize emblazoned in hot pink.

That was the feminine side of what I was seeing.

Then there were the multiple blades, a pair of rifles including the one that just looked like it would mow down a hundred zombies with one squeeze of the trigger, a spiked baseball bat, a shotgun with what I swore had to be an under-the-barrel grenade launcher attached, and a pair of scoped pistols slung low on her hips. Basically...I was looking at a real-life Laura Croft.

"Hey, buddy," the woman snapped her fingers in front of my eyes. "My face is up here."

"I wasn't...umm..." I stammered.

Had I been gawking? I think I was just blown away by the firepower she was carrying. Also, I was thinking back to when we'd first "met" and trying to figure out if I'd been aware my savior that day had been a woman.

"Marshawn King." I felt myself being nudged aside. "My friend here is Evan Berry…"

Marshawn rattled off the rest of the introductions, even going so far as to introduce both of the boys. "And this little guy is Toby Kennedy."

Huh, Toby. How come I hadn't even learned the kid's name yet? If I was the supposed leader of this band of misfits, I was going to need to tighten things up a bit.

"Yeah…that's all fine and good, my name is Alexandria Morris, but nobody calls me that. It's just Alex," the woman said with a shrug.

"Then why did you go through the trouble of telling us a name that nobody uses?" Tracy challenged.

I glanced over, more than a little surprised to see that both Tracy and Darya were standing shoulder-to-shoulder with a serious case of resting bitch face etched in deep on both their expressions. I had no idea what it was about, but now wasn't the time.

"Wait, let me see if I got this straight." Alex turned to face the other two women. "If this is the same lunatic I saw take your old compound down earlier, you are going all *Mean Girls* on me while there is some asswipe with a .50

cal mounted on a school bus looking to mow you down? How have you managed to survive this long?"

Not exactly how I would've put it, but she made a very good point. We needed to get moving and put some distance between us and Don Evans...for now. Once things settled and I was in better condition, I would seek him out as well as Natasha, and do my best to free Carl and the others if they were still alive, and end those two stains on civilization once and for all.

Running...again!

I was still trying to decide what to do—whether we should stay put or move out—when the terrible roar of a powerful machine gun caused everybody to jump. I noticed Alex jump a little, so I was bit relieved to see that she wasn't impervious to fear. That might seem like a neat trait to have but, in my limited experience, that is what led a person to be killed. I shuddered at my own brushes with death when I'd been running around thinking that I was going to die, and thus, had nothing to worry about.

"I think we need to move. He might not be the brightest bulb on the tree, but it's not much of a stretch to think he won't come over here and poke around," I said with a clap of my hands that was meant to get everybody's attention. I actually caused a couple of our group to jump.

"Where do we go?" Darya whispered. The fear in her voice was so thick, her voice dipped a register or two and sounded raspy.

"I think the idea of staying anywhere near the city is officially a bad one." I looked around and noticed that everybody except Alex was listening. She had sauntered over to the window.

I found my eyes following her and quickly forced myself to look away before anybody got the wrong idea. And that was another thing about a lot of the zombie stories that I'd had trouble with. The last thing I felt like doing right now was trying to hook up with somebody. I gave a covert sniff of my armpit to confirm that thought and my nose wrinkled at what hit me full on.

"So?" Tracy snapped, bringing my focus back to her and the others. My face felt a bit warm, but I pushed it away and wrote it off to nothing more than a surge of hormones in the midst of all the chaos.

"So?" I shot back. I had forgotten what point I was about to make.

"Where do we go if we can't stay here?" Tracy said with a tone that made me wonder if I'd missed something and she was now being forced to repeat herself.

I thought back to my idea of heading out to someplace like McIver Park. That was still close enough that we could perhaps slip in and raid some of the smaller communities nearby that existed on the outskirts of Portland while still being remote enough that maybe the zombie problem would be very minimal.

I laid it out for the group and said that I was open to other ideas if anybody had some other location in mind. I told them that there was enough open area that we could perhaps secure the location we chose and then go so far as to set up gardens and things along those lines.

"Whatever we are going to do, I think we need to decide now," Alex called over her shoulder from where she'd been peering out the window.

I rushed over and couldn't hear anything. I glanced at her, suddenly a bit self-conscious about what my breath must smell like at this close to another person.

"The shooting stopped." She looked at me for a second and then returned her gaze back out the window.

"Okay?" I pressed, not sure where she was going with things.

"They have been quiet for a bit." Alex returned her gaze to me for a moment with an expression that said she was waiting for me to connect the dots. Apparently, I failed. She huffed, blowing a strand of hair that had slipped from her floppy-brimmed hat and now hung lazily over one eye. "That means they either found something, turned around and left, or are now figuring out just where you ran off to. Judging solely on the little I've seen and heard, I would vote on the last one."

"Okay, folks, I hate to be the bearer of bad news, but we gotta go," I announced.

"Evan, these children can't keep this pace up," Darya moaned.

"We just got started," I shot back as I grabbed my bag and took Michael by the hand, leading him towards the back door of this house. "They are going to have to move or they are done for."

The moment I said it, I wished that I could take it back. The problem was...it was truth. Cold. But real.

"Jesus, brutha," Rickey whispered as he came up beside me as I unlatched the gate that opened up to a narrow alley that ran behind the houses on this block and those on the other side.

I had become so focused on what needed to be done and trying to figure out the best path for us to take that I'd stopped paying attention to my surroundings. I opened the gate and found myself standing before a zombie that had apparently been waiting for an idiot like me.

The girl was perhaps ten. Maybe twelve, but no older. She, like previous child versions that I'd encountered, did not just start for me, teeth gnashing and hands grabbing. She stared at me, her head cocked to the side like she was waiting for me to say something. Rickey started to reach for his machete, but something in me made me grab his arm. The sudden activity did have one reaction...the little girl zombie took a step backwards! I am guessing by the look on his face, and how it changed, that he was about to voice a protest regarding me keeping him from drawing a weapon, but I think that, by the time the words dripped from his mouth, it was likely about what he was seeing.

"The children are still frightened," Michael whispered.

I glanced down at him and wanted to ask how he knew, but when I looked back at the pathetic creature facing us, I had to agree that such an assessment was as good of an explanation as anything I could throw out there.

"How do you know?" I whispered. "Can you talk to them?"

Michael continued to stare at the ground, but he made

a sound that I am certain was him holding back a laugh. "Monsters can't talk, Evan."

"Jeez," Rickey exhaled more than spoke. "Everybody knows that, Evan. What are you thinking?"

I shot him my best withering glare, but I doubt Rickey even noticed. Instead, he moved laterally, keeping his distance from the zombie girl. Chewie was a different story.

As soon as she squeezed through the gate, her eyes locked on the creature. The hackles on the back of her neck and between her broad shoulders stood up and she let loose with a low rumbling growl.

Before the apocalypse, I could not recall hearing my big fur ball making any noises that could be remotely intimidating. Mostly she made noises that were very similar to her silver screen namesake. The sounds coming from her now were fierce and more than a little scary.

"Easy, girl," I breathed.

I was suddenly very glad that I'd slipped her collar on. She was already straining against it, and I am certain that, had I not held on tight, she would've laid into that zombie like nobody's business.

"There is a zombie child on the other side of the gate," I said over my shoulders so that the others would hopefully not be alarmed. Since she was now a good fifteen or so feet back up the alley, and making no attempt to come for us, I figured everybody would be able to slip by with no problems.

I was only partially correct.

The last person through the gate was Alex. She had one of her big blades in her hand and turned toward the child as soon as she saw it. In an instant, the creature was just like any other zombie as it made a hissing sound and began to stagger towards the woman who waited patiently for it to close the distance.

"Pay attention, Evan," she said over her shoulder without taking her eyes off the zombie girl that drew nearer and nearer, her teeth clicking in anticipation of tearing into the woman who faced her down.

Now Chewie was even more aggressive and yanked me back towards the scene of what was about to be a quick kill. Sure enough, as soon as the girl closed to within range, Alex leaned in and brought her blade down in a skull shattering overhand smash. As the child fell, Alex jerked the blade free, knelt, and wiped it off on the little girl's shirt before sliding it back into its sheath.

"At least your dog isn't an idiot," she scolded as she

91

stalked past me to catch up with Rickey.

"What the hell do you mean by that?" I said as I pulled Chewie around and jogged to catch up.

"The dog knows that a zombie is a fucking zombie."

"It wasn't attacking," I insisted.

"Did you see it change?" Alex spun on me. She wasn't yelling, but she was whisper-shouting pretty dang loud, and it made everybody stop and stare.

"It saw you pull a knife," I said.

Even as the words were coming out of my mouth, I heard the foolishness. But I couldn't help it. These were children...or at least they had been. And in each case, when I'd encountered them, they'd never attacked until I drew a weapon.

As that thought tried to entrench itself in my mind, I remembered the church. I remembered the feeling of absolute fear that dug its claws into my soul when those children had basically rang a dinner bell and brought on an onslaught of so-called regular zombies as I'd driven through them.

"Can you two do this later?" Marshawn stepped in between us. "We need to go...now!"

As soon as he said it, I heard it. The sound of what I

knew to be a school bus chugging up Johnson Creek Boulevard. It would reach the intersection and turn left, putting it at the gates of this once opulent neighborhood. We had to go.

I hated that I was not anywhere close to a hundred percent. If so, I would do everything in my power to put an end to this creep right now. The longer he floated out there in the world, the harder it would be to take him down simply because he would amass not only more firepower, but he would find other like-minded idiots just looking to take advantage of the unfortunate situations of others. I'd seen way more of the Don Evans sort out in the wilderness than I did people like Marshawn—and even Alex for that matter. She had saved my ass once.

We cut down the alley and emerged to discover a litter-strewn street with corpses decaying in what was promising to be a rather unseasonably hot early spring day. I kept the pace brisk, but tried to remember that we had little ones in tow and their legs could only go so fast.

By the time we reached the wall, the sound of the school bus was echoing off every surface, and impossible to pinpoint. We reached the end of the street where it split off in a tee-intersection. To the left was just a short distance before it terminated in a dead-end node of a street that went between two homes. A large sign announced the expansion of the neighborhood that would never happen.

As we reached the little barricade Rickey hopped up and turned to start giving people a hand over. Marshawn cleared the wall and waited on the other side to help everybody down and I hung back just a bit to keep an eye back up the street we'd jogged down in case the school bus from hell appeared. Rickey was just boosting Alex when our time ran out.

The nose of the bus was just creeping into view. I bolted, hoping that I'd managed to avoid being seen. I heard a few rounds of gunfire come from back that direction, but nothing to indicate it had been directed at me.

"Run!" I yelled, backpedaling to the barricade, hopping onto it, and following Rickey over.

I dropped to the ground and got my bearings. We were at the bottom of a moderately steep slope that would take us to another patch of forest. I was pretty certain that would take us to Altamont Summit, an upscale condo complex that sat on the far side of the residential neighborhood where one of my many nightmares originated.

The first night away from the group, I had stumbled

across a young man and an infant. He'd been perhaps thrown out of yet another gated community (I'd had no idea how many of those existed until this zombie thing started), but that hadn't stopped him from taking a shot at me. Thinking back, I guess he had his reasons considering what I'd encountered since that day. My last memory of that young man and the baby was what haunted me.

Zombies had come through the door and windows. I escaped out back, but he and the baby had stayed. I was almost across the open field beyond that home when I heard those first screams. I'd heard adults scream 'the scream' before, but that had been the first time I'd heard a child. That sound often echoed in my head, even when I was awake.

Part of me didn't really want to return to that scene, but our other option was to blunder forward through yet another neighborhood. At least this way, if we made it up the hill, we could take a moment to catch our breath in those woods before pushing on.

"Up there." I pointed.

"Evan…" Darya started.

Before she could finish, Rickey leaned over and scooped up Toby Kennedy in one arm and hoisted him onto his shoulders. Marshawn quickly followed suit with Michael. I held my breath, waiting for the boy to absolutely lose it. Instead, he leaned forward, crossing his arms and laying them across Marshawn's head like it was all perfectly natural and normal.

I was officially done trying to figure kids out. A quick glance at Alex made me amend my list and add women to it as well.

We started up the hill. Oddly enough (or not, considering everything that had happened these past several days), I was the weak link in the chain. I tried to play it off like I was simply doing my part to bring up the rear, but a few glances over his shoulder, and the look I was getting, told me that Marshawn wasn't even a little bit fooled.

We were halfway up when I heard the .50 cal on the school bus open up. I froze for an instant, certain that I was about to be shredded. When nothing happened, I risked stopping to get a look back towards the neighborhood we'd left behind.

I was almost relieved…no, who am I kidding? I was giddy. Apparently, Dumbass Don had brought out every single zombie trapped inside that gated community. Even better, he thought that he'd be able to just plow through them in that school bus. Scores of the undead were on all sides of the bus and more were coming from every narrow street of the grid.

Part of me, a sick part admittedly, wanted to stay and watch. I wanted to see the zombies pour into that bus. I wanted to wait until I saw that mohawked bastard come staggering out with a chunk bitten out of his ass. And if he was still dressed like he was last time I saw him, that wouldn't be a problem to see for real.

No such luck, though. "C'mon, Evan," Darya hissed as she reached the top of the hill.

I gave one last look, and felt all my joy seep out through my pores as the .50 cal cut a path for the bus to push forward. My last sighting of it as I reached the top of the slope was seeing it roll out onto the road. A team of at least ten people had pushed the cars blocking that particular gate aside, and the bus blew through it like it was paper.

I ducked into the woods and caught up to where everybody had basically collapsed onto the ground. Everybody, that is, with the exception of Alex. I decided to go over to her and put an end to whatever it was that was rubbing her the wrong way about me. If she was going to stay with us, we couldn't have this degree of animosity. Of course, I was putting the cart before the horse when it came to her really joining our group.

"Not now, buddy," Marshawn whispered as he caught me by the arm as I started to pass him.

"I can't have a bunch of attitude right now in the group," I insisted.

"No, you don't like that she is torqued at you specifically. She hasn't said a cross word to anybody else."

I opened my mouth to protest and just as promptly shut it. I glanced back at the woman who now sat under a tall pine as she dug through the small field pack she carried. She seemed absolutely oblivious that I was staring at her.

"I don't have any idea what you are trying to say…" I started to deny, and again shut my mouth. He raised an eyebrow at me and then shot a look back over my shoulder, presumably in Alex's direction. "I don't…I couldn't…" The protests were hitting the tip of my tongue and then falling like lead balloons.

What he was suggesting was simply not something that could be possible. As if to prove it to myself, I pictured my beloved Stephanie. I squeezed my eyes shut and brought her face to mind. The only problem was that it took a moment, and the first image that took hold was the one I had of her coming for me in the hospital. I shook that one off and tried to picture the image that had been captured in that photograph I'd had for the first several days, until…

That only served to piss me off. Again, my thoughts had to return to Don Evans. That picture had been in my bag that he and his people had taken from me. Nobody seemed to recall that I'd had it and I was willing to bet they had tossed it away without so much as a thought. After all, it wasn't theirs, so why should it matter.

But why couldn't I bring Stephanie's face to mind? Certainly, I couldn't already be forgetting her.

At last, a fuzzy image came to me. It wasn't very defined, but I knew it was her and I clung to that for all I was worth.

"You okay?" Marshawn asked, an uneasy look on his face.

I scrubbed at my eyes and felt the slightest bit of a suspicious moisture. Oh, hell no, I scolded myself. This was absolutely not the time, nor the place, for some sort of emotional outpouring. I quickly shoved all of those feelings aside and swallowed hard to clear the tightness in my throat.

"Fine." I could hear my lie, but I was counting on this guy not knowing me well enough yet to detect it.

I moved past him, but instead of confronting Alex, I walked over to where Darya and Tracy were fussing over the boy, Toby. I noticed that neither of them were even glancing in Michael's direction. Of course, unlike Toby, who was sniffling and acting like he was about to die, Michael sat next to Chewie and seemed no worse for the wear.

"Ladies," I said, and then wondered what else there was to say to them.

That thought was driven home when they both looked up at me with exasperated glares on their faces for all of maybe two seconds before returning their focus to Toby. I have no idea why, but I had a nasty feeling that the young man was not long for this world. As harsh as that thought was, I couldn't help but feel sorry for him. It was clear that he was terrified, and there simply was no relief in sight. Not in the near or distant future.

"Hey, I was thinking that maybe we could hang here for a few. We can catch our breath, and then try to find someplace to hide out for the night." I tried to smile, but it was a wasted effort since neither of the women glanced my way.

"I want my bed and my safe basement," Toby whimpered.

"I know, baby," Darya soothed.

I shrugged, unsure of what else I could say to these women. So, I turned and sought Michael. I walked over and plopped down beside him, my hands instantly drifting into Chewie's fur. Part of it might've just been habit, but I am also sure a good part had to deal with just getting that dose of comfort from her that I always gained from the simple act of petting her.

"How you doing, Michael?" I asked casually.

"Hungry," he whispered in response.

It struck me that we hadn't eaten since the previous evening. Everybody carried a canteen—even the two children. While adults might be able push themselves and stretch their water out, we had filled the boys' canteens and made it clear they were to tell us if they were empty. I'd simply forgotten food.

"I think I have a few things in my pack," I offered.

I looked inside and saw a few cans of soup that didn't

need water. That had been the staple of our camp diet. It was easy to fix and was probably the most well-rounded of our quick meals. Wanting to at least give him a variety, I asked, "What did you have last night?"

"Nothing." The answer was not spoken with any emotion. Michael was merely relating a fact.

"You didn't eat last night?" I said, just a little shocked. "How come?"

"Nobody offered to give me anything."

I felt my heart sink. The thought never occurred to me that not only would he not say anything if we were eating and nobody had given him a bowl; but it also hit me even harder that nobody had made that offer...including me.

I grabbed a can of basil and tomato soup. "I wish I could warm it up for you," I apologized as I opened the can and handed it to him.

I went into my bag to fish out a spoon, but by the time I found it and offered it, he was drinking it straight from the can. I took the time to pour some water into a bowl for Chewie and then scooped out a handful of dog food. She gobbled it down in a hurry and then looked up at me expectantly.

I briefly wondered if a day would come when I didn't

feel like an absolute dick. I looked into my bag and gauged how much kibble I had managed to take. I loved my big girl, but I was suddenly wishing she was more like a Chihuahua or some other tiny dog that didn't eat five or six cups per day. What I was carrying would not last more than three days, and that was if I only gave her enough to keep her strength up.

I knew she needed more. Looking around, I was certain that we all did. While we weren't yet starving, we were certainly eating much less than we needed to keep our bodies going at the pace we had been setting. All the more reason to find a spot we could secure and hide out for a while.

The next time I looked at Michael, the soup was gone and he was swiping his finger on the inside of the can to get every last drop. After he sipped some of his water, I got to my feet.

"Okay, everybody," I said, my voice naturally in a whisper considering everything going on. Between not wanting to be found by Don Evans or draw any of the undead, every sound seemed at least twice as loud as it probably was. "There is a condo complex just on the other side of these woods. If we can get into an upper floor of one and block the windows to keep any light from giving us away, I think we can take a couple of days to figure out a game plan."

"Game plan?" Darya squeaked. "There isn't a game plan. We get away, we hide, and as soon as we can, we get the hell out of this city. Maybe head to the mountains or even some island."

That last part sounded promising. If we could secure an island, we would be golden. The problem being the serious lack of such land features in these parts. A thought came to me and I snapped my fingers and pointed at her so sharply that it made her jump.

"An island...like Sauvie Island!" I almost shouted...at least it felt that way after working so hard to keep quiet. "Maybe not today or tomorrow...but that is not a bad idea."

Darya looked around at everybody else before returning her open-mouthed stare in my direction. "Do you have any idea how far away that place is from here?"

"Yep. But if we can find a vehicle—" I started.

"And have every single zombie for miles chasing us?" Darya shot back. "I've tried that little trick. We lost five people because somebody thought that it would be a good idea to try and raid a grocery store in a truck."

"And let me guess…" It was Marshawn who came to my aid. "You also left the engine running while you were inside?"

"We didn't want to tempt fate and have it not start when we came out." Darya spun to Marshawn, her tone as defensive as her posture.

"I've hooked up with a bunch of idiots," Alex muttered.

"Nobody asked you to come along," Tracy jumped in, stepping up beside Darya.

"Enough, for crying out loud!" I snapped. "Listen, everybody is hungry and tired and scared. We are all snapping at each other and acting like a bunch of assholes."

That made Toby gasp and cover his mouth, but I swear I heard Michael chuckle and mimic the word 'asshole' in what I guess was his impersonation of me.

"We are going to need each and every one of us to start thinking straight and acting like we are all on the same side." I made sure not to let my gaze linger on anybody too long lest they think I might be singling them out.

"Then you have to understand that you aren't out here

by yourself anymore, Evan," Tracy said calmly, obviously trying to make her point without sounding pushy. It was a start.

"And as nice as this little come-to-Jesus moment must be for all of you, the reality is that there is nothing resembling the old ways anymore." Alex stepped forward now and, like Tracy, she was doing her best not to sound confrontational. "The kids are going to have to grow up in a hurry if they are going to have any chance at survival. It isn't pretty, but it is the way of the world now."

"I can help carry them," Rickey offered. "I know they are tired little soldiers, and they barely weigh a thing, so I can help that way."

"Me too," Marshawn offered.

"Another thing." I had to bring this up, there was no way I couldn't. "Did anybody realize Michael hasn't eaten since we found him?"

"You mean he found us," Darya sniffed.

"Whatever. The fact remains that he is going to require a degree of attention that might make things even more difficult. Nobody thought to offer him anything when we ate last night...including myself." I made sure to add that last bit to be sure they knew I shared in the culpability.

"Why didn't you guys feed him?" Alex asked. Again, she wasn't challenging, she sounded more curious than anything else.

"We think he might be *autistic*," I answered, reflexively whispering that last word like folks used to do when they spoke about some serious illness that they were probably more ill-equipped to deal with than the person they were talking about. "I think people just tend to forget he's here because he doesn't make any fuss."

"You know that's not really an acceptable answer," she muttered. Now it was obvious she was trying to keep her comments in check.

"It's the only one I have right now," I replied. "I'm brand new to this whole dealing with kids thing."

I realized the irony of my statement as it fell out of my mouth. I'd just been certified as a school teacher. Wasn't dealing with kids part of my job description? I could dwell on that later, right now, we had much bigger problems.

"Okay, the way I see it, we need to find a place to hide that is going to allow us some safety for at least the foreseeable future," I started.

"Good luck with that," Darya sniffed. "We thought we had someplace like that until you and your people showed up."

"Can we do this later?" I snapped. "If we are going to pick each other apart every chance we get, then maybe we should all just go our own ways."

"Perhaps you and your kid think you could do better on your own?" Marshawn stepped up beside me. "Nobody's making you stay with us. You've been bitchin' up one side and down the other almost since you fell in with our group."

Darya opened her mouth and then shut it with an audible click. To her credit I didn't see any tears welling up. But the red flush to her cheeks told me that she was probably pretty pissed off. Honestly, I didn't have the energy to care. I was done with trying to make everybody happy. If I was, in fact, the leader of this little band, then it was time that I started acting like a leader and take control of things.

"Here is the deal," I said after it was clear that Darya wasn't going to keep pressing her luck. "There is a nice condo complex just beyond these woods." I saw Alex start to open her mouth, but I kept going. "Beyond that, there is a gated community. I'm not sure if it is still occupied. But that seems like the next best place to check. If we can find a defensible location, we can hold up there. If even only for a couple of weeks until we can make better plans that can perhaps be more permanent."

"Do you think such a place exists?" Alex asked quietly. "I saw that massive pack of zoms that were heading toward the overpass. I don't know what made them change direction, but I was in the process of getting ready to run right before they just went and turned away."

"That was us," Marshawn said.

"What do you mean?" Alex turned to face the man. "You made them change course? Seems a bit far-fetched."

"Actually," Rickey moved up beside Marshawn, "a few of our guys jacked a police car and led them away using noise. Lost one of our own on that run."

Now wasn't the time to discuss what Neil may or may not have done. "Look, we can tell you all about it later." I gave an apologetic nod to Darya. "But right now, we need to get on the move."

I slung my pack over my shoulder and reached down to get Chewie's leash, but Michael already held it. It would only be a concern if she tried to charge after something, but something in my gut told me that wouldn't be a problem.

We started through the woods and emerged on the edge of the condo complex just as I remembered. The place looked like it was totally empty. Where we popped out, I didn't see a single zombie. At least not one that was moving. There were quite a few corpses rotting on the pavement of the driveway as well as around a few of the covered parking spaces. A couple of the units had burned down, and I could see what I thought might be a basketball court. It was fenced, and somebody had tried to make a stand there. A few zombies were impaled on some sort of crude barricade made from what looked like sharpened table legs or something of that nature.

"Somebody didn't think things through," Alex quipped.

Looking at the scene, I understood her assessment. While it was true that the courts were completely fenced, and somebody had put up some tarps as cover, it was still much too exposed. Now, there were a few of the undead inside that had been trapped; likely survivors that learned the hard way of their folly.

Then we saw them.

On the far side of the courts was an open park area. There was a big, sandy rectangle-shaped playground complete with a climbing structure and a swing-set.

If not for what I knew I was seeing, it could've been an absolutely ordinary scene. One child sat on a swing, gently swaying forward and back. A few were just standing around the play structure as if they were waiting for somebody to show them how to climb up on it.

"No fucking way," Alex breathed as she edged past me.

They had not noticed us yet, and that allowed me to get in a quick count. Nine. Nine children between the ages of perhaps three and no older than twelve. I had no idea why, but I was now very certain this was important. There was something very different about these zombies. Despite what Alex had done earlier, as well as what she'd said about them simply being the undead, the children were not like a regular zombie.

I had to stifle a chuckle at that thought and the absurdity of it. Was there anything "regular" about *any* zombie? Absolutely not.

I stepped up beside Alex and pointed out one of the children in particular. She was a little girl and might be the oldest of the bunch. She had red hair that still managed to stay in the braids on either side of her head. She was wearing a tattered pair of jeans and a tee shirt with a face on it.

I didn't have to look to know that it was that over-processed pop star, Shari. It had seemed in those last few days before it turned into "all zombies all the time" television, that you could not turn around without seeing her face on the screen. Something about a scandal involving her little sister and her manager was all the rage. I think that the manager had fled the country or something considering that he was like forty and the little sister was perhaps fifteen.

The red-haired girl was walking in a circle around the play structure. Every so often, she would stop and look around as if she had some sort of realization as to where she was. It was creepy, but what added to the eerie scene were the dozen or so cats slinking around her ankles. Adding to my confusion was that she did not seem to mind. She made no attempt to grab one.

I was puzzling over that when a dark shadow emerged from the nearby shrubs. After a moment, the shadow separated from the thick bushes that had once acted as a barrier between the playground and the driveway and parking area for this part of the complex.

A Golden Retriever.

There was a moment when I thought nothing would happen. The dog looked like it had been living in filth. It instantly dropped to its belly and even from across the distance that separated us, I could hear when it let loose with a pitiful whine. The cats reacted first, every one of them darting away and vanishing without a trace.

The dog didn't seem to notice that, and instead started to do that belly crawl dogs sometimes do. I could see its tail swishing in the grass every so often as it obviously hoped to find some form of human interaction. After all, it was a Golden Retriever. In my experience, they are almost glued to their people and bathe in the lavishing of affection they get.

The girl with the red braids noticed it almost as soon as the cats bolted. She turned to it and cocked her head first one way, then the other. She seemed to be regarding it with curiosity. As it drew nearer to her, it began to make little yipping noises mixed in with its whimpering.

Alex stepped past me, a machete in each hand. I reached for her and she jerked away.

By now, the Golden had crawled to the feet of the little girl. It rolled over onto its back, another pitiful whine escaping it as it seemed to writhe on the ground at the zombie girl's feet in hopes for some form of human contact.

The problem? That wasn't a human it was trying to entice to give it some form of affection.

Things seemed to slow down as the zombie girl suddenly dropped to its knees. The Golden actually rolled into her. I realized that I'd stepped away from the group as well. While I hadn't ventured as far out into the open as Alex, I was a good several feet away from the rest of the group that had stayed put this entire time.

The zombie girl's head dropped, and I knew instantly what she was going to do. I was too far away to do anything, but that was also when I noticed that the other zombie children gathered around this playground had obviously spotted us.

There was a yelp and a howl that cut deep into my heart as the little girl bent all the way over, her face burying itself in the exposed belly of the Golden. That yelp was enough to send Alex charging.

"Get away, you evil bitch!" she yelled.

The little red-haired girl's head popped up and turned almost in slow motion to confront her oncoming attacker. A fresh smear of red seemed even brighter as the sun hit her face and almost seemed to focus on her. The dog had struggled away and had gotten to its feet. Tail tucked between its legs, it darted into some nearby shrubs, its pained yelps fading, but still seeming to echo in my head.

I broke into a run as the children all changed like a switch was flipped. Alex reached the girl first and swung one arm, her machete taking the top third of the girl's head off in an attack that was as brutal as it was anti-climactic.

By now, all of the other children had turned and began advancing.

5

No Right Answers

If it was only the few we'd first seen when that nightmare began, I doubt things would've gone so bad. I know all of us would've walked away from it alive. I wouldn't be listening to the sobbing. And I wouldn't have to sit here and wait for one of our very finite numbers to close their eyes one last time so that I can end their life before they awaken to join the legions of the walking dead that are outside.

We're trapped. And I have to shoulder the blame. If I am the leader of this group, then I have to accept that it is my responsibility.

I'm still trying to let it all play out in my head and catalog my mistakes. If we survive this, I don't want to make them again.

I won't.

***

I veered toward the swing set and cut off three of the little horrors that were so focused on Alex that they didn't turn to face me until I buried my own machete in the top of the first one's head. I didn't even notice if it was a boy or girl.

I spun and kicked out at the closest of the two remaining children that were near to me. That gave me enough space to stick the other child in her eye socket. By then, the one that I'd kicked was coming for me once more.

A part of my brain screamed that there was something very different about the children despite what was happening at the moment. I ended the third of the swing set trio and spun just in time to see at least ten more undead children emerge from the bushes.

I froze. I knew that Alex had ended the red-haired girl. I'd seen it with my own eyes, yet there she stood. She had been almost decapitated.

"Don't just stand there," Rickey snarled as he pushed past me and brought his own weapon to bear.

I hadn't seen it until now, but he had what looked like one of those old-fashioned executioner's or headsman's axes. I'd seen something over his shoulder that had some sort of leather cover on it but had never thought to ask what it might be. Anybody else trying to wield such a weapon would probably have struggled with its apparent size. And judging by the sound it made as it cleaved through the air and then buried itself in the first zombie child unfortunate enough to come into range, this was not just a decorative item.

His swing came at an angle, but chopped into the head of the little boy that had foolishly stepped towards the big man. It cleaved through the head and split the body all the way to the hip in a horrific explosion of gore. With amazing agility, he brought the weapon around, spinning it by its long handle and driving the spiked end of the axe head into the side of the head of the next child.

Three children came at him from the side, and I was certain that he would go down, but he side-stepped and then brought the weapon up and across his chest. Using the haft as a barrier between himself and the oncoming little zombies, he caught all three across the chest, and with one massive shove, sent them tumbling onto their backs.

119

He planted his weapon into the ground and drew a knife, quickly dispatching his would-be attackers.

I'd watched too long and now had two of them within striking distance. The closest was a little girl, maybe four years old. I caught her by one of her outstretched arms and slung her past me, then stuck the second one. My machete went too deep and the tip of it ended up bursting from the back of the little boy's head I'd just ended. I tried to jerk the weapon free, but it caught on bone and would require more effort than I had time for at the moment.

I yanked a large knife free and spun to catch the girl who had, unfortunately, not fallen over. I grabbed her by the hair, my skin pebbling as she opened her mouth and let loose with that baby cry sound before snapping her teeth together in the empty space where my hand had been just a second ago. I shoved the knife into her milky, tracer-riddled eye and just as fast tossed her aside.

I took a step back and felt something solid collide with my shoulder. I spun to discover Alex with her hands both cocked back, each holding a blade that dripped with dark blood and gore. She had a crazed look on her face, and blood trickled down one cheek. It was dark enough that I knew it wasn't hers, but my eyes couldn't help but track the rivulet as it reached her jawline. The drop grew fatter and eventually lost its war with gravity, landing on the collar of the heavy jacket she wore.

"I told you," she hissed. "They aren't children...not anymore."

With that, she moved to my left and started for another group of zombie children that emerged from the bushes...this group had several adult versions on their heels.

A bark from behind me made me spin around. Chewie had obviously jerked free from Michael, or the boy had simply let go of her leash. Whatever the case, she had bounded out from the woods and came charging toward me. People often thought that her size and easy, swaggering gait meant she was a slow dog. That was not the case, and as she came on the run, I couldn't help but be impressed.

A low moan to my right made me spin back to the situation at hand. What I saw made my heart jump to my throat. Coming around the corner of a nearby unit were another thirty or more of the walking dead. And this group were all of the adult variety. That put them between us and the direction we wanted to go.

I thought things were as bad as they could get...until the single report of a pistol echoed in this canyon of abandoned condos. A scream came on the heels of it and I had to back up to get a look over my shoulder. Chewie wasn't the only one charging out of the woods. The rest of our small band was coming like bats out of hell. I could only guess as to why, but unfortunately I didn't have the time to wait and find out.

I turned to face the leading edge of adult zombies coming for us. The first one looked like he'd been working at a service station. He had grimy coveralls that were stained with oil (I hope) and a face that sagged with age and undeath in a very ugly combination. His jowls seemed to sway like a Bassett Hound's. What was worse was the freshness of the blood that stained his lips. When he opened his mouth and moaned, I could see that his teeth were also coated in a crimson sheen.

I ended his existence as I backed away. As I did, I could see that somehow we'd gotten ourselves surrounded. Zombies were now spewing forth from the trees we'd just come from—which explained why the others had come charging out—and more were coming from between another pair of long, rectangular buildings that might be garage complexes.

Even worse, we were spread out now. Alex had drifted away in her own fight. Marshawn was over by the basketball court holding off a batch while Rickey was in the bed of a pickup truck, his executioner's axe acting like a scythe as it cut into the zombies gathered around him. Darya had her son Toby at her side as she turned first one direction then the other, waving the pistol she held like it might scare away her would-be attackers. She was babbling something through the sobs that were consuming her as several of the zombie children closed in, creating a noose-like circle of undeath. Tracy had made it on top of a Dumpster and was methodically driving her blade down into the tops of the heads of the zombies that could only come at her from the front since the Dumpster was in a walled-off garbage area that had eight-foot-high concrete walls on three of the four sides.

I had my own problems with the ten or so adult zombies that had managed to back me into a covered parking area. A row of hedges at my back wouldn't be impossible to dive through, but they were thick enough that it would not be an easy escape route. I could hear Chewie barking off to my right, but it was unlike any sound I'd ever heard from her before. My eyes darted that way out of reflex.

If I wasn't careful, I felt like I would eventually vomit my heart up. It was as if I could feel it climbing ever higher in my throat with each new terror I beheld. My beloved Newfie had backed onto a porch of one of the ground-floor units. Maybe she'd seen it as a cave or den. I have no idea, but she was now trapped by a wall of several child and adult zombies. It was also clear that she was going to die if I didn't help. She was darting back and forth, her ears and tail down, and even from here, I could see the whites of her eyes

I took a step towards her just as a scream of terror snapped my head in the other direction. It took me a second to realize what I was seeing, and to be honest, I thought it was just a new and nasty trick of the undead children. After a second, it was clear that what I was seeing was an actual living child.

As soon as her eyes found mine, she reached in my direction and screamed for help. She had come out of one of the units and stood just outside of the sliding glass door. Three adult zombies were closing in, but that was only part of the problem. If it would've been just those three, she could've ducked back inside and maybe shut the door until somebody could get to her. Unfortunately, I could see the stirring behind her, and while they were only dark, shadowy figures at the moment, I had a good idea what waited for her inside that condo.

I took a step towards the child...again, it was simply a reflex action. The whining bark of Chewie froze me in my tracks. The child and my dog were in almost perfectly opposite directions from each other. In the blink of an eye, I could see that I was the only one who could respond to either at the moment.

"Nooo," I moaned, realizing that there was no way possible I could get to both.

"I'm sorry, I'm sorry, I'm sorry," I cried as I took off at a sprint. I reached the zombies and dropped the first one before the scream rent the air and cut through every shout and moan with its intensity.

Chewie darted through the opening I'd created when I'd killed the first zombie. Just as fast, she spun around and sank her teeth into the back of the leg of one of the zombies as I made short work of another. The entire time, the screams continued. Hearing that little girl's screams for her mommy...shrieking "No, no, no!" over and over drove spikes of guilt pain into my ears until a sickening gurgle

125

ended them.

I turned to see a cluster of the undead on their knees around the child I'd just sentenced to a horrific and painful death. There was no comfort to be found in that I'd saved my Chewie. The reality was that I'd just made a choice that ensured the death of a child. Would I have made the same choice if it had been Michael? Would it be different if I'd been a parent?

I didn't want to spend any more time in that dark place. If I did, I would end up throwing myself on the ground and letting the zombies have me next. Instead, I rushed over. I wanted to at least keep the child from joining the ranks of the undead...as one of the zombie children.

That thought spurred me forward. As I neared, I was greeted by yet more horror to stoke my guilt. One of the child's legs was kicking out still. Weakly, sure, but those weren't muscle spasms I was seeing. That was confirmed when I saw a tiny hand swat feebly at the side of the head of one of the kneeling undead.

At last, I reached the cluster of zombies. All of them had their back to me, and it was easy to grab the first one and jerk it back by the hair as I plunged my blade into the side of its head. Maybe it was an unconscious choice, but I'd grabbed one of the zombies at the girl's feet.

I would never be ready to look that child in the eyes. Maybe I was hoping she would expire before that happened. Whatever the reason, I grabbed the next one and ended it as well.

I did this in a state of shocked autopilot. But at last, I had no other choices. The two remaining zombies both turned; whether it was because of a newer, fresher potential food source, or a simple case of realizing they were being attacked, I didn't know, and I didn't care.

I attacked the first one swiftly and ended it as it started to get to its feet. And that was when I got a really good look at the frail body sprawled on the ground.

She hadn't even been five if I had to guess. Her blond hair was matted and filthy, and now it was fouled with blood from the expanding pool she lay in. Her torso was splayed open and a few splintered ribs jutted from the gore. How she had not yet simply died was beyond me. Maybe the adrenaline of fear kept her from the relief she would now only find in final death.

I managed to avoid her face as I ended the last of her attackers, but now I had no place else for my eyes to go.

Her face was a rictus of pain and contorted in a way that no child should ever express. Her eyes were squeezed shut so tight that her forehead had creases and her lips pressed so tight they'd gone white. Blood had splattered her face, but tears had carved their own tracks, expanding the crimson with rivulets of pink in a hellish mask.

I knelt, switching the grip I had on my blade so I could just very quickly end her existence with one swift plunge. As I brought my arm up in preparation to strike...her eyes fluttered.

I was already fighting the urge to be sick as I faced the consequences of my choices. When those eyes fluttered, I had just a fraction of a second to hope to any deity that might exist that they would be filmed and tracer ridden. Instead, they were bloodshot in black, but there was no film...only more tears that leaked from the corners. She opened her mouth, but only blood came out in a misting spray.

There was no way she should still live. Her body had been savaged. I was already going to live with my guilt for an eternity, but the powers-that-be obviously decided that wasn't good enough. A sickening gurgle came from the little girl, and I realized that I'd been just standing over her doing nothing but feeling sorry for myself while she suffered.

"I'm sorry," I breathed as my arm drew back in preparation to come down with one swift swing and end her suffering.

And that would be the next horror to add itself to the agonizingly frightening slide show that played every single time I shut my eyes these days. Despite her pain, despite all that she'd endured, despite how close to the brink of death (and then undeath) she teetered, she still had enough presence remaining to be afraid of that blade as it came down.

The machete struck with finality, the tip of the blade making a 'chink' sound as it struck the concrete pad of the porch that would serve as this child's final resting place. By now, the figure inside the condo had emerged. It was a woman, and I didn't need to look closely to know that she was the dead girl's mother.

I was about to step over the body at my feet when another scream sounded. This was close. Chewie had not left my side since I'd rescued her, and she actually ducked behind my legs when I turned to face whatever fresh hell awaited. Of course, that now put her between me and the undead mother moaning and shuffling toward me from the open sliding glass door, but I didn't have time to give that any thought.

Darya was in a tug-of-war with a pair of undead children. The rope was the outstretched arms of her son, Toby. The little boy was thrashing and jerking, trying to get free of the zombie children, but he was only making it more difficult for his mother to keep her grip.

I took off at a sprint and felt Chewie loping at my heels. I could feel the elation rising in my chest as I realized that I would make it in time to help. I leapt over a few of the scattered bodies on the ground and slammed into the pair of zombie children, sending them flying backwards.

I heard rather than saw Toby and his mom crash to the ground behind me. I rolled over and came to my feet, spinning around to see that I hadn't been completely successful. There were still more of the undead moving in, and now, both Darya and Toby were on the ground, basically helpless since the gun Darya had been holding had gone spinning away someplace.

One of the adult versions fell on Toby and I didn't need to see the jet of blood that came; his scream said it all.

For the second time in moments, a child was shrieking for his mommy. I sprinted, but not for the child. Darya was still able to be saved since the two zombies coming for her hadn't managed to get their hands on her yet as she scooted back and kicked out with her feet.

A blur of black sped past me and Chewie reached her first, leaping and catching the first zombie with the full force of her hundred and twenty-plus pounds. The child zombie never stood a chance and landed on its back so hard that its head slammed into the blacktop with an ugly crack.

I reached the second one and drove my blade into its open mouth, angling up and punching through the roof of its mouth. Unfortunately, it fell, taking my knife with it, but I still had another machete and came around to finish the one Chewie had knocked over. It had enough time to make a hissing sound before I chopped down and buried my machete into the forehead of the child monster. I spun and plunged the point of my weapon's sturdy blade into the back of the head of the zombie mauling Toby. I kicked it away as Darya shoved past me and knelt over the boy.

I didn't need to see more than the glimpse I'd gotten. The little boy had a chunk torn from his shoulder, and blood was gushing from the wound. I doubted he would live long enough for his eyes to show the symptoms. His screams were not letting up, and he was thrashing against his mother who kept trying to soothe and comfort him to no avail.

Chewie barked once and took off again. I turned to see where she was dashing to and caught sight of Michael standing at the edge of the playground all by himself. His expression gave no hint that he was even remotely aware of what was happening around him.

"Evan!" Alex screamed from behind me.

I turned to see another dozen of the undead stumble through the bushes and into the playground that had quickly turned into a killing field. I could hear moans from someplace off to my right and left. That meant we were now some sort of bullseye for every zombie in who knows how much of a radius.

What I knew for sure was that we could not keep this up. When I found Rickey and Marshawn, they were back-to-back and fighting off several of the child and adult versions. Even in that quick glance, I noticed that Rickey was focused on the adult versions and seemed to skim right past the child zombies. He'd also lost his headsman's axe someplace and was now wielding a very plain looking machete.

I looked around, but couldn't see anyplace close that we could run to with the exception of one. The building where the little girl had emerged.

"Everybody follow me!" I shouted.

I didn't wait to see if anybody followed, I sprinted for Michael. By the time I reached him, he already had Chewie's leash and appeared to be waiting for me.

"C'mon, Michael," I said, reaching down for his hand to lead him to what I hoped would be someplace safe for a while.

I started for the scene of carnage waiting on the back patio of the condo where the little girl I'd basically allowed to be brutally killed had emerged. The dead bodies everywhere did not begin to paint the picture of the terrible things that had just occurred.

"You saved Chewie," Michael said as we rushed past the little girl's body. "I'm sorry."

I didn't know what exactly he was apologizing for, but I could hear the choked sound of a near sob in his voice. Was it possible that he understood what had happened here? Also, where had he been while this took place? My one solace was that this would be my own personal guilt. How would the others react if they'd seen what I'd done?

I stepped into what had once been the dining room. What had probably been a pretty fancy dining room table was broken into several pieces. It looked like somebody had flipped it over and busted off the legs.

The smell hit me at the same time the middle-aged man with his guts hanging from the savage rip in his once protruding belly came around the corner of the entrance to this area from what looked to be the living room. His low moan was so deep that it felt like my teeth vibrated. I pulled free from Michael and stepped in to cleave the man's head, but I hadn't taken my surroundings into account.

My machete slammed into an overhead lighting fixture that was supposed to look like a bunch of brass candle holders. The crash was tremendous, and also enough to elicit even more moans from what I had to assume were the rest of the family lurking someplace inside the condo.

Something collided with my back and I found myself sprawling into the open kitchen to my right. Even worse was discovering what looked like a two-year-old staring at me from where he sat in the corner, his milky, tracer-riddled eyes gazing into my own as his mouth opened and a dark stream of drool dribbled down his chin. He made no move toward me as I lay on my stomach, staring him in those milky, horrible eyes.

"Evan?" Marshawn's voice said from close by, letting me have a good idea who'd just slammed into me.

"Umm…yeah," I said, my voice barely a whisper.

"What are you d—" he started to ask, but his words cut off suddenly. No doubt he was able to see what I was seeing.

I heard a moan, and then a heavy, wet thud as somebody obviously finished off the zombie that had been coming into the dining room. Marshawn moved past me and stuck his knife in the top of the little child's head. I swore that, in the seconds before it was put down, it glanced up at the knife and started to moan or make some sort of zombie noise. But a split second before that, I was almost positive that I saw…fear? Surprise?

The sound of the sliding glass door came right on the heels of what sounded like Darya and Toby crowding into the dining room. I got up and did a quick head count. Six plus Chewie meant that everybody was present and accounted for.

I got up and was almost to my feet when Darya launched herself at me. "This is all your fault!" she screamed as she came at me with hands like claws.

I barely staggered back enough to avoid her attack. She tripped over her feet and some of the remnants of the table still scattered on the floor. She hit hard and I heard her make a pained sound that cut off her ranting...at least for the moment.

"Whoa!" Rickey barked, catching her by the collar as she scrambled to her hands and knees and tried to come at me again.

"My son..." her voice died out, replaced by hitching sobs. I swear I could feel her grief pouring from her in waves of heat that plunged flaming daggers of guilt into my heart.

I turned to the heap on the floor and could see a pool of blood already spreading under him and darkening the hardwood floor. Chewie was standing over the small figure, sniffing around his head.

"Get that animal away from my Toby." Darya shoved past everybody and shooed my big Newfie away.

Michael hurried to the big dog and whispered something in her ear as he led her away. I wanted to tell Darya that Chewie wouldn't hurt her son, but this wasn't the time to be confrontational.

"He's going to turn," a voice breathed in my ear. I glanced over to see Alex standing beside me, her expression almost completely blank.

"You all stay away from him," Darya spat. She locked eyes with each of us one at a time, almost daring any of us to challenge her.

"Look at his eyes." Alex stepped forward, apparently undaunted by the angry mom who now hunched over her son, his head in her arms as she brushed his hair from his face.

"Toby is gonna be one of the monster people, huh?" Michael said, his voice seeming uncommonly loud in that moment of silence.

"All of you stay away!" Darya repeated.

She scooted back against a wall and hauled her son with her. She pulled him around so that he was in her lap and she could look down at his face.

Now that I could see him better, I noticed the unnatural paleness of his skin. His eyes were closed, squeezed tight against the pain. But as I watched, I saw that tightness start to lessen. His breathing got shallow and rapid. I wasn't the only one who noticed. Marshawn had drawn the knife he'd just sheathed, and Rickey had backed up a few steps.

Even Michael had turned his head slightly and looked to be watching the other little boy out of the corner of his eye and Chewie was standing between Michael and Toby like a furry, black wall. The only person who did not seem to notice was Darya.

"Sweetie," Tracy whispered, stepping toward the mother and child with her hands out and open in a placating gesture, "I think you need to let me help you."

"You stay back, too!" Darya spat.

I was suddenly very thankful that she'd dropped her gun. I had no doubt she would be waving it around at us if not just opening fire; namely at me.

There was a heartbeat or two where we all just stood there, nobody seeming to know what to do. Darya continued to hold and rock her son. And then it started.

First it was one leg beginning to twitch. That twitch spread to both legs and then Toby's entire body began to convulse with violent spasms.

"Baby...no...sweetie...Toby, honey..." Darya started

sobbing as she sought to give comfort to her child.

There was nothing she could do, but none of us could tell her that as her son's spasms continued for what felt like an eternity. Then, he arched up, his back bowing in an impossible curve. I felt like I should hear bones popping. But just as fast as it began, it ended and he collapsed in a heap with a rattling, wheezing exhale that sounded exactly what you would think a death rattle should sound like.

Part of me wanted to jerk that child's body from his mother's arms and put a spike in his head. Only...I was frozen. Not from fear. I think it was more sorrow than anything else. I was still trying to decide what to do when I saw the little boy's eyelids flutter and then open.

"Evan?" Alex hissed.

"What?" I shot back, perhaps a bit angrier than I meant to sound as all the stress and tension building in me came out in that one word.

"Kill it."

Two simple words.

I turned to her. She wasn't looking at me. Alex had her eyes locked on the mother and son. I could see the knot undulating in her cheek from where she was clenching her teeth so tight.

Darya's sobs were suddenly muffled, and I looked back to see that she'd buried her face in her son's chest. Her shoulders shook as she cried, but that wasn't where my eyes locked. It was a single twitch. Just a single finger.

I took a step forward, my gaze locked on the one hand when I saw a second flexing, this time it was all the fingers. They flexed and then closed into a tiny fist. Darya didn't seem to notice as she continued to cry.

"Darya," I whispered. "You need to come here."

She didn't respond at all. But Toby did. His legs began to move almost like he was trying to ride a bicycle, but very jerky and uncoordinated.

"This isn't going to happen," I heard somebody say from behind me.

I felt a hand ease me aside, and Tracy moved to Darya, grabbing her under one arm. The grieving mother lifted her head and stared up at the woman trying to get her to move, but it was immediately clear that she wasn't seeing anything. Her eyes had that distant, unfocused look to them.

I saw that little hand open and the arm start to raise. That was also when I was finally able to see Toby's face. It was pale, the skin slack. His cheeks that had still held a trace of baby fat had sagged to become jowls. His lips were twitching a bit and his mouth opened just enough so that I could see his teeth and a sickening looking gray tongue that swiped back and forth.

"Toby?" Darya looked down and saw her son moving in her arms. "Baby, it's mama."

Toby's eyes opened. The pus-colored film was an ugly yellowish color and the black tracers were stark in contrast. There was no doubt as to the condition of the boy. Yet, despite the obvious condition of the child, his mother held him in her arms. When he opened his mouth and let loose with a deep moan, that was enough to propel me into action. I stepped forward; my intention was to grab the woman and jerk her away from the creature that was no longer her son.

"Don't touch me," Darya hissed, leaning back away from me.

I ignored her, my eyes watching as Toby's gaze shifted to me. He opened his mouth again and moaned even louder.

In my mind's eye, I saw how this would play out. It was almost too cliché. The grieving mother refusing to accept the horrible reality of her child's fate. The child would sink his teeth into her and then we would have to kill them both.

Tracy obviously saw the same thing that I did and lunged to grab Darya away from the zombie child. Darya moved faster. She had a blade in her hand in the blink of an eye and drove it into Toby's eye socket before the child could turn back to her.

"This is your fault." Darya pulled the weapon free, wiping the blade on the leg of her jeans and slipping the knife back into its sheath.

"How do you figure?" I shot back.

Personally, I was carrying an awful lot of blame already. Most of it was well-deserved. What I wasn't going to do was willingly shoulder more that didn't belong to me.

"You and your people came barging into our little secure area. You brought zombies on your heels and ruined everything we'd set up." She hugged her dead child close. "My baby had a nice, safe room in the basement of our house. We had a good thing going."

"Umm...yeah, that's bullshit," I said with a tired sigh. "You and your people were trying to hold out in the middle of what had been a densely populated neighborhood full of zombies. We were being chased by living raiders. You attacked us first. Maybe if you and your people would've just stayed low and let us pass, we wouldn't even know you were there. But noooo, your people lobbed a freaking Molotov at us. And just an added bit of information for you to swallow... if you'd let us pass, chances are you would've met up with the people we were running from, and let me tell ya, you wouldn't have liked that. I can assure you that your fate ends up much darker."

Darya opened her mouth to say something, but I have no idea what it was because there was a loud crash behind me. I spun to see Rickey face down on the floor. That was also when I saw the rip on the back of left leg of his pants. There was a dark stain, and the material had started to become glued to his skin as the blood dried.

I hurried to him and rolled him onto his back. He was breathing heavy in short bursts. I was about to pry his eyelids open when he opened them himself very suddenly and made a wet gasping sound.

I skittered back solely out of the perfect combination of fear and surprise. His eyes told me everything I needed to know. The dark tracers were just now starting to spread from the corners. If you stared—which is exactly what I was doing at that moment—you could see them spread oh-so-slowly.

"Dammit," I breathed.

"So…looks like I'm not one of the lucky ones," the big man wheezed with a half-hearted laugh that ended in a fit of coughing.

I didn't say anything, but I didn't see the need to. He knew what was up. His eyes flicked down to one of the knives I wore on my hip. He looked back up at me and pressed his lips tight. I wasn't sure he was going to speak until he actually did.

"Soon as I give it up, you'll put me down, right?" His eyes returned to my blade.

"Sure." What else could I say?

We went through the house to make sure there were no nasty surprises. The last thing we needed to do was get careless. Once we were sure, we hoisted the heavier furniture to the sliding glass door, stacked it, and did our best to make sure it would hold up.

The front door was locked, and I managed to wedge a coffee table and love seat in the entry hall to ensure nothing came through that front door. Once that was done, we made Rickey comfortable in the upstairs master bedroom.

The people who lived here drank some expensive, top-shelf booze. We brought him up a bottle of tequila that I'd never heard of before, but Marshawn assured me that it was pretty expensive stuff.

He nursed the bottle for about an hour and I sat beside the bed the entire time. As he drank himself into oblivion, we managed to have a decent conversation. He told me that I had to stop taking the blame for everything that goes wrong. I learned that he played bass in some local metal band, and that he was married.

Like me, he saw his wife turn, but things had progressed to the point where he knew what was happening, and so he actually waded into a small group of zombies to put her down. He said that part of him had hoped he'd be bitten then, that way he wouldn't have to go on without her.

He said he changed his mind when he reached her and grabbed her. At that moment, he hadn't been certain if he was going to put her down, or let her take him. He said he made up his mind when he looked into her eyes.

"She wasn't there...at all. Whatever that thing was that looked a little like my baby...it wasn't her. It was just some...*thing*. And that's what all of them are..." His voice trailed off, and I thought he was done, but then he continued. "Except for the kids, man. Something's seriously wrong with them. They don't act like regular…monsters." I had noticed that he'd stayed away from using the word zombie this entire time. "They look at you like they are trying to figure you out. They do stuff that ain't normal for one of them things."

I knew what he meant. I couldn't help but look at the child versions of the zombies as something different. I just wasn't the guy who was going to figure it out. "They hunt you, man." Rickey's voice was barely a whisper. "I don't care what that girl was sayin' about them just being one of the monsters, and how they weren't no different. Don't you believe that, brother."

I guess I felt some sense of relief that I wasn't the only person seeing that there was something about the child versions of the walking dead.

"And you gotta give yourself a break, man." Rickey patted my arm. "I don't know how you will keep the group together, but you gotta try. Nobody was ready for this. Stop beating yourself up if something doesn't go exactly as planned. There ain't no right answers. And…"

Once more, his voice just faded out. I looked over to

see if maybe he'd finally passed, but he was looking up at the ceiling, and there were tears in his eyes that reflected the light of the portable, battery-powered lantern we'd found in the garage while we were searching this place.

I sat quietly, waiting to see if he would add anything else to his statement, but he was done. After another long pull from the bottle that drained the last of its contents, Rickey Lipinski closed his eyes. His breathing got fast, then it slowed way down. Finally, after one deep in-hale...he just stopped living.

I heard somebody behind me start to cry as I stood and drew my knife from my belt. I realized in that mo-ment that I hadn't even asked him how he'd been bitten. Did it matter? Were we reaching a point where death was now just the way of things?

I didn't have any answers. All I knew was that we'd just lost two people in our group. The problem I was fac-ing now was keeping a promise. Rickey had made it clear that he didn't want to come back as one of those things. I'd asked him if he wanted me to be sure first, and he'd told me in no uncertain terms that he did not want to spend a single second as one of "those unnatural monsters." And I realized again that, at no point in our conversation, had he used the term zombie.

I didn't wait for his eyes to open. I eased the bottle from his hand, pulled the pillow from under his head, put it over his face, and then drove a knife into it. The person behind me that had been crying made a gasp to punctuate my strike.

I jerked the blade free and wiped it on the bedding, then grabbed the comforter and threw it over the pillow so that I wouldn't have to look at the dark stain blooming around the puncture hole.

After a watch rotation was set, I went into the living room and stretched out on the couch. Surprisingly, I felt my eyes sliding shut within moments.

6

Yet Another Move

Nobody was more surprised than I was at the fact that we were able to stay put for five days with almost no problems. On occasion, one of us would have to slip out and take down a pesky zombie that decided to paw at our door for some unknown reason.

The best thing about this place was that one of the upstairs bedrooms had a window that gave a great view of a large portion of the parking lot. It also let us see that, while there were zombies wandering the area, it was surprisingly thin.

The cupboards gave us plenty of food to glean, and there were five cases of bottled water in the pantry. It looked as if maybe things went bad for this family just after they stocked up to hunker down. We each even had the luxury of having our own brand-new toothbrush still in the package.

The only down side was that we had to use cold water from the tank on the backs of the upstairs and downstairs toilets since obviously the water service plants were all off-line. But that still allowed each of us to dunk a large wash-cloth into a bowl and clean up.

Also, I had to venture out to a few of the nearby resi-dences to try and find dog food for Chewie. That had some other unfortunate consequences. She'd grown up on a pretty strict and regular diet. Sometimes, our grocery bill for her was as much as mine and Steph's. Now, she was forced to make do like the rest of us. That wreaked havoc on her stomach. Also, it wasn't like I could just take her outside to do her business anytime I wanted.

What I ended up doing was breaking in to the condo next door. At first, Chewie was not having any of it, but I had to get her to use the bathroom indoors. I was forced to use a trick that I'd learned in a book about potty training. It involves inserting something in a delicate place which forces her to expel it, hopefully along with going to the bathroom at the same time. The look on her face was pa-thetic, and I could almost hear her trying to ask me "What madness is this?"

I made it a habit to take her before and after each watch shift. The only time I made an exception was if she started sniffing around the door. That had always been her tell in normal times. Usually, she would sleep at my feet during my shifts.

Twice during my own watch, I spotted a living person move through the area. Once, it was just a single person—it was almost impossible to tell with all the gear they were wearing if it was male of female—and they didn't venture into any of the buildings. Judging by the backpack, I'd say the individual was pretty well stocked up for just one person. I had to wonder how long it would be before that burden either became too heavy, or was depleted to the point where scavenging would be necessary.

It was the second time that was more interesting, and told me what we would be facing out there when we eventually moved on. It was a group of five guys. None of them were shy about whooping it up as they strutted through the complex like it was just a normal day. I was only forced to wait for a short period of time before I discovered they were doing this on purpose.

The first zombie that wandered out to them had been

a young woman. I doubt that it made a difference to them in regard to the gender. To these individuals, the zombies were now sport. It was easy picturing this same group before the dead got up and put us on the menu as they hung out on some downtown street corner. These were the ones who thought your walking was in the way of their skateboarding. These were the ones taking video of each other going over jumps, grinding on metal railings, and wiping out in spectacular fashion. And those wipeouts were always greeted by jeers and laughter. Very seldom did you see somebody rush in to see if the injured rider was okay.

Apparently the zombie apocalypse had simply offered them a new venue for their general jackassery.

I watched in fascination, unable to look away. One of the five peeled off, making quite a show of being the first to do so as he swaggered up to the first zombie to arrive…the woman. I found myself holding my breath as he caught her by the wrist as she swiped at him. In one fluid motion, he swept her legs out from under her and plopped down to straddle her chest, effectively pinning her arms to her sides.

For whatever reason, he thought it was a good idea to dangle his fingers over her snapping teeth. Twice, I was almost certain it got him the way he jerked back and screamed, only to turn and wave to his gathered audience.

By now, a few more of the undead had wandered into the area. They all started toward the lone individual who had grown bored with his first game and now got to his feet. As the zombie stood, he went into some sort of elaborate faux-martial arts demonstration as he taunted the creature with harmless slaps and sloppy spin kicks. Twice he lost his balance and ended up on his butt. Both times, he jumped up and assaulted the zombie like it had caused his fall.

By now, the rest of his group had spread out into a circle around their comrade. If the zombie wandered towards one of them, they would punch it or kick it and shove it back towards the middle of the improvised ring. They seemed unconcerned about the newly arriving zombies until the creatures were almost upon them.

Apparently the first one reaching their little game was the signal that the fun was over. In a sudden explosion of violence, these young men unleashed the real ferocity as they drew a variety of bladed weapons and set upon the undead. They didn't go for the quick kill, but instead contented themselves with hacking off limbs, gutting, and even beheading.

For whatever reason, they saved the first zombie, the woman, for last. She was systematically dismembered, disemboweled, and decapitated. Once they cut off her head, they broke into a sadistic game of soccer as they booted the head around the lot until it finally broke open after being punted into a curb one too many times.

The twisted soccer match finished, they set about smashing windshields and headlights on several of the abandoned vehicles littering the parking areas. One of them produced a can of spray paint and set about tagging the area with profanity and a series of images which I guess were supposed to represent the stages of a penis from flaccid to fully erect.

They all swaggered off like drunk pirates, elbowing each other and carrying on at full volume, no doubt relating some highlight of their recent exploits in case it had been missed. I very briefly wondered how long that particular group would survive.

It must've been that racket that brought the herd that arrived about an hour later. The group was large enough that we heard them first. I slipped outside with Marshawn and we made our way to the entrance to see that the road was clogged with zombies all trudging this direction.

We could've hidden and hoped that they continued on their way, but I wasn't in the mood to risk it. Tracy suggested that we maybe try to lure them past our location using noise, but the truth was, I knew this would never be a place where we could stay permanently.

That was another thing that always made me crazy about the old zombie stories. Nobody ever stayed put. I blame George Romero. Ever since he let that bunch of Savini-led bikers raid the mall, no group had ever found someplace that they managed to keep and hold. I was determined to find us a location that we could secure and fortify. It would need to be big enough that we could add to our numbers, but considering how bad things were, I doubted we needed to be concerned with more than a hundred or so people if we got lucky.

That had been my focus while we hunkered down in the condo. I wanted to find us someplace to retreat to that would give us an environment suitable for growing fresh fruits and veggies; plus, we needed a relatively clean water supply. For some reason, my mind kept returning to Milo McIver State Park.

When I'd been younger, that was the place me and a

bunch of friends used to go and camp. Mostly because it was close enough that we could pop into town and replenish the beer supply. It was one of those places that ended up packed during the summer with families. It was what my friend Marley called "glamping". That was his word for fake or "glamour" camping. He refused to accept anyplace with power outlets and showers as actual camping.

It had the Clackamas River running through it. While I am sure there is some degree of pollution in pretty much every river in the world, this one always seemed to feel cleaner. Chewie loved it, and she could swim all day and not come away with an ear infection like when we went to the Willamette, which runs through the Portland industrial district.

Also, I seemed to recall this small island in the middle of the river. It wasn't anything special, and it was pretty minute, but I was willing to bet we could set up on the banks of the river and have that island set up to be a fallback location. The main reason for not just hunkering down on the island was that I had no idea what the flooding situation might be like. And there wouldn't be any National Weather Service announcement to warn us.

I shared my thoughts and got a mix of reactions rang-ing from complaints about the distance to how we would be able to come back and look for our missing friends. Interestingly, that last response came from Michael...in a way.

"Are we gonna let the bad man have Selina and Carl and the others?" he asked innocently.

I knelt in front of the boy. His gaze continued to be fixed on the ground, but I'd come to learn that he listened despite not making any eye contact. "I am going to do everything I can to get them back. But before we can do anything...we need someplace safe."

"We're gonna live in a park?" he asked in a whisper.

"Sort of." I did my best to sound cheerful. "Sort of like camping."

"Can we have s'mores?" His voice was tinged with that hopeful, child-like anticipation and excitement that kids used when talking about something they saw as enjoyable.

I scratched my head. While his request wasn't crazy, it was simply the matter of being able to break in to someplace and grabbing what we needed. The thing is, I couldn't deny him, but it wasn't something that I could guarantee either.

"I will do my best to make that happened," I finally promised.

That seemed to be good enough for him. I wish the adults could be half as agreeable. Tracy was almost vehemently against it and Darya was nearly as resistant to the idea. I was not making any headway when Marshawn stepped in.

"How about you ladies just figure out what you want to do and go on your way. I'll go with Evan, the dog, and the kid. All this arguing is gonna end up getting one or all of us killed. Honestly, I'm tired of listening to it."

With that, he grabbed his pack and then knelt to help Michael with the small tote that he'd rigged with straps so the little guy could be like one of the group and have his own backpack. I clipped Chewie's leash and then shouldered my bag which was loaded a bit on the heavy side with a huge, sealed container holding a few days' worth of dog food.

We went upstairs to check the layout one more time and ensure that we weren't walking out into the leading edge of a group of undead. Once we were certain we had a window of time to slip away, we hurried downstairs.

Through all of this, Alex remained silent. I had no idea

which way she might lean. Hell, she might've decided by now that it was preferable to return to being on her own.

I was only mildly surprised when Tracy and Darya followed on our heels. After moving the furniture out of the way, we took one more look out the sliding glass door before opening it. The smell of undeath had become so prevalent that I barely noticed it on the gentle breeze.

It was there, but not overwhelming. The smell of actual death and decay was far more pervasive. There was also a deep hum. It took me a moment to realize that it was coming from the clouds of bugs swirling around the corpses sprawled out all over the warming pavement. The shimmer of heat waves rose off the all-black surface, a visible indicator of how hot it was as the sun sat almost directly overhead.

It struck me as we stepped outside that we hadn't heard another peep from Don Evans and his people since that time several days ago. Part of me began to build this story where he and his lackeys were overpowered by a mob of the walking dead. We would come around a corner and find the school bus sitting there. A zombie version of Don would be pawing at the door, his mohawk stiffened with dried blood, and a huge bite out of his butt where his assless chaps left him vulnerable to such an attack.

"What's so funny?" Marshawn gave me an elbow to the ribs as we all stood huddled on the back porch of the condo that had been our home these past few days.

I opened my mouth and shut it just as fast. That last bit was probably best only spoken by my 'inside' voice.

"Nothing, just nerves," I lied.

We ventured out and saw a little movement in pretty much every direction. There would not be a way we could go and not have to deal with a few zombies. The thing now was to find a vehicle and the keys to start it. I didn't want to risk trying for the one we'd abandoned on the interstate during our diversion ploy. Also, I thought it would be best if we stuck to back roads and side streets as much as possible.

Despite the fact that neighborhoods were probably death traps if any of my past experiences were any indication, they would likely be our safest route of travel. As we slipped along the side of the building, I heard the occasional moan or slap of a dead hand on a wall or door.

When we reached the end of the building, I moved ahead of the group and to a look around the corner. What

I saw gave me just the smallest surge of hope.

It was like my vision became telescopic for just a moment. Sitting on the pavement behind a nice-looking Suburban was a huge keyring. It had a length of chain still attached to a hunk of a leather belt. If those keys went to that vehicle and it actually started, we might have a really good chance of making it to the Milo McIver site.

Of course, nothing in the zombie apocalypse is ever going to be easy. Sitting beside the keys was a man who might've been in his late twenties. It was odd to see a zombie just sitting there. He wasn't really doing anything. That didn't make it any less creepy that he was snacking on an arm. Looking around, I tried to see if maybe there were any people in the area. This was a fresh kill. I could see the legs of the victim jutting from a nearby shrub.

There were a few zombies staggering off, and I had to wonder how we'd missed the scream. A death-by-zombie event always came with the scream. To me, that made this whole scene appear even more ominous. There was something wrong here.

"So, which of us is gonna make the dash?" Marshawn whispered into my ear.

"Dash?" I was momentarily confused as I continued to

try and process what I was seeing and figure out what I was missing.

"Yeah, one of us should run for those keys. The other should get everybody ready to jump into the rig once the runner gets in and starts it."

Marshawn was also looking around. That told me that he was probably thinking some of the same things that I was.

"Okay," I turned to face him, "how do we decide?"

"Duh!" he snorted. "Rock, paper, scissors."

I thought he was kidding until he extended one hand palm up and made a fist with the other. He looked at me expectantly until I sheathed my blade and did the same thing. Honestly, if, at any time in my life, somebody would've told me that I would be playing "rock, paper, scissors" in the middle of the zombie apocalypse...well, I just don't know what I would've thought or said.

"Ready?" he asked, glancing up at the rest of the group that were now way too fascinated by what was happening. "A three count and choose."

I nodded. He did the countdown and stayed with rock...which crushed my scissors. For emphasis, he actually pounded my fingers with his fist.

"I win." Marshawn got up to his feet and drew a machete from the collection of assorted bladed weapons dangling from his belt.

"I have your back," I insisted. "You just focus on the keys and getting to that Suburban. I will have everybody ready to make a dash."

"Why don't we all go?" Darya asked.

"If that baby doesn't start, then we are all exposed...and there is something off about the situation," Marshawn said, basically voicing my own concerns.

"Let's just hope those are the keys to that vehicle," I whispered. "It seems a bit too convenient."

"Can you not jinx this worse than it already is?" Marshawn quipped before turning, taking a deep breath, and then sprinting across the open expanse of parking lot. He was halfway there when a muffled report of a gunshot shattered the relative silence.

I saw Marshawn fly forward and my heart lurched at the thought of him having been shot. He rolled over twice and came to a stop against the rear wheel of the Suburban. I breathed a sigh of relief when he scrambled around so that he was sitting up with his body shielded by the vehicle.

Now that I knew Marshawn was okay, or at least seemed to not be wounded, I looked around for the shooter. There was no sign of anybody, then I felt a hand on my shoulder. I glanced back to see Tracy; she was looking off to my right at a condo. At first, I didn't see anything, then my eyes caught movement in an upstairs window. A dark blanket or towel had been draped in it, but the barrel of a rifle could be seen at the bottom. It was scanning back and forth, obviously the person was looking for another target.

I made a gesture for Tracy to stay put and keep Michael, Darya, Alex, and Chewie with her. Once I was certain she understood, I waved at Marshawn and pointed to where the shooter was hiding. Next, I made a gesture letting him know that I was going to try and slip around the back. If I could get to that building, then I might be able to find a way in and take this person down.

Alex stood back until I was ready to go then grabbed my shoulder and pulled me close. I couldn't help the reaction that rippled through me as she whispered into my ear. Seriously, I could feel her warm breath and even the occasional brush of her lips on my ear as she whispered.

"I'm coming with you. I have a little something that will make this much easier." With that, she reached into the bag slung over her shoulder and produced a bottle with cloth at the top and liquid sloshing around inside. "Molotov."

I nodded. That was a much better idea than me trying to sneak into a building where who knew what waited inside, then having to sneak up on a person and shoot them.

I was very aware that killing people was going to be part of the way of things—at least for the foreseeable future. That didn't mean I felt good about it or was eager to engage in that sort of thing.

We slipped down the side of the building adjacent to the one our target was in. We reached the end and I peeked around to discover a trio of undead trudging away from us. From the looks of things, they were headed for the general area of our shooter. Sure enough, they turned in and started pawing at a window of the building where our intended target resided.

I was considering just letting them do what zombies do best when I heard the sound of a window sliding open. Instantly, all three zombies lunged for the opening. I heard the telltale 'thunk' of a blade chopping into the skull. It took me a moment to realize that meant there was more than just one person inside. Alex was not as slow on the uptake. She drew one of the pistols she carried on her hips and pulled something from a pocket, screwing it into place at the end of the barrel.

I was still trying to figure out how to move in when she ducked, scurried up to the window, shoved the larger zombie corpse out of the way, grabbed the smallest of the three to bring up with her as cover, and then threw an arm over its shoulder before firing off two quick shots.

Just as fast, she threw herself to the ground. A heartbeat later, the loud boom that could only be a shotgun sounded and a chunk of the window frame exploded in a shower of wooden shrapnel.

I started forward when the chatter of what had to be an automatic weapon came in a staccato burst of high-velocity lead that punched out holes in the wall of the house just a few feet from where I crouched.

Instinctively I threw myself backwards and landed flat on my back...to find myself staring up at the slack, empty face of a zombie child. I was able to take it all in with the blink of my eyes.

She was about seven years old. Not only was her left eye missing, but almost that entire side of her face had been ripped away. Her mouth was smeared with very old, dried blood which told me she hadn't bitten anybody recently. As all of that registered in my mind, I was hit by how she was just staring down at me and not attacking.

That lasted until I moved my arm and brought the machete into view. In an instant, she let out a moan and dropped on top of me. Her cold, undead hands pawed at my face as she tried to get a grip on me and take a bite of my nose. I shoved her aside easily enough, but I still winced when I heard her tiny body slam into the concrete foundation of the building we were beside.

Rolling over, I scrambled to my knees as another round of weapons' fire came from inside the condo. More chunks of wood and siding exploded out from the wall in a line that crept towards me.

Despite my potential immunity from a zombie bite being a plus right now, I shuddered at how I'd just come terribly close to having a bite taken out of my face. Also, I was certain I wasn't immune to bullets. Without giving it another thought, I grabbed the squirming body of the little zombie girl that was trying to get to her feet. I pulled her body to me to act as a shield for my torso. I had no idea if this was an effective tactic. But I think I'd seen it done in movies so often that it was probably a reflexive action more than anything else. Not that I would've ever considered using a child as a human shield; but, perhaps a part of my brain was starting to let go of the idea that these were still children.

I felt my pants leg tug as the last rounds sounded. I also felt a burning sensation on my right leg, but by now the adrenaline was dumping into my system so fast that it was giving me a nauseous feeling.

Getting to my feet, I was just about up when Alex popped up and fired off another half dozen or so rounds through the window. I had no idea if she hit anything, but I used the opportunity to make a dash for the door that would open up in to the condo.

Naturally, the door was locked. I stepped back and kicked. A nasty jolt of pain shot up my leg and I saw a dark stain around a rip in my jeans that told me I was bleeding. It wasn't much, but all I could think of in that split-second was how screwed up it would be to get what used to be just a simple infection. That is not how I wanted to die in the zombie apocalypse. Not that dying was on my "to-do" list.

I was still sort of hopping on one foot as I processed the pain when Alex elbowed past me and kicked the door in with surprising ease. I would deal with that blow to my ego later, but at the moment, I had to follow her and give support.

The two of us were in the entry hall, and I heard the sounds of feet stomping up the stairs. Alex poked her head into what turned out to be the kitchen and then waved me forward. Spent shotgun shells and assorted brass casings littered the floor. There was also a small pool of fresh blood and a trail of droplets that led from this area and up the dark hallway. The stairs were at the end of that hallway.

"You ready for this?" Alex asked as she knelt and ran a finger through the blood on the floor.

"If I ever say yes to that question, you might want to put me down." I checked the pistol I held and quickly swapped out the magazines since I couldn't recall if I'd even fired the damn thing.

After giving me a peculiar look, Alex started up the hall. She reached the stairs and raised a fist in the universal signal for me to stop. I could hear my heart pounding in my skull as my mouth went dry and my vision seemed to narrow.

I swear it seemed like she moved in slow motion, but

with a great deal of caution, Alex slipped around the corner and, staying in a low crouch, started up the stairs. Halfway up, she paused and produced the Molotov. She glanced over her shoulder and motioned for me to back up. I retreated to the bottom of the stairs and watched her light the cloth that dangled from the top. She didn't toss so much as fastball the thing.

There was a crash and the 'whump' of flames erupting to life. I heard shouts of at least three people. A heartbeat later, the first of the attackers appeared. I cleared my mind as my arm rose with the pistol in it. I heard muffled pops as I squeezed off three shots. The man staggered back a step as my first bullet caught him in the shoulder. The second hit him pretty close to dead center in his chest—probably a direct hit to the heart. Later I would tell myself he was dead before the third round punched a hole in his throat, sending a spray of blood across the wall to the man's left.

The second guy had the misfortune of being in the splatter zone of the Molotov. I guess he forgot about the "stop...drop...and roll" advice when you are on fire. He stumbled to the stairs and received mercy in the form of two rounds to the chest from Alex.

Apparently, anybody that remained chose to leave out the window. I heard a crash, and then I heard gunshots from outside. All I could do was hope that it was our people doing the shooting.

I didn't even hesitate as I spun and headed back down and out the front door. I arrived to discover a man sprawled on the postage stamp-sized front lawn of the condo building. He had three crimson blooms spreading on his shirt.

"Well, that was fun." Marshawn got to his feet from where he'd been taking cover behind the Suburban.

I was about to ask how this guy had met his ending when Tracy and Darya emerged, each of them holding hunting rifles. Both still had wisps of smoke drifting from the barrels.

"I think we should get moving," Tracy said as the two women, Michael, and Chewie came up to us. She gave a jerk of her head over her shoulder.

I looked past her to see a few dozen figures staggering through the dense foliage that surrounded this complex. We'd once again become a bullseye for the undead due to all the noise.

I agreed, and Marshawn scooped up the keys. He

opened the front door, climbed in and jammed the key into the ignition. I don't think I was the only person holding their breath as he turned it.

There was a cough, a sputter, and then the big motor of the Suburban turned over. I know for a fact that I wasn't the only one to erupt in a spontaneous cheer. We all poured in. Alex hopped in front with Marshawn and I opened the rear cargo door for Chewie.

In that one instance, the zombie apocalypse faded away as she bounded in with what was left of her tail wagging furiously. I'd almost forgotten how much she loved going for a ride.

7

About Alex

We had an easy start to our trip. It was almost like a normal afternoon drive during the pre-apocalypse...minus the fact that we were the only moving vehicle.

We reached Johnson Creek Road. I knew from my own trips out to McIver Park that we could cross over to Highway 224 via SE 142nd Avenue. That street was becoming a recurring theme for me. It was on the corner of 142nd and Johnson Creek that the church where I'd first encountered Don Evans existed.

We were rolling past, nobody really talking. Michael had climbed into the very back to sit with Chewie and I was just staring out the window as the scenery drifted by when I saw her.

"Stop the car," I said.

Perhaps I just thought the words had come out of my mouth, but when we didn't so much as slow down, I tapped the headrest on the back of the driver's seat.

"Stop the car, Marshawn." I was already gripping the door handle in anticipation of stopping.

"You do see all those zombies, right?" Alex looked back at me, her expression almost empty. "Why would we stop here?"

"Just stop the damn car." It came out surprisingly calm. Thinking about it, that might be why Marshawn hit the brakes.

The Suburban jerked to a halt eliciting cries from pretty much everybody. Even Chewie barked in what was probably the doggie equivalent of "What the hell are you doing?"

I opened the door and climbed out into what was quickly becoming a warm spring day. My eyes scanned the surroundings, but most of my attention was dialed in to one zombie staggering alone along what remained of the bushes that bordered one side of the church parking lot.

I stepped up onto the sidewalk and paid almost no attention to the closest zombie that I grabbed by the shoulder and jammed my blade into the temple of before shoving it away. Twice more I had to put down an approaching zombie, but never once did my eyes really stray from my objective.

When I reached her, I stopped about five feet away. Currently, the zombie was more interested in trying to push her way through a ragged looking shrub. I looked at her, and felt my guilt try to rise up and crush what remained of my soul.

No, I thought, *Don Evans made a choice to do this. Chances were, he was going to do it anyways, and likely add me to the menu.*

"I'm sorry I couldn't help or protect you, Ariel," I whispered.

It must've been loud enough, because she turned to face me. She had a huge stain of dried blood down her front. Her shirt was long gone, and if she'd been wearing a bra, that had also been torn away. She had bites taken out of her shoulders, and it was no surprise that her abdomen had been ripped open and the insides pulled out. My gaze locked onto some large, dark piece of viscera that dangled from the open gash. If I was forced to make a guess, I would say that was the liver. Strange, the things you focus on when you are almost too overwhelmed with emotion to think straight.

I stared into her filmed-over eyes and tried to see any of whatever had made her human…Ariel. All I saw were empty orbs with a milky, pus-like film that was shot full of black tracers. If there was anything remaining inside, it did not show up in the eyes.

"I won't let you stay like this," I said to her as I grabbed her shoulder and pulled her closer so that I could drive the tip of my blade into her eye socket.

I pushed the tip of the blade into her eye, turning away as it burst, sending a gooey, jelly-like substance trickling down her cheek. She collapsed the moment my blade found whatever part of the brain it is that allows for this unlikely scenario to play itself out.

I laid her down on the ground and turned to head back to the Suburban. When I climbed inside, things were surprisingly quiet. Not even Alex had a snarky comment or even so much as an eye roll.

Marshawn popped us back into gear and nudged through the handful of zombies that had managed to make it to the vehicle during my brief excursion. We rolled through the residential area where I could still make out some of the spray-painted markings from where Evans' people had already scavenged.

We rolled past the pirate-themed monster truck that had chased me, Edmund, and Miranda. The dead bodies where still right where I'd left them, only, it was clear that some local wildlife or perhaps a pack of feral cats or dogs had gotten to them. There was a lot of damage to the softer bits of the face on the one young man I got a good look at.

"Sorta back to where we started," Marshawn quipped as we rolled past the entrance to the neighborhood where I'd feasted on freshly grilled steaks and downed a couple of chilled beers in a time that seemed an eternity ago.

That memory made my mouth start to water and I looked inside my pack. It was with a begrudging sigh that I ripped open a pouch of jerky and bit off a piece. I had to wonder if I would ever have steaks fresh off the grill or ice cold anything ever again. My stomach weighed in with a loud rumble and I did my best to push those thoughts away.

Once we reached the highway, I was pretty confident that I knew how to get us to Milo McIver State Park while keeping to the backroads for the most part. I did seem to recall one stretch that ran through the heart of one of those duplex-riddled pop-up neighborhoods where all the homes look the same and you can almost reach inside your neighbor's kitchen window to borrow a cup of sugar from the comfort of your own kitchen. Also, I knew of at least one mobile home park. From everything I'd seen, that was likely not someplace we would want to get caught unaware. Lots of people plus a small area equaled bad news.

We rolled up to a bit of a fork in the road. I knew we needed to veer right, but just as we slowed down and started to edge around a small, two-car wreck, the sounds of gunfire came from ahead...in the direction we needed to go.

"Big machine gun," Alex said. "Maybe your boy?"

She turned to look back at me and for a split-second, I found myself caught up by her green-gold eyes. They weren't really hazel. It seemed that the light had some influence over what color they were. They could look more green like they did now in the shadows, or more golden when the sunlight hit them.

"Well, Evan?" Marshawn spoke up, and I looked up to catch his gaze in the rearview mirror.

"We can go straight. It is a longer route, but we can get there that way as well." I had to speak up over the sounds of what was now obviously a very powerful machine gun with an apparently endless supply of ammunition.

"I gots no place else to be," Marshawn chuckled as he eased us to the left and drove over the curb to put us back on the road heading uphill and away from the gunfire.

We started up the gentle slope, but it was also a wide, sweeping curve that gave us little advance warning of what lie ahead. The first surprise came almost right away when we rounded the second bend in the road.

The school bus looked to have been run off the road by an old pickup. Before the nightmares became real, lots of folks used to like to talk about what absolute badasses they would be if something like this were to happen. I don't really know what happened here, but from the looks of it, that truck came up behind the school bus and somehow ran it off the road.

The nose of the pickup was snagged in the metal of the rear quarter of the bus. The former driver was staring out at me...sort of. His undead eyes tracked us as we went past, but he was probably trapped in that cab forever. He had a visible wound on his forehead from where it had cracked the steering wheel or something, but I had no idea how he'd turned. Maybe he'd been bitten beforehand and was trying to escape to someplace.

The bus was another story. I could see adult versions wandering about inside it. What I didn't see were any children. That lent to the possibility for countless scenarios, none of them were pleasant to dwell on for more than just a minute.

We had to swing out into the oncoming lane, and, while there was no danger of oncoming traffic catching us by surprise, there was still a very deep ditch on that side of the road and we had to almost drop into it to get around the accident. The problem was that this was that sort of ditch that was maybe a few feet deep and really steep on the sides. If we dropped in, we would be walking.

Once we cleared that obstacle, we were on open road again for what felt like a good distance. Most of what we were driving past consisted of farmland. I knew we would eventually run out of luck, I just kept hoping it was later rather than sooner.

By the time we got close to the little town of Damascus, I'd started to breathe easier. That was pretty stupid.

There was a sudden and sharp lurch as the Suburban jerked to the right. Fortunately, we were only driving about thirty miles per hour. Marshawn had no problems slowing us down and coming to a stop. No sooner had he done that when I jerked instinctively as the glass, just inches from my face, exploded. I felt something sting my upper lip, but I was already trying to figure out where the shooter was hiding, and so I didn't really feel it for more than a few seconds.

"Heads down!" Alex barked at the same time I was realizing that we were being shot at.

"And hang on tight," Marshawn added.

I heard him stomp his foot to the floor, sending the Suburban forward with a jolt. I could also hear the wheel grinding away at the pavement. Fortunately, we were angling away from the culvert on the driver's side and in no danger of dropping over the edge.

When the second shot was fired, I heard it. Of course, I was amped up from all the adrenaline that had just dumped into my system. I also knew that the shooter was on my side from the bullet that had come frighteningly close to hitting me.

I risked a look as we continued to chug along. That was also when I realized we had to bail out of the Suburban as soon as we could manage. The noise from that rim grinding away on the asphalt was excruciatingly loud.

Fortunately, Marshawn was not stupid. He yanked the wheel to the left at the first side street he reached. As soon as we passed a few homes, he angled us for the curb and brought the big SUV to a stop.

"End of the line, folks!" he called out with far too much cheer in his voice for my liking.

I hopped out and hurried to the back hatch to let out Michael and Chewie. They both came pouring out like their behinds were on fire. Each for different reasons. Chewie always got excited when we stopped after a ride in the car. I could take her around the block and, when we arrived back home, she would jump out acting like we'd gone on some incredible journey. Michael's reason was something else entirely.

"I think Chewie needs to potty," the little boy said, holding his nose for emphasis.

I had no need to wait around for the funk to hit me in the face and grabbed Chewie's leash, pulling her down the side of an old home that had the front door wide open. I resisted the urge to duck inside because I had no idea what might be waiting within and did not want to become trapped inside by any zombies that might be lurking.

I could hear footsteps behind me, and glanced over

my shoulder to see the rest of the group in a single-file line. They were all right on my heels, and it was a comfort to see that Michael was holding Darya's hand.

We all made it into the backyard of the potentially abandoned residence. Once everybody had a chance to collect themselves and we got a look around, I spied a road through some trees. That was also the direction I heard a low rumble coming from.

I signaled for everybody to stay put and hurried to the tree line in a hunched over crouch. I watched as a school bus crept past. The entire thing was covered in absolutely filthy graffiti. On the top, in the front and rear, metal posts and a railing had been welded into place. Each of those spots had a man holding a rifle. Next to each of the gunners was another person with binoculars scanning the area.

"Little early for the wanna-be *Road Warrior* types, isn't it?" Marshawn whispered.

"Apparently not." I hoped that I'd been able to conceal the fact that he'd just scared the piss out of me...literally.

"Those are just kids," Alex said from the other side of me.

This time I am certain I jumped enough to be noticed

by my companions who apparently did not understand the universal gesture for 'stay put'. I shot her a nasty look, but she was paying me no mind as she peered through her own set of field glasses to get a better look at the bus and its occupants.

"I count seven," Alex whispered. "The four on top, the driver and two more moving around inside."

"You think those are the ones who shot at us?" I turned to her.

"Probably." She gave a nod and opened her mouth to say something else when an electronic squeal echoed off the trees lining the road the bus had been prowling along.

"To the people who thought they could just roll into our area," a voice belonging to what sounded like a kid in maybe his late teens called out. "We have laid claim to this area. You are trespassing. This is your only warning. If we catch you, we will show no mercy."

The bus continued to prowl along the road away from where we were hiding. All the while, whomever had spoken, continued to repeat his message.

"He's reading it from a script," Marshawn snorted.

"How do you know?" I turned to the man with an eyebrow arched in curiosity.

"He is saying the same thing over and over...word-for-word."

"You wanna take them down?" Alex hissed.

I glanced over to see her gripping and re-gripping the rifle she had unslung at some point and now held in her hands. There was a dangerous expression etched on her face, and I was beginning to wonder if having her along was a good idea.

"Why?" I asked as calmly as I could manage. "What would the point of attacking those kids be? We need to get out of here as quickly and quietly as we can manage. If we stop and pick a fight with every person we encounter, we will either take forever getting to our destination, or we won't get there at all because we will all be dead."

"They shot at us first," Alex snapped back. She turned back to face me, her eyes glittering with either anger, hatred, or a nasty combination of the two.

"We are in their area. They are protecting it. You don't think we will be doing the exact same thing when we get to McIver?" I shot back. "Once we get settled, I plan on us holding our place. Anybody who comes into what I consider our home will face the same...if not worse."

She opened her mouth, and I thought she was going to

argue. I seriously didn't have the time, nor did I possess the extra energy it would take. Instead, she shut her mouth and gave a barely perceptible nod.

I waved everybody over and we waited, huddled close while we let the bus slowly rumble away. Just when we thought we could get up and start moving, the damn thing did a U-turn or something and came sputtering back up the street. It made a few more passes, the entire time, the person on the megaphone kept reading the exact same warning.

Eventually, they must've gotten bored. The bus rolled away and about five or ten minutes later, we heard distant gunfire and the muted and now undecipherable sound of somebody speaking on an amplified megaphone.

"Okay, we still need to find a vehicle if we want get out of here fast and also reach our destination sometime today." I stood up and stretched.

All the little aches and pains stacking up on me were beginning to really add up. I did a very quick inventory and realized that there were fewer places that didn't hurt than those that did.

"Let me duck inside this house real fast," Marshawn said, not waiting for a reply as he jogged to the back porch and gave the doorknob a twist.

It opened, and he ducked inside after drawing a weapon from his belt. I took that time to check on Michael and Chewie. Both were sitting in the grass. The boy was feeding small pieces of jerky to my dog.

As I watched them, something inside me felt like it changed. I was not seeing them as two separate beings anymore. In my mind, Chewie and Michael were almost as one. It didn't make any sense to me. I had no feelings I could relate this to, but there was something different.

I needed to care for them both. Everybody else would be able to take care of themselves, but if push came to shove, I needed to be able to take care of the two of them at any cost. Chewie had always been my responsibility. But now, there was just something about the boy. Not in a mystical "chosen one" sort of way. No, these two were my family.

"Hey!" Alex snapped her fingers in front of my face and I glanced up at her.

"What's up?" I asked with a yawn, realizing that I was much more in need of sleep than I'd been allowing myself to realize.

She stared down at me for long enough that I began to

get uncomfortable. And by that, I mean even more uncomfortable than I was already just being around her. I didn't know why, but there was something about Alex that...did it for me. I wasn't sure what that was, but I knew I was in no way ready to have those kinds of feelings for anybody else. The loss of Stephanie, while now several weeks old in a world where every day seemed like a lifetime, still felt fresh. Or, at least it felt to me as if it should.

"You and I need to be on the same page if we are going to make this work," she said as she sat down beside me. "I have no idea what your problem with me has been, or why you are always giving me dirty looks, but maybe we just start from scratch and let everything before just be like water under the bridge?" Her voice rose just a bit at the end, making that last bit seem like more of a question than a statement.

"Why would you think I have a problem with you?" I asked after I made certain to wipe away any sort of edge to my tone and hopefully any sort of expression that might come across as a dirty look. In fact, when I gave it two seconds of my time, I decided that I had done no such thing. I was about to open my mouth and tell her those exact words when she started talking.

"It's just been really hard for me, and you guys coming along when you did almost felt like too much of a good thing. Maybe I wasn't very friendly in those first few minutes..." Her voice trailed off, and I thought that she was done, but after a moment, she started talking again. "You have no idea what had just happened literally minutes before I ran across you guys."

I looked up to see Marshawn poke his head out the door and give me a wave and then a gesture to just stay put. Obviously he'd found something inside the house. Either that, or he wanted to look around a bit more. I saw Darya and Tracy had both moved to the porch steps of the house Marshawn was searching. Chewie and Michael were still sharing jerky as well as a bottle of water. I looked over to see that Alex had a faraway look on her face. I could see something warring across it, but I didn't know her well enough to know what those feelings might be. Then...she spoke again.

"I was at my sister's house getting dressed for my wedding when it all fell apart..."

***

189

"The dress looks beautiful, Allie," Samantha Lynn, my baby sister gushed as she stepped back with her phone and took a few pictures — as if she hadn't taken enough already the past few hours, and I wouldn't be forced to stand in ridiculous poses and take a bunch more over the next two or three hours.

She also used the name 'Allie' which she knew I hated

"I feel like I am being squished," I snapped, giving her both middle fingers as she tapped her phone to take still more pictures.

"Alexandria, we have discussed this."

Great, now my mother was going to start, and she was using my full name...which I hated even more than being called 'Allie'. I silently swore that I would get them both back for doing things they knew would only make me more annoyed.

"No, Mother, you have lectured," I shot back.

"It is not every day that a mother gets to see her oldest daughter married," my mom retorted with almost as much gruffness in her voice as I managed. "You will do this one thing and then you can go back to being — "

"A giant lez," Samantha Lynn whispered.

"Samantha Lynn, you will not use language like that

in my presence," Mom scolded. "You shouldn't be using it at all. It is not decent, nor is it ladylike."

My mother was about to replay the same argument she'd been having to one degree or another with first me, then my sister in some form over the past two-plus decades when a shriek came from what sounded like right outside the door. I started to step off the stool I had been forced to perch on for the past hour when a loud thud sounded. Samantha was close and held up a hand to signal she was going to check it out. Before I could tell her to get away from it, she opened the door and squeezed outside. Less than a few seconds later, the door flew open with a crash.

Stumbling into the room came a scene I will never forget. A man was riding on my sister's back, his face buried in the crook of her neck. Despite looking strange due to his eyes being messed up with the tracers and the skin of his face being so pale and slack, I recognized him, and knew he was some friend of my soon-to-be husband's only brother. He was some military guy home from the Marines. Apparently, he'd come just for the wedding. I might've been able to recall his name if not for the geyser of blood that was pumping from my sister's throat as this bastard ripped it out with his teeth.

Samantha Lynn let loose with a gurgling scream and my mom started yelling something unintelligible about how this son of a bitch needed to get off her daughter. And that was what froze me for just a split second and probably saved my life.

I'd never heard my mom swear until that moment. She was on this guy before I could move. She kicked him in the side of the head, but he didn't even seem to notice as he tore into my sister's throat again and came away with another huge chunk. Her screaming had stopped, but now she was making this horrible gurgling noise that I know will haunt me forever.

My mom grabbed one of the heavy crystal candlestick holders that sat on the table. Oddly, she had just chewed Samantha out not more than ten minutes earlier for not having taken them downstairs yet. She smashed the man in the back of the head hard enough that the crystal broke. When my head would eventually clear, I would realize that is what saved us. A big chunk of the candlestick holder jutted from the back of the man's head.

Unfortunately, my mom also cut her hand really bad. I would look back on that later and kick myself. In the moment, we didn't give it any thought.

By now, there were more screams coming from down-stairs. I had to hike up my dress, but I still managed to run out into the hallway. Looking downstairs, I saw the front door open and two people I didn't recognize stumbling through it. At first, I thought they were drunk. They kept bumping into each other as well as the door frame, but then one of them looked up and I saw the eyes.

The news had been talking about it for a few days, but I hadn't heard of anything to do with the 'Blue Death' making it out this way. Last I'd heard, it was a few limited cases globally and that town in Kentucky or something that had been quarantined. It was like any other supposed illness that the news over-dramatized. It was a problem someplace besides here, so I didn't really think about it.

By now there were more screams and strange moans coming from not just downstairs, but also outside. I reached the landing on the stairs and could see that there were three fights taking place just inside the house. I also realized that I was not dressed for the situation. One of those things at the bottom of the stairs was now coming up.

I glanced at my mom and realized that the shock had

finally crashed down on her. She was just standing at the top of the stairs a few steps behind me. She kept staring back and forth between the room where I knew my sister lay dead, and then to me. Her mouth would open and shut, but she wasn't saying anything. I looked back down to the entrance and saw my fiancé, Paul Morris, go under a pair of the creatures as they pushed through the congestion in the entry hall. He never even saw me. He was just trying to save everybody and rushed into the fight like the former Marine he was.

When I heard him scream that terrible scream, I rushed back up the stairs. I reached my mom and had to physically turn her around and shove her back to my sister's bedroom. Imagine my surprise—at least in that instance—when I slammed the door behind me and turned around to see my sister standing up.

That was also when the smell hit me full force. Of course, my mom threw herself at Samantha, hugging her and babbling. That thing was not my sister. I knew it the moment its head jerked in my direction and then back to my mom. It wasn't just the eyes or the terrible rip in her throat and all the drying blood down her front. I can't explain it other than to say there was nothing left of my sister when I looked at that monster.

Having not lived under a rock my entire life, I got an inkling as to what this might be. I grabbed the other candlestick holder from the table and charged at the creature that was now looking down at my mom, its mouth opening as a guttural moan escaped it right before it was about to take a bite from her shoulder.

My swing caught the thing in the nose. That hadn't been enough to kill it, but it did knock it back so that its teeth clicked together when it missed the flesh of my mom's shoulder.

Now my mom was yelling again. This time, she turned her anger on me. That plays into part of my theory as to why this happened so fast and wiped out so many in those early days. Nobody was prepared to embrace fiction as reality...especially when it came to having to turn on your former friends and loved ones.

"Alexandria Marie Ramsey!" she hollered. "What on earth do you think you're—"

My sister lunged at Mom, her teeth once again clicking together loud enough to get my mom's attention. She knew right then and there that her daughter, my sister, was not okay. She might not have been quite ready to accept that she was one of the walking dead, but she knew danger when it tried to take a bite out of her.

She couldn't put her down, but she was smart enough to step behind me and let me do what needed to be done. And that was my first zombie kill. My own sister.

It took a few minutes, and the screams from outside the room were getting fewer, but the moans were also getting louder as the undead began to outnumber the living. We needed to get the hell out of this place. My mom had shut down and was just staring at the ruined thing that used to be Samantha's head.

I grabbed her by the hand and pulled her to the window. Taking a look outside, I saw where the problem had come from. An ambulance had crashed up the street. From the looks, it had rolled into a power pole. Not hard enough to take it down, but certainly with enough force to end its days as a useful vehicle. There were three cars all stopped around it.

Doing a quick guess of events, I'd say that it started in the ambulance. People pulled over to help and ended up becoming part of the problem. The folks that lived at the end of the street probably came out as well. That would add to the numbers in a hurry. And if they'd sat up as fast as my sister, then the dozen or so people downstairs had given the numbers another big boost.

I reached back and pulled down the zipper to my dress and shed it in record time. I heard the gauzy fabric rip as I yanked and tugged to have it off me in a hurry. I grabbed my jeans, tennis shoes, and the flannel shirt I'd slipped into this morning before heading over to be squeezed into my wedding gown.

I was about to put on clothing more suited to running for my life when the sound of something at the door caused me to turn around. Standing there was my niece, Caitlyn. She had just turned four. I still remember the amount of crap I'd given Samantha Lynn for getting knocked up at twenty-two. But my niece turned out to be more like me than my sister. That meant she was already a bad ass tomboy. She threw a fit every time they tried to put a dress on that little girl. I'd already found the mini-dirt bike I was going to get her for Christmas this year.

Her chestnut brown hair was almost black with blood. Her left arm was gone...nothing more than an ugly stub of bone jutting from the tattered sleeve of her favorite football jersey. (I'd told her she could wear it under her flower-girl dress.) She stood in the open doorway and stared at me.

I heard my mom try to hold back a sob. I felt sick to my stomach when she cocked her head to one side and then the other as she just stood there staring at me with her goo-filmed eyes full of those hideous black tracers. While she was not making a move towards me, there was still nothing about this thing that resembled my Caty Cat.

She took a step into the room, her head jerking around to look down at Samantha's corpse. Then she looked back up at me. Her expression never changed. I opened the window and told my mom to crawl out onto the roof. Never taking my eyes off what was left of my niece, I followed. Just as I slipped out, there was some movement out in the hall past the little zombie. In walked three of the adult versions, and they made a beeline for me as soon as their eyes found me.

They pushed past the little one, actually knocking it to the ground. One of the three was what was left of my fiancé. His insides were spilling out from a huge rip in his belly and when he reached out with his hands, I saw fingers missing from both.

I climbed out onto the roof with my mom and slammed the window shut behind us to give me enough time to wiggle into my jeans, throw on the shirt, and slide my feet into the shoes.

I'd come over in my pickup and knew for a fact that they keys were still dangling from the ignition. It took some effort to get my mom to start moving. In the time it took to put on my clothes, she'd just stared at the window. Twisted versions of Paul and Caitlin's faces stared out at us. He was trying to gnaw on the window to no avail, but she just stared out, her head doing that creepy bird-like twitch.

I had to guide my mom to the tree that grew beside the house. I was worried I might have to shove her off — which might've been a mercy considering things — but she started down after just a simple nudge and a few whispered pleas for her to get moving.

Once we were down, I pulled her along to my pickup, shoved her in the front and then climbed in after her. The engine roared to life and I saw figures starting to stumble out the busted in front door as I backed up. I stomped on the gas and got us out of there in a big hurry.

We came home...I lived back in that neighborhood where we ran into each other. I arrived to find the place was already a mess. A bunch of people were already packing up and planning on heading to one of the FEMA shelters. A few chose to stay behind and we got together and closed the gates, parking cars in all the exits and entrances.

Things were okay until some of the idiots made a run and came back with two members bitten but didn't tell anybody. When they turned and took out their friends and families a few of the remaining families decided to make a run for it, they left one of our entrances open and a bunch of those things got in.

That was the last day I saw any of the others. Unfortunately, by then, the cut on my mom's hand from the crystal candlestick had become infected. Twice I tried to get her antibiotics. I made runs at that medical center down the hill. I finally came back with a bag of stuff...but I'd never heard my mom say that she was allergic to penicillin.

***

"Time to roll," Marshawn said, interrupting Alex and causing us both to jump.

She wiped her eyes, got up, grabbed her bag and walked over to where the rest of the group stood. Marshawn watched her go and then turned back to me.

"Everything okay?" he asked, his voice laced with concern.

"Will the answer to that ever be yes?" I replied as I slung my own pack over my shoulders.

Amen

"I found the keys and there is a car in the garage," Marshawn announced to the group. "Also, I found a few things we should bring with us."

"Sounds great." I went over and stood with Michael and Chewie. "Anybody else have input?"

I glanced around at the group and saw confused faces. Tracy finally stepped forward.

"We still don't really know what the plan is. You say that McIver Park is our goal. Only...well...why? Isn't there a better choice for a place to call home?" She glanced over at Darya who nodded. Something told me they had been discussing this topic at length.

"The reality is that we will need water. That is our biggest priority when choosing someplace to fortify.

Houses are great short-term ideas, but the plumbing is or will be offline. Also, if there are houses, there will eventually be scavengers. We will no doubt have to deal with the living, but finding someplace that will get the least amount of traffic possible is ideal. I can only speak for myself when I say that I want to put down roots and try to rebuild some kind of life." I looked around at the group for any indication that they might be on the same page. Only Marshawn appeared to be nodding along.

"But McIver?" Darya pressed, joining in the conversation. "That seems a bit random."

"Here is why it makes sense." I realized then that I'd gone over this idea all by myself. I hadn't given any reasons or explanations as to my choice. They were well within their rights to ask. This wasn't a dictatorship. And certainly people should have a clue as to why I'd made this choice. "It is on the Clackamas River and I think that is our best and least fouled river in the area. There are a few basic amenities that we can use. Wood is going to be our source of heat in the coming months. There is also a small island that I believe we can fortify as a fallback location. And it still keeps us in proximity to residential areas. That will allow us to continue to scavenge goods for the time being until it becomes either too dangerous, or else we tap everything out."

"But why McIver?" Tracy pressed. "We could go pretty much anyplace and do this. Instead, we are traveling out to Bum-fuck, Egypt. I don't know why we don't just find someplace closer."

"Water." I did my best not to get agitated. After all, I was basically asking these people to just follow my lead. "We need water to survive. That is one of those things where you don't realize it until you don't have any. I always used to talk to friends about how living in the Pacific Northwest would make it easy to survive the zombie apocalypse. Hunting…fishing…and that is great. But without water, we are done. And we need to boil it before drinking."

"So why not just find someplace on the Willamette?" Darya pressed.

"Too much of the industrial district dumping crap in it for years. Who knows what is lurking in that water," I said. "Yeah, we could boil the water there too, but it isn't some kind of magic wand. I have no idea what might still exist in the waters of the Willamette."

There was a moment of quiet where everybody just

stood there. Finally, Tracy nodded. "Okay then. I guess you have a plan. We're in, Evan."

"What about Selina and Carl?" Michael spoke in a voice that was barely above a whisper. "Are we leaving them?"

"No." I knelt in front of the boy, resisting the urge to tip his chin up so that he was looking me in the eye as I spoke. "But we have to have someplace to bring them back to if this is going to work. So we will just have to hope and pray that they stay safe until we can come help."

"Will you?" The question came so quick, and was so open ended that I had no idea what he was asking or how to answer.

"Will I what?"

"Will you pray that Jesus will watch over them and make them safe?"

I felt my mouth open, but nothing came out. I don't think I'd ever actually prayed for anything unless you counted my occasional, but quite loud, vocalizations for my favorite teams to win.

"Sure we will," Marshawn said, stepping up beside me. "Ladies, care to join us?"

I looked up and saw Tracy shrug. Darya simply

walked over and knelt beside Michael. The bigger surprise for me was when Alex knelt beside her. Tracy got down beside me and Marshawn took his place at Michael's side.

"What do you want us to pray for, Michael?" the big man asked.

"For Selina and Carl and everybody the bad people took to be safe until we can come get them and bring them back to our new home at the park." Michael's voice was absolute innocence.

"Okay." Marshawn gave a raised eyebrow to me as if asking to go ahead. I nodded. "Dear Lord, we ask for you to watch over our friends in our absence. Place your hedge of protection around them and keep Satan's hand from them. Nourish their hearts, souls, and bodies and guide us to them when the time comes. We ask this in the name of your son Jesus who died for our sins."

"Amen," everybody said in fairly close unison once it was clear Marshawn was finished.

"Amen all the way to Heaven," Michael added in a whisper.

As everybody followed Marshawn inside and started pitching in to get us ready, I couldn't help but think maybe we were coming together as a group. There was a sense that perhaps we could unify and carve out a life in this living nightmare.

As I helped Marshawn load a very large tool box into the back of the dark green Durango that sat in the garage and had already been turned over to ensure that it started, I could not help but ask, "Were you religious before all of this?"

Marshawn gave a grunt as he shoved the toolbox against one side and then turned to me. "My pops was a preacher. He could lay down the gospel." A faraway look came to his eyes for a moment, and then he shook his head as if to clear it. "I used to listen to him when I was little and think I was going to follow in his footsteps."

"But you didn't." It wasn't really a question. Marshawn was a nurse. Was he both?

"I just didn't feel like I could ever give people what they came away from his sermons with every Sunday. The day he had his heart attack and I visited him in the hospital, I met a guy who was one of the nurses taking care of my dad. I watched him do his thing, and then I saw this sour-faced lady who had the exact same job. I started nursing school two weeks later." He smiled. "My pops was so proud of me. That was the best part. I'd been worried that he might be disappointed when I didn't follow in his foot-steps."

With that, we had a few things from the residence that would come in handy as well as anything edible. I was perhaps the most excited to find a medicine cabinet with some A & D ointment, a 1000 count bottle of ibuprofen that hadn't even been opened, a tube of toothpaste, and a razor with four refill cartridges.

I had to force the garage door open once everybody was in the vehicle, and in a stroke of luck that I would take as a good omen, nothing waited for us on the other side. There were a few zombies in either direction on the street, but nothing that was going to be a problem. I thought I heard a distant bit of noise that might've been the mega-phone announcer and his school bus, but nothing that would give cause for concern.

The SUV rolled out and onto the street, I hopped in to join the others. Marshawn took a look when we hit the in-tersection of whatever side road this was and Highway 212. Once he was confident that the coast was clear, he rolled out, turning left and into the heart of the tiny town of Damascus. We rolled past a Safeway, a gas station, and a Dairy Queen on one side of the highway with a Bi-Mart, some small shops, and a Mickey Dees on the other.

Just as we rolled past the Dairy Queen, Marshawn slammed on the brakes causing everybody to yelp or curse in surprise. Once I managed to untangle myself from Chewie and Michael who had ended up in a jumble at my feet and in my lap, I smacked the back of the driver's seat.

"What the hell, man?"

Marshawn pointed out the passenger's side as he cranked the steering wheel over and pulled off the road. At first I didn't understand, then the small sign jumped out at me.

"Lost most of your stuff back there at the other place." Marshawn put the SUV in park and turned back to face me. "Not sure when or where we will get another shot like this. Might be worth a quick look."

I jumped out after reminding Michael and Chewie to stay put and behave. The gravel of the parking lot made a loud crunch as Marshawn and I walked to the small window that looked into the reception area of Village Vet.

I tried the door after we were fairly certain nothing was waiting in the lobby area. It was locked. No big surprise.

Using my elbow, I gave the window a solid shot. It

exploded inward with a deafening crash. As soon as it did, the smell of death rolled out to greet us. On the positive side, it wasn't the telltale smell of undeath.

I climbed in and then unlocked the front door for Marshawn. He hurried in and the two of us started grabbing bags of dry dog food stacked against one wall.

It didn't take us long, and after the first trip, Alex and Darya both pitched in to help. Tracy stayed put outside the vehicle with a rifle at the ready. As soon as we grabbed what we could, I hopped the counter and took a peek in the back. I quickly located a locker with a notice that it was not to be opened without authorization.

Hurrying out to the vehicle, I found a clawed hammer and rushed back. It was harder than I'd expected and made a great deal of noise in the process. At last, I managed to manhandle the door open. There was a variety of medications, so I searched around until I found a bag and loaded up as much as I could, having no idea if I was even getting anything useful. Still, many of the prescriptions had instructions. I could look through them later and try to make my best guess as to what each might be used for.

Once more, we were on the move. We passed through a very rural area with a good mix of sprawling farms, dilapidated trailers sitting on cinder blocks and a few green-house/nursery locations. We noted these as we passed. These would be the kinds of locations we would likely make scavenger runs on once we were settled. These places would help us establish our farms. That was one more lucky break I gave thanks for. Spring was right around the corner. That meant many of these places would probably have a plethora of gardening supplies. A few had large flatbed trucks parked in them that we could hopefully get started and then make bigger runs.

We reached the tee-intersection of SE 232nd Drive. Turning right, we found ourselves on a gently rolling two-lane road. There were certainly more houses along this road, and I noticed everybody sitting up just a little bit straighter as our level of vigilance increased.

"Heads up!" Marshawn hissed as he let off the gas and very gently applied the brakes to bring us to a stop.

Despite seeing nothing up ahead, I knew why he'd stopped. To the left was a parking lot with rows of school buses. Just beyond that lot was an elementary school. I instantly flashed back to the school I'd passed what seemed like an eternity ago. My gaze drifted across the street to what appeared, for all intents and purposes, to be a fallow field of some sort.

The road we were on was lined with trees, so this had sort of snuck up on us. We could back up, but there was no guarantee that we wouldn't encounter something similar in another direction. Also, just because there was a school did not mean there were child-zombies.

"Well?" Marshawn asked, meeting my gaze in the rearview mirror.

"I say we roll through. Doesn't have to be anything up there," I replied.

"Of the five elementary schools I have come across, four of them have been like zombie children hives."

"Then maybe we go really fast," Darya offered. "The road is empty right now. I haven't seen the child versions show themselves to be any quicker than the normal ones."

"She makes a good point." Alex opened her front passenger door and stood, taking a look ahead with her binoculars. "I say we rocket through. There is movement for sure, but there is also some sort of fence in place. I think we can skirt past without a problem."

She climbed back in, shut the door, and gave Marshawn a slight nod. He seemed to take that as good enough and stomped on the gas. There was a short chirping squeal as the tires spun a few times before gripping the road, then we were moving.

As we sped past, I had my face pressed to the window. Sure enough, I saw several small figures moving in the shadow of the building. For whatever reason, it seemed that the child versions of the zombies were drawn to schools. That would be good information to store.

We eventually came out onto Highway 224. That would take us towards Estacada. I'd only been there a few times, and not any of those being recent. It had been known as a logging town once-upon-a-time. I also recall it Having a reputation for being a bit of a 'No Man's Land' when it came to the surrounding forests. If you believed the rumors, there had been some large pot growing operations back in the day, and then meth moved in. Honestly, I have no idea as to the truth to any of those stories, but I also knew we would pass through the heart of it on our way.

Maybe I would get an idea as to how possible it would be to make some supply runs to the houses and small shops or stores in the area. We started along the road and had to avoid a few bad accidents on the way.

We came out of the winding curves and saw what was

left of a small gas station/convenience store that had suffered a terrible fire. It looked as if the fuel tanks had blown. The only reason we knew what used to be there at the location where a huge crater now dominated the landscape was because of the toppled sign that we had to weave around as we drove by.

Just past that we came upon what I initially thought to be just another small roadside church. That changed when Marshawn cursed and brought us to a stop as we crept around a particularly nasty three-car wreck. From the looks, somebody had come through and either pushed or drove these vehicles into the deep ditches that ran alongside the highway in this area. The zombies had been dispatched some time ago—via machete by the looks of things, I noted.

Up ahead, the church was also apparently an elementary school. Several zombie children could be seen just standing in the open field that had once served as the school's playground. They definitely saw us. All of them were just standing there, but a few had come to the fence that lined the front of the school. They weren't doing anything but watching…and that was incredibly creepy.

"You still say that the kid versions aren't any different?" I mumbled, giving a tap to the back of Alex's seat.

"They're still zombies. They might behave different, but the end results are the same." She turned in the seat to look at me. "And I never said they weren't different. Only that they are still just walking dead and will bite and turn you like any other of its kind."

"But what if they do have some sort of awareness?" I shot back. I couldn't explain why this was sticking with me, but it was, and I couldn't just let it go. "Maybe there has to be something else we can do when dealing with this kind of zombie."

"Can you two do this later?" Marshawn snapped. "We need to get past them."

A low rumble sounded and I turned to see Chewie straining against Michael's grip as he struggled to keep her in the back with him. This was a new behavior, and I tried to look in the direction she was focused.

At first, I didn't see anything beyond the distant zombie children. Then a flash of black caught my eye. I was leaning over Darya, and I heard her breath catch at the same moment I saw it.

"We need to go," I hissed.

"What?" Marshawn started to turn around, and then

he saw it as well. "You've got to be kidding."

Emerging from the woods were at least a hundred zombies. Leading them were a pack of coyotes and three huge dogs that looked at least related to the Pit Bull.

"How the hell…" Tracy started, but her voice choked off to a whisper as a sob escaped.

This little mob was coming from our right, just a few yards from the school. I leaned forward, straining my hearing. There it was. Faint, but after the second time, I was certain of what I was hearing.

"You need to go…NOW!" I smacked the back of Marshawn's chair and he stomped the gas in response.

I rolled my window down as I shifted back to my seat. There was a house mostly hidden by the trees along the front. The chain link fence had been folded down. From the looks, I would say a large group of zombies had trudged through at some point. The ruined fence was fouled with strips of cloth as well as a few chunks of things best not looked at too closely. From beyond those trees, the sound came again. It was a metal on metal noise like somebody was smacking a pole into a sheet of corrugated metal. It was distant enough, or muffled perhaps, so that I had to concentrate to really hear it.

"What is that noise?" Alex whispered.

For the first time in our short acquaintance, she sounded a little frightened. I very briefly related my own prior experience with a similar situation.

"So they set up and wait for people to pass and then ring the dinner bell?" Tracy gasped.

"Something like that," I said with a nod as we rolled past the church/school.

"How are we supposed to fight this? What's next? Rats...birds...fucking mosquitoes?" Tracy snarled.

"I have only ever seen it jump to dogs," I said, doing my best to sound calm and like I wasn't just as terrified.

We cruised down the highway, and I couldn't help but get to my knees and look back. Sure enough, zombies were just starting to stagger and shamble out onto the road. The dogs were still with them, but only a few turned our direction. Most of them kept going into the yard with the busted fence. We were just going around a slight bend in the road when I saw two zombie children emerge.

They came out to the street and might've looked our direction, but I am certain that I saw them cross the street. The problem with what I saw came from the fact that one of them was carrying something long and slender...like maybe a metal pipe? The other was dragging a square of what I am certain had to be metal.

Could the children be growing this coordinated in their ability to drive the adult versions? This was every kind of bad. I turned back to face front and gather myself. Once I was certain that I had my emotions under control, I shared what I'd seen with the group.

We were back up to speed, actually close to the posted speed limit of 55 miles-per-hour on this stretch of the highway, when the next distraction came into view. It was Alex who saw it first.

"A gun club?" Her voice had a tinge of excitement to it, like a kid anticipating a visit from Santa. "There has to be something there worth a damn."

"Or…" Marshawn let that word draw out and then paused before continuing. "They could be heavily armed and waiting to shoot looters."

"We aren't looting," Alex retorted.

"And I am sure they are going to be the sort to wait and ask us our intentions." Despite his words, Marshawn was slowing down.

"Home of world and national champions," Tracy read from the sign as we came to a stop at the turn-in. "You know, this doesn't mean they actually have stuff on the premises. I imagine most people bring their own gear. It is a rifle *club*, not a shop."

Marshawn eased the steering wheel over to turn in when a muffled report sounded. It was almost instantly followed by the 'ting' of a bullet striking the hood of the big Durango. The vehicle jerked to a halt as Marshawn stepped hard on the brakes.

"Yeah...I don't think so," he said as he cranked us around and floored it so that we accelerated away rapidly.

"What the hell!" Alex exclaimed, looking back at the entrance to the rifle club as it faded away. "Why would they do that?"

"Maybe they've met the wrong sort," I offered with a shrug as I sat back and watched the scenery zoom past. "I can't say I'm all that angry...or surprised, considering what I've bumped into out here."

Alex opened her mouth to say something, but instead just sighed and turned back to face the front. I couldn't help but notice all the farmland passing us by. Much of it looked to have already been tilled and perhaps even planted. Maybe we would have to return to this area over the next several weeks. If we could just reach our destination and it panned out the way I was hoping, we might be able to make a halfway decent life for ourselves.

A small voice in the back of my mind started whispering to me that I might never see it come to fruition even if it was a success. As soon as we got settled, I would take a few days, and then I had to go find Don Evans and rescue Carl, Selina, and anybody else who didn't want to live under his rule.

At last, we passed a Ranger station on our right as we came to a sweeping bend in the highway. Estacada was right around the corner which was one of the places that I intended to use as site for scavenging supplies.

"So much for that," I whispered to myself as the small town came into view.

The small shops and eateries that sat to our left had been torched. It had been very deliberate from the looks of things. Whomever had done this had used a mountain of tires from the Les Schwab Tires, setting them on fire and using that fire to bring down all the other establishments at this end of town.

We slowed to a crawl as a series of spike strips became visible in the road ahead. Then we noticed the collection of fire trucks that had been parked to form a giant square around an already fenced in tower at the other end of the small town. That was also where a line of RVs were parked, sealing the road off that would allow us to turn into the little downtown area. Along the roofs of the RVs, a group of people stood, all of them with a variety of weapons either slung over the shoulder, or cradled against the chest.

"If anybody has any ideas, now is a good time to share them," Marshawn called out as we rolled to a stop.

"Attention vehicle occupants," a voice called out. "We ask that you please step out of your vehicle. Do not display or reach for any form of firearms."

I looked between the front seats and took in what waited for us. I could count ten people on the RVs and there was movement on the tower. Now that I got a better look at it, I could see that it was some sort of fire department training structure. This small town was apparently faring better than the big city. I couldn't say I was all that surprised. The population in rural areas such as Estacada were known for being much more prone to owning a variety of weapons.

I opened my door and stepped out first, making a point to raise my hands above my head. "Everybody else just stay put. If this goes bad, try to get away," I said from the side of my mouth, doing my best not to move my lips as I spoke.

I walked around to the front of the vehicle and stopped when I saw a group of five individuals climb down, converse briefly, and then saunter over with the casual confidence of a group that at least feels like it has the advantage. I wasn't going to dispute that at the moment.

The man leading the 'welcoming committee' had a serious no-nonsense look about him. Wearing what looked like a felt cowboy hat, he stood around six and a half feet tall. I would guess him in the two-hundred-and-fifty-pound range. His gray beard was probably well-kept during the pre-zombie era, but it was just starting to show signs of being a bit scruffy with a few hairs jutting out and starting to curl. He was barrel-chested and looked maybe a touch larger than he really was due to the heavy sweatshirt, leather jacket, work boots, and faded coveralls.

He held a shotgun casually in his hands as he approached. I noticed a pair of pistols dangling from his hips as well as pouches that most likely held more ammunition. He carried some sort of scoped hunting rifle over his shoulder and had a nasty-looking knife strapped to one leg.

"How many more folks you got in that rig?" the man asked by way of greeting when he came to a stop about ten feet away from me.

"Just a few." I wasn't going to just start handing out information. "And a dog."

"And what brings you out here?" the man pressed, looking past me and eyeing the Durango with a concentrated squint.

"Actually just making our way out to the hills," I answered. Again, I wasn't going to tell this man a thing. If he thought otherwise, then he was sadly mistaken. "And we don't want any trouble. We just want to move on...hopefully set ourselves up someplace safe and ride this out."

"Safe?" the man barked. "How long you been out? If you've been hiding out in one of them shelters, then you might've missed the news, friend. Ain't no place safe these days."

"Yeah...well hanging around the metro area is a bit worse than out here. If we are gonna have a shot at making it, then getting away from Portland was a priority."

As I spoke, I let my own eyes do some drifting. Unless I was mistaken, a couple of the guys backing up this fella were carrying grenades. I knew that folks living away from the city might own a few less-than-legal weapons, but I absolutely did not expect to see grenades.

"What do we have here, Ken?" a dark-haired man wearing jeans, a dress shirt and tie, and shiny, black boots asked as he strolled up.

If this was a movie, I'd just found the bad guy. This man screamed 'politician' from his clothes to his way-too-friendly nature as he sauntered up. I noticed he only carried a single pistol on his hip.

"They say they're passing through...leaving the city and heading out someplace safe," the man, apparently his name was Ken, replied, sounding a bit derisive when he said that last bit.

"Where exactly is this safe place?" the politician asked, his smile not slipping in the least as he stepped up beside Ken and gave me a nod in greeting. "Before everything went south, word had it that most of the Asian countries were simply gone. Both Koreas blew each other up if you believe that happy-crappy. India just imploded. Their population density and poverty made them fast food for them infecteds. Russia denied the problem all the way up to the end, but YouTube exposed that lie before the internet crashed for good. Big cities and small towns all went the way of the dodo for the most part."

"You seem to be doing okay." I gave a nod to the tower and the RVs blocking the main entrance to what I assumed to be downtown Estacada.

"We lost our share. Just had a few people that weren't fooled by the media denials early on and set ourselves up to defend against the infection getting a foothold is all. That..." he paused and looked over my shoulder at the Durango, "...and the fact we also figured on the living becoming more of a problem than the infected."

"Well, we don't want to be a problem," I insisted, taking a step back when I saw this man turn his attention back to me. There was a sudden hardness in his eyes that did not match the smile he still wore. "We honestly just want to move along and find our own place."

"You all don't really have any idea what your doin', do ya?" Ken chortled. "There been a few groups try to pass through here, then sneak back in and try to take from our people."

"I can't speak for any of those folks." I took a step

back. "We've had enough of our own troubles with some bad people wandering these parts. In fact, if you see a school bus come rumbling along, you might be best served just shooting first and asking questions later."

The two men glanced at each other and then the one named Ken leaned over and whispered something to the politician. After a moment, the two men finished their whispered conversation and Ken gave me a slight nod.

"One of our citizens said something about a bus. Actually, we have a 'shoot on sight' order out for any such vehicle that might come our way." Ken took a step back and ushered me forward with his arm. "We would like for you and your people to come to our checkpoint. We want to take down names and the information on that vehicle. If you don't prove to be a problem, and if for some reason you need to come back this way, it will make things easier."

That seemed like a reasonable request. I could understand their caution, and as long as that was all this was, then I didn't see the harm.

It took a total of about an hour, but my crew all signed the register they were handed. They even treated us to a jar of beer. Apparently the one guy, Ken, owned some sort of local brewery.

Also, I'd been right about the politician. I discovered that he had been the mayor of Estacada. His name was Sean Drinkwine, and while he came across as a bit smarmy, he turned out to be a gracious host. He even explained the logic behind their register. "Let's say you folks decide you want to come back this direction and maybe ask to become a part of our community, this way, if any of us here today don't happen to be on sentry when you come back, who knows what could happen."

He then showed me a large register with names of people, a few vehicle license plate numbers and descriptions, and even a few photos of people that were either welcome or not. They added all the information we had about Don Evans and Natasha Petrov to the list.

While this community did seem to have things on the ball, I also noticed an undercurrent of unease from some of the people that had gathered around us during the entire process. Whether it was because of our presence or some internal strife, I had no idea.

By the time it was all said and done, we'd even been given a few boxes of venison. I guess they had a surplus of meat and were feeling exceptionally generous. A part of me wondered if they would come to regret that gesture as time ticked past. There were going to be those who had a very difficult time putting the 'old ways' behind them. I was of the mindset that food would become a very precious commodity much sooner than some might believe.

By now, nothing perishable that had sat in bins or on shelves was still edible. This was just another reason we had to get settled and get a garden in place. We would be living out of cans for a while, and I knew that was not the most ideal dietary situation. One of the things I was going to put at the top of our scavenging list was vitamins. There were a number of illnesses that would start to manifest as things progressed. Right off the top of my head, I thought of scurvy. I didn't actually know what it was, but I was pretty sure it was something pirates used to get because of lack of vitamin C or something.

At last, we said our farewells and loaded back into the SUV. Michael and Chewie both collapsed. I'd seen them both being lavished with attention during the early part of our arrival. Once I spread the word about Michael's situation, many people gave him space, but there was nothing I could say that would keep them from Chewie. That had been an issue before zombies. Anytime I took her anywhere, people just couldn't get enough...and she absorbed the attention that came her way.

One of the RVs was moved, and we rolled past the blockade, taking a right on what the sign said was Highway 211. Next stop...Milo McIver State Park.

Hopefully.

9

Getting Situated

I ducked under the outstretched arms of the zombie staggering towards me with dried blood smeared on its mouth that did not look more than a couple of hours old. Its teeth clicked together as it bit down where my arm had been just a few seconds earlier.

A dull 'thunk' sounded, and its head split at the top. I stepped back to see Marshawn yank his machete free. He gave me a nod as he moved past me to take on the next closest zombie.

Tracy was on her knees pulling her knife free from the temple of a girl that had to be in her mid-teens. She wiped the blade on the tattered tee shirt and stood. Only a few of the undead remained, and each was being engaged. It was over. At least this phase was in the books. We hadn't got-

231

ten much past the main park section of the campgrounds.

"Looks like we weren't the first to think of this idea," Tracy quipped as she sauntered over.

I looked around at the two dozen corpses that littered the ground. Most were dressed in what I was starting to recognize as basic post-apocalypse gear. A mix of leathers, baseball catcher's gear, football pads, and helmets, adorned many of the zombies we'd taken down.

The football helmets proved to be the most problematic as it protected the only vulnerable location on the undead. The one I'd taken down had also been close to the three-hundred-pound range. I was almost willing to bet that the kid had probably played for an area high school. His gear had fit him far too perfectly. I'd had to switch to a Ka-Bar knife I carried strapped to my right thigh. I'd driven it into the cage that protected most of the face, but it had taken a few attempts.

"Probably came in that big van," Darya sniffed as she wiped her own blade clean on a swatch of cloth. "And was it me, or did every single one of the girls have a damn 'Shari' shirt on?"

"Right?" Tracy sniffed.

"I think she was in concert here a few weeks before all

hell broke loose," Marshawn said as he came over and plopped down in the grass.

"Yeah?" I chuckled. "Big fan were ya?"

"Some of her stuff was okay." Marshawn gave an unapologetic shrug. "So, what next. This place is a bit more open than I imagined. And I'm not sure how you expect us to set up any sort of decent perimeter. This whole place is dangerously hard to control. Zombies could come from just about anywhere. And then there are the living."

"That would be my bigger concern," Tracy piped in. "Zombies are a problem in numbers, and even though we had more than a few here, it wasn't too bad."

I wanted to tell her to speak for herself. I'd been in danger a couple of times as we'd cleared the area. Of course, I'd been dumb enough to just hop out of the car and mosey up to the cluster of five that were gathered around an outhouse, pawing at the exterior. I didn't expect to find two more zombies inside the damn stink box.

"I say we do a sweep of the place." I wiped off my own blade. "The road winds through the park. We should follow it down and get in the general vicinity of the actual river. I don't want us too close in case it overflows during the flooding season. But having this ready water source close at hand will be a game changer."

"So what do you think happened to that other group?" Darya waved a hand at the corpses scattered around.

"Could be anything." Alex gave a shrug as she pulled her canteen from her pack and took a drink. "Maybe one or two of them were infected when they got here. It wouldn't surprise me. That's a big reason the FEMA shelters fell. Once somebody turned inside, it just went downhill fast. Or, maybe a small pack came through and caught them off-guard."

Michael and Chewie got out of the Durango after Darya opened the door for them. Almost instantly the two started chasing each other around the open grassy area of the softball field. I noticed they stayed well clear of the dead bodies.

"I'll keep an eye on them here," Darya offered. "You guys take a look around."

"Tracy?" I motioned the woman over. "You wanna hang here? Marshawn, Alex, and I can head into the camp grounds and see what we have to work with."

"Sure." She gave a shrug and walked over to sit on the picnic table beside where Darya had plopped down.

"You think splitting up is a good idea?" Alex mumbled as we climbed into the SUV.

I looked out at Michael and Chewie as they ran around chasing each other. I could hear Chewie's deep 'woof' and the boy's laughter.

"I don't think it's the best idea, and if this were a movie, the big nasty would show up right after we disappeared from view. But those two have been cooped up and kept quiet for too long. I think they both need this." I turned the key and started the big vehicle. "If we don't give them a little time to blow off some steam and run off some of that energy, I think they will explode. Besides, I believe we need to get out of the car and search around down by the river."

"Yeah? So?" Alex shot back as I followed the arrows that pointed us towards the campsites.

"Every time we stop and get out, that dog barks," Marshawn answered for me. "If there is anything in these woods, I'd like to get the jump on it."

That seemed to satisfy her. She sat back with only a slight huff and stared out the window. I know it was just my imagination, but it seemed like the shadows grew ominous and much darker the moment we turned the corner that put the open field where Chewie and Michael played out of view.

We hadn't gone far at all when the first zombie staggered out of the trees and shrubs that lined the narrow access road. This one was in full police riot gear; the only saving grace was the shattered face shield. I didn't recall seeing any police cars in the parking lot when we'd rolled up into this place.

I stopped and Marshawn climbed out. He pulled his machete from its sheath on his hip and let the zombie approach him. As soon as it was close enough, he plunged the tip of the blade into the zombie's face. It dropped to the ground almost anticlimactically and Marshawn turned to come back, wiping off his blade. He took two steps and froze.

Just as he turned, obviously hearing something that I wasn't, a gunshot sounded. That I did hear.

I threw open my door when a second shot sounded, quickly followed by the sound of a bullet hitting the metal of the big Durango. I was momentarily torn between getting back in the vehicle or exiting and rushing to help my friend. In that span, another shot sounded and the driver's side window shattered, the glass spraying me.

I threw myself to the ground and rolled underneath. I

heard the passenger door open and saw Alex's feet hit the ground. She took three fast strides toward the scrub that line the road. Another shot rang out and I could see her fly through the air and vanish into the thick greenery.

"Evan!" Marshawn hissed.

I looked out the front and saw him sprawled on the road. I could also see a dark stain on the pavement around his left shoulder area.

"Are you okay?" I hissed.

"No, idiot, I'm freakin' shot!"

Another shot rang out and I heard it puncture the metal of the SUV almost directly above my head. A second later, the hiss of what had to be the radiator started. A steady drizzle of fluid that began to spatter just in front of me confirmed my suspicion.

"C'mon out or the next round hits that fella lyin' in the middle of the road," a voice shouted from up ahead and to my left.

I considered staying put, but one look at Marshawn told me I couldn't. He needed help right now.

"I'm coming out, but I need to get to my friend. He's bleeding," I shouted back.

I'm pretty sure I heard somebody mutter "Oh shit!"

but I was already rolling out from under the damaged SUV. Staying low in a crouch, I rushed over to Marshawn who had managed to roll onto his back.

As soon as I reached him, I could see the large dark stain on his shoulder. He was bleeding heavily, and his eyes were squeezed shut in pain.

"It looks worse than it is," Marshawn managed through clenched teeth.

"Oh, good...because it looks like you are going to bleed out," I snarled as I pulled a knife and cut away his jacket and shirt.

Marshawn was a pretty big guy. He had a broad chest and shoulders. Those shoulders were both capped with humps of shoulder muscle that would make a camel jealous. From the looks, a bullet had gone through the left trapezius muscle. There was a puckered hole that was oozing blood in a very steady stream.

"My bag is in the car," he said. "Grab it."

I jumped up, almost having forgotten about the shooter. I was quickly reminded when a figure in full hunter's camo stepped out from the trees. He even had the hat with a veil over his face so I couldn't see him. As soon as I jumped to my feet, he brought the nasty looking hunting rifle up to his shoulder. From the looks of it, I guessed it to be a -30.06. It had a scope, but at this range, he wouldn't miss.

"I don't have time for this," I spat. "My friend is bleeding out. Either shoot me or let me go to our rig to grab his medical bag."

"He's a doctor?" the voice behind the veil gasped. "Oh...crap."

I decided that the time for talking was done and turned my back on our attacker. I rushed to the Durango and threw the door to the rear cargo area open. A black bag shoved off to the side jumped out at me and I unzipped it to be sure. Sure enough, I saw bandages, some tubes of whatever, and a few bottles of alcohol and such.

Grabbing it, I rushed back and knelt beside Marshawn. "Tell me what to do."

I registered the fact that our shooter had moved closer and was now kneeling on the other side of Marshawn's body. He'd lifted his camo veil and I almost dumped the medical bag. I grabbed one of my filthy gloves by the fingertips and jerked it from my hand then repeated the gesture with my other glove.

"A fucking kid," Marshawn hissed. "I got shot by a

kid?"

"I'm seventeen," the boy said defensively. "And are you really a doctor?"

"Not right now," I snapped as I pulled out some gauze and one of the bottles of alcohol.

Popping the lid, I pressed the wad of gauze to the mouth of the bottle just as the acrid smell singed my nostrils. I felt the cool liquid as it saturated the bit of gauze. I leaned forward to make a swipe at the wound.

"Wait!" Marshawn barked. "Kid, get over here. When he puts that on this wound, it's gonna hurt even worse than it does now."

The kid glanced at me as if seeking permission. I just shrugged.

He quickly shouldered his weapon and scrambled forward on his knees. "Okay, now what?"

Marshawn swung so fast, it was little more than a blur as his right fist connected with the kid's nose. A nasty crunch sounded followed by a yelp that was probably more pain than surprise...and I had to imagine he was pretty dang surprised, so I had to guess the punch hurt.

"What the—" the kid began.

"That's for shooting me," Marshawn snapped. "You're

lucky that's all I'm doing."

"So I don't get to shoot him?" a voice said from the bushes.

Alex stood up and slung her rifle over her shoulder. For his part, the kid hardly flinched. He did glance over his shoulders briefly, and when he turned back to me, I am pretty sure he breathed a near silent whistle.

Alex strolled over and nudged the kid out of the way. "I've got him. You've done enough."

"You ready?" I held up the alcohol-soaked gauze.

Marshawn nodded. Without any delay — or warning — I slapped the wadded material on the wound. I probably could've done it differently, but I wanted to just get to it. For his part, Marshawn made a long hiss as he sucked air in between his teeth.

I wiped at the bleeding hole and then swapped out the first bit with another. After two more times of doing that, Marshawn directed me to soak the next one and then push it into the wound. Next, I repeated the process on the exit would. I cleaned it as best I could and then packed in some more fresh gauze soaked with alcohol. After that, I slapped a square of the stuff on front and back, taping it into place.

As soon as I had that done, Marshawn sat up. He shrugged himself into his coat and then reached up to have me help him to his feet.

"You wanna tell me why the hell you shot at us?" Alex said as Marshawn flexed the hand on his injured side.

"Umm...well..." the kid stammered.

"You make it a habit of shooting at people?" I pressed.

"No, but there were these people here two days ago. They were crazy. Tried to set fires in a bunch of the campsites. Running around making a bunch of noise. Almost like they were trying to bring zombies down on this place."

I described Don Evans and Natasha and asked if any of the people fit that description. He didn't even hesitate before saying that nobody fitting those descriptions were part of the raiders. Once he described the first person as being black, I knew this group were not involved with the Evans crew.

"Name?" Alex snapped, apparently bored with the banality of the conversation.

"Todd...Todd Burns."

The kid removed his hat and I could now get a good look at him. He still had a smattering of teenage acne marring his face. His teeth were a bit widely spaced. This was even more pronounced with his front upper teeth to the point I would swear you could fit a drinking straw between them. I had a brief thought that it was now beyond realistic to think he would ever see an orthodontist to correct the problem. His blondish hair was cut down to a crewcut. He had thin lips that barely amounted to a dark slash where his mouth was, and his blue eyes were close set. His nose was upturned, and his nostrils constantly looked flared. He was perhaps about six feet tall; and if he had a few rocks in his pocket, might weight a hundred and seventy.

"And I take it you're alone?" Alex asked as she made a show of slinging her rifle over her shoulder.

"Yeah...why?" Todd Burns answered meekly.

"Idiot." In a flash, Alex grabbed the kid by the arm, tossed him over her hip and onto the ground and dropped onto his chest with her knees on either side of his head. She held a knife I hadn't seen her produce with the pointed tip just scant centimeters above the kid's rapidly blinking left eye.

"You don't ever give yourself up like that," Alex hissed as the kid began to both babble and whimper; almost simultaneously begging her not to kill him and asking what he'd done wrong. "As far as we knew…until just now…you might have a dozen people hiding in the woods with guns trained on us. Now we know it's just you. I could gut you and leave you for walker bait right now with no worries."

"And I would put a bullet in the back of your head," a female voice called from behind us.

I turned to see a girl who also looked to be in her teens. She had a rifle pressed to her shoulder and it was obvious that she had Alex in her sights.

If I wouldn't have been staring at Alex's face, I would've missed that very slight twitch of her lips that suggested a smile. It was there and gone in the blink of an eye…but I know what I saw.

She raised her hands, making a demonstration of pulling that blade away from where it had just been pointed at Todd's eye. Turning slowly, she faced the girl who now had her at gunpoint.

"And who might you be?" Alex said softly.

"The person with the gun…that's about all you need to know right now." The girl stepped over some tall grass and edged around so that she had an unobstructed view of all three of us, but her gun never came off Alex.

"Are we gonna stand here and have a pissing contest until something comes along and takes a bite out of all our asses?" Marshawn growled. "In case anybody forgot...I was the one who just got shot."

"And how do we know you aren't part of that group of assholes that just rolled through here the other day, shooting the place up and causing trouble?" the girl snapped back.

"I guess you don't." I stepped forward, raising my hands a little higher to hopefully demonstrate that I wasn't trying to cause a problem.

"They weren't doing anything like them other guys," Todd said, wiping at the blood that dripped from his nose. "And they got a girl with them." He made a gesture to Alex.

"I'm a woman." She sheathed her knife and made a nod towards the girl still holding the gun pointed at her. "*That*...is a girl."

"I didn't mean..." Todd began to sputter and stammer, but Alex actually laughed.

"I'm just busting your chops. All that crap people used to get so excited about is really low on the list of things to get worked up over, wouldn't you agree?"

"Ummm...I guess." Todd shrugged. "Margaret, put the gun down."

"Don't call me that," the girl huffed as she lowered her weapon.

"I'm really sorry about shooting you, mister." Todd turned to the man he'd injured, his neck turning scarlet as the blush of embarrassment crawled to his face and came into full bloom on his cheeks.

"Well, it seems to have passed through," Marshawn said with a shrug that turned to a wince. "Just gonna have to keep it clean so infection doesn't settle in."

We made hasty introductions where we learned that Margaret Burns preferred to be called 'Maggie'. We still didn't reveal anything about the others back at the main campground, but with what we'd learned about things that had happened, I suddenly very much wanted to get back to Chewie, Michael, and the ladies.

And then we heard the baby-cry sound.

As one, all of us spun to face the source of that hair-raising noise. A single zombie stumbled from the woods. He looked like he might've been a park ranger or whatever they have stationed at McIver. His uniform was shredded and most of his right arm looked like it had been thrown in a wood chipper. Strips of meat hung from it in dried strands that resembled beef jerky. His mouth was a dark stain, and when he opened it, that awful sound came out looking very wrong as it came from a man easily over two hundred and fifty pounds.

"I've got him," I said as I stepped past Marshawn and drew my blade.

Just as I plunged the blade into the side of its head, a crash came from off to our right. Several more of the un-dead were fighting their way through the woods to get to us. They had reached an area dense with foliage and were now making a lot of racket.

"Maybe we should bail," Todd whispered, sounding far too nervous for somebody who'd been out in this envi-ronment for as long as it appeared he'd been.

"There aren't that many." Alex gave a dismissive wave as she stalked past the uncertain boy who was now looking over at his sister for an indication of what to do.

Maggie pulled what looked like little more than an axe handle with a metal spike attached to the end and fol-lowed Alex into the scrubby brush. I was on their heels after I put up a hand to keep Marshawn from joining in.

"Oh, now you want to be all worried about some-body's injuries," he grumped as I took off at a jog.

Once we had them put down, we looked around the boat landing and found a few good places to start a base. One of the first things we would need to do would be to erect a barricade.

"There is a backhoe or something along those lines back behind the park manager's office," Maggie said as we all walked up the road back to where the rest of our group waited.

"Great, hopefully we will be able to get it running." I gave my machete a pat. "But something like that is going to bring the undead. We will need to have basically every-body else ready to fight off anything that heads our way."

Alex gave me a slight nudge and raised her eyebrows and then gave a slight nod in the direction we were head-ed. I was pretty sure I understood her intent.

"So, we do have other members in our group," I said as conversationally as possible.

"How many?" Maggie asked.

"Two women, a little boy…and a dog." I had paused for a few breaths before I said that last part.

"A dog?" Todd showed the first real excitement I'd

seen from him.

In just the brief time we'd been around this brother and sister, I'd figured out in a hurry that she was the one calling the shots. She'd really ripped him a new one for shooting Marshawn. The kid looked a bit beat down the whole time we walked back to the main area where the others waited. Now, at the mention of a dog, he was almost a new person.

"Yeah...a Newfie," I answered.

"What is a Newfie?" Todd pressed, the excitement leaking through his voice.

"They are big and black—" I started.

"Like me," Marshawn joked.

"They are known for being very lovable."

"Me again," Marshawn snickered as he popped in with another comment.

"And are amazing swimmers." I paused and glanced over at the big man.

"Don't look at me," he scoffed. "I'm black. Me and swimming don't jive at all."

"You suck," I shot back with a laugh and a shake of my head.

"Okay...I was just screwing with you. Actually, I

swim pretty well. Used to spend the summers kicking it with my buds on the river. We'd hook up and take out the Jet Skis, then cruise around all day. We'd grill at night and catch a buzz."

"Sounds like fun," I said with a wistful sigh as I thought back to the previous summer.

Steph and I had spent two weeks camping with friends beside a river in the Coastal Range. It had been the first time we'd taken anything resembling a vacation together. By the time we got home, neither of us wanted to even mention the word 'camping' again. That had been when we discovered that the most we could tolerate was about three days. After that, it lost any of its appeal. Now, here I was, about to basically spend the rest of my life doing something along those lines.

We walked in silence for a bit. It hadn't seemed nearly as far when we'd been in the SUV. It was Alex who asked what I think had been on my mind since meeting these two.

"So...what's your story?" she said to Maggie.

"We came up from Corvallis for a concert with our high school choir. Shari was in Portland, and a bunch of us got to be part of the choir that sang back-up for her. After that, we were supposed to stay in Portland for three days and our show choir was supposed to do a few performances. Next was a trip to Canada to sing in a competition in Vancouver. We were on our way home..."

Her voice cracked just a bit and she swallowed to get her composure back before continuing. I glanced over and saw Todd's face had become an unreadable mask.

"The bus driver literally abandoned us on the highway. He pulled over and I guess had called somebody and they pulled up, he got out, jumped in the car, and vanished.

"He'd taken us off I-5 and so nobody knew where we were. One of our chaperones had grown up outside of Portland, so she drove us here. She said that we needed to get away from the heavy traffic areas." Maggie stopped talking and a sigh escaped her that sounded like all of her spirit had just fled from between her lips.

"But out here?" Alex pressed. "McIver? Hell, this entire area? Why would anybody come out here?" She shot a quick look at me. "No offense, but I don't see what the big deal is about the place."

"None taken," I said with a shrug. "I think it is just remote enough to be off the beaten path, plus a lot of folks made this place an annual ritual for holidays like Memorial Day and the Fourth. Maybe it just has a connection with good memories."

"I think that's what Miss Bordal said," Maggie sniffed and then wiped at her eyes. "When we got there, the place was almost totally empty. The only other person there was the park manager guy and his family. He tried to make us leave, but Miss Bordal and Mister Geddes pretty much told him that we weren't going anywhere. The freeway was closed heading south and Portland was crazy with what were initially being called rioters…but we all know what they really were. Then martial law was put in effect and we were stuck."

"Tell them about the police man," Todd piped up suddenly.

"Oh yeah," Maggie drew that one word out like she had forgotten. Although, as she related the story, I didn't see how.

"This police car showed up one night. The officer was this big guy. His arm was all bandaged and he only made it two steps from his car when he fell flat on his face. Miss Bordal and Mister Geddes helped carry him to the office. That night, we heard screams from the little building. We were all still sleeping in the bus at that time. I was one of the few people that went to see what was happening."

"One of the idiots," Todd muttered under his breath.

Maggie gave him an elbow to the ribs that didn't look very gentle, but to the boy's credit, he didn't show any signs that it hurt.

"We got to the door when it flew open and the manager guy's wife stumbled out. She was holding her throat, but even in the weak light of the lantern somebody was carrying, you could see all the blood. We could hear fighting, and then the worst scream I ever heard in my life...up until that day...came from the building. I still can't believe that noise came from Mister Geddes.

"We ran back to the bus and shut the doors, but a few minutes later, Mister Geddes came out of the building and came to the bus, trying to get in. It was Miss Bordal who went out and killed Mister Geddes. Although...I guess he was already dead. But none of us were ready for it and we shut her out of the bus."

Now Maggie's voice choked off. Tears started to run down her cheeks and Alex put an arm around her in what seemed like a very awkward gesture for her.

"That policeman, the park guy, and his wife attacked

her, and we just watched."

My head turned, and I could see that Todd also had tears leaking from his eyes. He stared back at me without any shame. I was kinda jealous. I didn't think I could do that in front of the others right now...much less total strangers.

"We all hid at the back of the bus while she screamed...screamed that terrible scream. She begged us...called some of us by our names as they tore her apart. In the end, she said terrible things...and we deserved it." Todd sniffed. "Then...what was left of her got up and joined the others pawing at the bus trying to get in. At some point, the lantern had been dropped and we were in the dark. It was so black you could hardly see your hand in front of your face. When the sun came up, I think most of us wished it hadn't. There was so much blood."

We walked in silence a while again. The only sounds were our feet crunching in the gravel of the access road. Sun filtered through the trees and illuminated the dust motes that were still settling from when we'd driven through.

"I finally couldn't take it," Maggie whispered. "And so those were the first zombies I ever killed. I put down

Miss Bordal, the park guy, his wife, and the policeman."

"By yourself?" Marshawn asked, a bit of awe leaking through in his voice. Maggie nodded, and I noticed a flush in her cheeks that had nothing to do with the tears leaking from her eyes. "So, you're kind of a bad ass."

That last remark was said with sincere respect. I had to agree. Considering she was a teenaged girl and had taken down a handful of the undead on her own while everybody else that had been with her did nothing...bad ass was the tamest thing I would think to call her. But that brought up something.

"What happened to the rest of your group?" I asked. "You said there were a bunch of you from this choir, right? Where are they now?"

There was a long silence as we continued to walk along the gravel road with its two distinct ruts where countless sets of tires had rolled. I shot a look Todd's direction, but he was staring at his feet as he walked. Obviously he wasn't going to talk, Then I realized I couldn't blame him. I'd just scolded him recently about giving up his numbers. Of course, his response had been a lie, but still…

"We're all that is left." Maggie sniffed and wiped at

her running nose with one sleeve before she continued. "Some of them vanished in the night, a few got bit and…are gone. The rest either died or were taken when those…*animals* came through the other night."

"We came here thinking to fortify it and make a safer place to stay," I explained as I could see the opening in the trees up ahead. We were almost back to Chewie, Michael, and the others. "If you don't have a problem with it, this is where we want to make our base."

"Why?" Todd blurted. "Wouldn't it be better to find a house?"

"Not really." I gave a shake of my head. "For one, without power, they are only going to be good for shelter. They will be cold and, unless we find one with an adequate fireplace, offer nothing in the way of heat. But even with a fireplace, the results will be negligible. Also, there will be no ready source of water. And sewage would quickly become a problem."

"But why here? Why this place?" Maggie took up the question.

I explained the dire need for water as well as being someplace remote to hopefully prevent the likely reoccurrence of more raiders like the ones they'd already encountered. I told them about the little island I recalled and how we could make it into a fallback location in an emergency.

Once I finished with my explanation, I saw them both nodding. They understood, or at least were pretending to.

"And we can be a part of your group just like that?" Maggie pressed.

"I don't see why not."

The pair stopped and stepped away from us, heads bowed together as they whispered back and forth for a moment. After a few minutes, they broke their conference and Maggie turned to face me.

"We accept your offer."

It hadn't been much in the way as an offer, more like a suggestion, but I was glad. Something told me that we needed to try and bolster our numbers.

While it was the norm for most of the zombie stories I watched or read to have just a few people band together, I was discovering a steep learning curve that required more than what I'd learned from the fictional versions of such a thing.

A thought came to me and I realized that the only times there were large groups in these things, they tended to be the bad guys...the raiders who hit the small cluster of "good" guys. Heck, up to this point, that part had been correct. The people like Don Evans and his sort were banding together in large numbers so they could hit groups and take their stuff.

It was time to flip the script. My group was going to grow, and we weren't going to be a bunch of heartless raiders. We would grow into a force that could repel attacks as we brought in more survivors that allowed us to become an outpost of humanity.

There were still so many questions. Were the zombies going to eventually wind down as their food source depleted? From what I was seeing, the undead were not looking like they were weakening. They simply continued to exist.

One thing I had to cling to if I was going to keep my sanity was the simple fact that all of the rules from the society we'd all known just a few months ago were null and void. Setting up this new community was going to be a trial of errors. I could only hope that I wasn't going to get somebody killed by making the wrong decision.

As we neared the end of the road, and the open field of the actual park portion of McIver became more clearly visible, I felt a lump in my throat.

I hadn't realized I'd stopped walking until Marshawn gave me a nudge. "You okay?"

I kept staring straight ahead, my vision on the verge of blurry as a hint of moisture congregated in my eyes. I watched as Chewie bounded through the grass that was already a few inches high in a sign of the coming spring. Running along beside him was Michael. The boy was laughing. I could hear it from where I stood. It was an incredible sound. That laughter was occasionally punctuated with a deep 'woof' from the bounding Newfoundland.

In that moment, everything was as close to normal as we'd probably ever see for the foreseeable future. We were about to embark on building what we hoped would become a stronghold able to shelter us and assist in keeping us safe from those who wished us harm.

Suddenly, Chewie stopped. She sniffed at the air, and then turned our direction. With the same deep bark I'd come to know and love that greeted me every day in the 'Before' when I returned from work, she came for me at a gallop.

10

Kids and Kitties

The next few days, we scoured the riverbank. We selected a location not too far from the boat launch area and
got to work. We had some basic tools, but it also became
very clear that we needed more than we had managed to
scrape together. We found more implements in a shack by
the groundkeeper's place.

Marshawn found the keys, and the best news we'd
had early on was that the backhoe had a full tank and
there was even a barrel with about twenty or so gallons
left, a pump, and three five-gallon tanks. That meant we
would dig a trench first thing.

The zombies were a very infrequent problem unless
we were running the noisy machine. What was worse
were the occasional gunshots echoing throughout the

countryside. Twice, I'm sure I heard screams. The one thing we didn't hear were any vehicles.

At last, we had a nice trench that was about ten feet wide and at least eight feet deep. We'd set ourselves up far enough back from the river that we didn't have to worry about water flooding in. We'd wanted it a bit deeper, but we hit a nasty layer of rock that Marshawn said was probably old volcanic stuff and decided we would be happy with what we had.

We'd put up a single six-person tent, and always had one person on watch as we got started. Once the trench was finished—a two-day job—I decided that it would be good for us to start hitting the very few residences along the road where the entrance to McIver ran. The houses up here were the multi-million-dollar types, and I didn't hold much hope that the group that had come through and attacked Maggie and Todd's group hadn't already stripped it. Still, if we didn't at least look...

It was decided that Alex and Todd would come with me. We all agreed that we needed to have at least two people running the foraging missions together. Since I'd suggested this particular run to see if we could find anything useful in the gigantic homes, I got to choose my team.

It was also made clear that either Alex, Marshawn, or I would have to stay behind each time. We had that particular conversation away from Darya and Tracy since we didn't want to rile them up or make them feel like they couldn't be trusted.

Because Marshawn was nursing his having recently been shot, I chose Alex to be on this run. Also, I wanted to get a better grasp of Todd's capabilities, so I added him to the team. Maggie had protested, insisting that she be the one to go, but I explained that I had no worries about her ability to handle herself.

"So you're taking my brother because...?" Her tone was hard, and I felt the challenge coming through loud and clear.

"Because we need to know he can handle himself," I answered.

"He's handled himself fine so far."

"Yeah," Marshawn snorted, "tell that to my shoulder."

"He thought you guys were those raiders returning for more," Maggie hissed. "You have no idea what those people were like."

I thought of my encounters with Don Evans and Natasha. "Actually, I think I do."

She tried to insist that she'd be a bigger help, but I shut it down and made the plans for Alex, Todd, and I to head out at first light the next morning.

***

Light was stretching things. We woke to a steady rain and a frigid wind that cut through to the bone. Part of me wanted to put it off for better weather, but I didn't feel like debating with Maggie for another day. Plus, our food stores were getting thin already. While I did not expect to find much, there was always the possibility we'd find something that looters hadn't scooped up.

The three of us headed up the long, paved entry drive as the blackness was pushed back by the gloomy gray. We all picked out our own version of what we felt made good survival gear the night before, but had to modify things a bit to compensate for the rain.

I didn't like wearing a third layer of clothing. I felt as if it made me even less maneuverable, but getting sick was a situation made much worse given the current situation of the world.

By the time we reached South Springwater Road, I was already soggy and my nose was stuffed up. We had two immediate choices. One of them was an older residence that looked like it had been around forever. That one was directly across from us. The other was one of the huge mansions with the great view of Mount Hood that folks paid millions for. It had a heavy iron fence with an electric gate, but oddly enough, that only ran along the front of the residence.

Thick woods lined both sides, but all that they bothered to put up along the sides was a simple barbed wire strand fence. We tossed some of our gear over, and then just ducked between the top and middle strands.

I held onto a little hope since the gate and front fence looked to still be intact. When we were all on the actual grounds, I heard a soft moan.

Looking around, at first I didn't see anything. Eventually, a cluster of bushes moved, and out crawled a man. What was left of him.

"No way." Todd started toward the zombie, drawing his machete. He was a few steps from it when he stopped and glanced over his shoulder. "He ain't got no teeth."

That made Alex laugh. After a moment, I joined in.

265

When you thought about it…a toothless zombie was kind of funny.

"Should I kill it, or just let it be?" Todd asked.

"Never leave one behind you if you can help it," I said as our laughter sobered.

The zombie was now out on the grass of the expansive yard. Judging by the response of the other two, I think we were now realizing that our laughter was coming at the expense of a man who had obviously suffered horribly.

A filthy strand of his insides were dragging behind him. They had long-since dried, but that didn't make what we were seeing any less disturbing. His arms were covered with tiny bites. There was a near-perfect set of teeth prints on his shoulder that was visible since most of his clothes looked to have been ripped away from his body. Most likely, the crawling around on the ground had done a majority of that work.

His right leg was almost entirely intact, but his left one had been gnawed down to the bone. That struck me as a bit strange, but I didn't have any ideas. I'd not seen zombies work at something to the point of taking it clean to the bone like a drumstick; that didn't mean they didn't…that just meant I'd not yet seen such a thing.

I gave a nod and Todd walked over and buried his machete into the top of the poor old man's head. He jerked his blade free and was kneeling to wipe it off when a new sound reached our ears.

I looked around, but couldn't find the source. When it came again, the cause of the eerie yowling noise had either moved…or there were more than just one.

"I've never heard a zombie make *that* noise," Todd breathed.

"That's no zombie," I said without moving my lips. I don't know why, but despite knowing that the source of the noise wouldn't understand me, much less read lips, I'd adopted that manner of speaking. I think it was simple fear.

I pointed to a collection of shadows under one of the fuller bushes. Both Alex and Todd turned slightly in the direction I indicated. At least ten cats slunk out from the bush. They weren't coming at us in an aggressive manner, but they were certainly eyeing us in a way that made me very uncomfortable.

"Are they z-z-zombies?" Todd stammered as he took a step back.

"I don't think so," Alex hissed as she actually took a

step towards the felines.

As if a cue had been given, the entire group of cats scattered. They bounded away in the grass, most of them retreating directly towards the sprawling home that sat as the crown jewel to this piece of property. Adding to the creepy feeling I was getting, a distant rumble of thunder sounded.

"That was a bit cliché," Alex scoffed as she started towards the home.

I fell in and then looked back when I realized that Todd wasn't following. He was standing, frozen in place. Perhaps I'd been wrong in insisting that he join us.

I snapped my fingers, but his eyes were looking past me and over my left shoulder. I turned with no idea what to expect.

"Fuck me," I breathed.

Alex must've heard despite how quiet I thought I was being. She stopped her advance and looked over her shoulder at me with an eyebrow cocked that I could see despite the ski goggles she wore for protection.

Standing in the shadow of the trees that ran down the side of the property were perhaps three dozen zombie children. They weren't advancing, but they weren't leaving either. They were just standing there…watching us.

To add to the creepiness of it all, many of the cats had fallen back to them. For whatever reason, the children made no attempt to attack. That oddity was amplified when I swear I saw one of the cats tug at a piece of loose flesh dangling from the leg of a little girl wearing a tattered and blood-stained dress.

I made the connection between the old man's injuries and this band of children. That brought an entirely new level of horrible to the situation. I had to shut my brain off as it tried to create the scenario that would lead to the results we'd encountered.

"He saw them as children and couldn't bring himself to do what needed to be done," Alex said as if reading my thoughts. "And you need to wrap your brain around that idea the next time you consider *not* killing one of those things right away."

Without another word, she started towards the rag tag pack of diminutive undead. Once again I noticed that the moment the zombie children became aware of the weapon she brandished, they reverted to regular zombies…in a manner of speaking.

The thing was, there were so many. I took off at a jog

to help, but she was on her own for the first few seconds. Not that it appeared to matter as she swung her machete at one while kicking another away at the same time.

I arrived just as a trio of the creatures all lunged from Alex's right flank. She would've never had a chance to take them all down. Later we would discuss being reckless, but for now, I struck fast. My own machete cleaved into the side of the head of a little boy as I swept the feet out of another young lad. The girl managed to grab Alex by the elbow with her tiny hands, but the woman shook the monster off, spun, and had a knife in her other hand that I hadn't seen. She drove the point of it into the girl's eye socket and let go of the blade as she side-stepped another few coming from the left.

I stepped around her and lowered my shoulder as I charged at another pair. I could only hope that Alex had the three handled as I sent my two flying. They didn't go far, and I was able to hurry over and end them both. I spun and saw that Todd was still standing stock-still. His face was a blank mask.

"Crap," I snarled, "the kid checked out."

"Did you really think he wouldn't?" Alex grunted as she ended another little boy with a jab of another magically appearing blade that drove into the zombie child's temple.

I jumped back as two children lunged for me just as I chopped down into the crown of the skull of a girl that had been no older than five or six. From the looks of it, her fate had been sealed by the nasty bite that had torn out most of her tiny throat. Or maybe it was one of the bites on her right forearm.

Both of the children tumbled to the ground in a heap, and I stomped onto the back of one while ending the other. I had just enough time to glance around and get a look at how many remained. Eight more, and they were spread out in an arc around me and Alex.

Correction…eleven more. A trio of the zombie children had, for whatever reason, adjusted their course and were heading towards the still frozen-in-place Todd Burns. A quick assessment told me that there was nothing I could do. If I drew a gun and tried to shoot them, I risked hitting him.

"Todd!" I yelled as I skipped to the side of one of the approaching zombies and swung backhanded at the creature. I felt the machete bite into the skull and I jerked the blade free just in time to swing with a forehanded sweep at the next one approaching—a little girl again. Why did it seem I was drawing all the little girl zombies? I took this one's hands off just below her tiny wrists, but did nothing to end her attempts at attacking me. I had to kick out at her and scuttle backwards a few steps.

That gave me just enough time to re-orient my blade and line up an overhead swing that would be much more effective. As I swung, I heard a yelp from behind me in the direction of Todd. Unfortunately, I didn't have time to look as I stepped in to finish off the last of the child zombies within reach of me.

Alex and I both put down our last threat almost simultaneously. I spun to see that, thankfully, the young man had snapped out of his trance. He was backing away and not attacking, but at least he hadn't simply stood there and been pulled down.

I took off at a run, coming up behind the straggler of the group, and swung my machete with all my might. The attack was a shade low and decapitated the little boy. His head flew away, rolling a few feet in the grass before coming to a rest on one ear. At least it was no longer a mobile threat. I grabbed the next one, another little girl, by her ponytail and jerked her backwards. She fell unceremoniously, but I was able to cleave the remaining one before returning my attention to the girl.

By then, Alex arrived and was finishing her for me. As soon as she yanked her blade free, she walked up to Todd and clocked him with a vicious backhand that sent him staggering a few steps before losing his footing and landing hard on his butt.

"I'm only going to tell you this once," Alex seethed. "You do your part. If not, you endanger my life and that of anybody around you. These things will rip you apart and chow down on your guts the first chance they get." She shot an angry glare my direction, then returned her focus to the young man staring up at her with a mix of fear and pain etched on his young face. "I don't know who or what put the thought in our head that these things are any different behavior-wise than any other stinking meat bag. They are zombies…flesh-eaters…whatever you want to call them. What they *aren't* is living." She turned and stomped away, intentionally bumping my shoulder as she passed me.

I watched her for a second before returning my attention back to Todd. "I don't want to pile on, but you need to shape up. This is the way of things now. Can you handle it?"

He nodded as he got to his feet. I turned and followed after Alex. I wanted to watch over the kid, but I didn't have time to baby him. By the time we reached the end of the driveway with a paved parking area in front of the four-car garage with enough room that it could double as a full-length basketball court, Alex had cooled down — or at least appeared to. She stopped at the wide walkway that led to the front door and waited until we caught up.

"Not sure what to think about this," she said by way of greeting.

I looked past her and saw a very large house cat sitting on the single step that led to the front door. Several small-er kittens were scattered around. Some were snoozing and other were wrestling with each other, but making it a point to stay under the overhang and out of the rain.

"Cats." I scratched my head in confusion. "What the hell is the deal with all the cats?"

"Maybe it has something to do with all the zombie children?" Todd finally said with enough meekness to make it sound like a question.

"Why would it…" Alex started, but then stopped. She turned to us with a puzzled expression. "Did you see how they wove in and out between the children? I swear I saw a few of them nibbling on exposed flesh. And not once did any of those kids try to attack them."

"Whew!" Todd gasped. "I thought that I'd imagined that."

"I saw it, too." I looked around Alex at the mother cat and her kittens.

I gave the house a closer look. It had a front that looked like it had been constructed with stone. Judging by what this place probably cost, I doubted it was fake. This place was one of those houses so far beyond anything I could even begin to imagine. It was the kind of house you put on your list when you had a nine-figure bank account and a seven-figure annual income. As nice as that first place was that I'd stayed at with Carl, Michael, Selina, and Betty, this place made that one look almost low-rent.

The cat on the porch seemed to be studying me as much as I was studying the house. Every time my gaze passed by it again, it was staring.

"Doesn't look like it's been bit," Alex said quietly.

I glanced at her and saw that she was staring just as intently at the cat. From the sound of her voice, I would say that the feline had her unsettled.

"Then let's go inside and see what we can find," I said as I pulled out the flashlight I'd packed.

This house had a lot of windows, but as overcast as it was, I knew it would be shadowy inside. I took two steps toward the front door and was greeted by the mama cat standing, arching its back, and hissing. It made a low mewling growl in its throat and I paused.

"So, you can take on swarms of the undead, but a little cat has you scared?" Todd scoffed.

Before I could say anything, he stepped past me. He'd drawn this odd-looking blade that he had been carrying on his back. It had a hooked blade attached to a three-foot handle like you would see on a sledge hammer or splitting maul. In one swing, he cleaved the animal in two.

"What the fuck!" I yelped as I grabbed him by the shoulder and spun him around.

"It's a cat, dude." He shrugged away from me with an ugly scowl on his face and an expression that made goose bumps rise on my arms.

"Exactly," I snapped. "It was just a cat. It wasn't doing anything except protecting its young. We could've gone around it. There was no need for that."

"Jeez, make up your mind," he said in an over-exaggerated tone that reminded me of every smartass teen I'd ever encountered. "Do you have a list of what I should and shouldn't kill?"

"I thought you had some shred of common sense." I shoved past him and approached the front door. "Just...just keep your eyes open for zombies. And don't pull another stunt like that again."

He muttered something under his breath, but I chose to ignore it. I stepped over the gory scene and tried not to hear the mewling of the kittens that were now probably doomed.

No surprise, the front door was locked. It was also extremely sturdy. It would take a huge effort and make an incredible racket to break down. I moved over to one of the gigantic windows and peered inside. Just as expected, it was shrouded in shadow, but I could tell that it was extremely opulent. Hell, just the furniture in this massive room probably cost more than mine and Steph's house.

I stepped back and looked around, quickly finding what I wanted in the shape of a stone a little larger than a softball. It stuck out because it was almost black and sitting just a little distance away from the meticulously placed ones in the flowerbed that ran down the entire front of the house.

When I picked it up, I paused and then started to chuckle. I tossed the stone up and down in my palm as I stepped out of the flowerbed.

"What's so funny?" Alex asked, looking at me like maybe I'd finally cracked under the pressure.

I fiddled with the stone for a moment and then flipped open the hidden hatch where a key sat. I tossed the fake rock and returned to the front door. When I turned the key and heard the tumbler, I realized how quiet the world had really become. That also made me think about just how loud shattering a fifteen foot or so tall window would've been. Since I knew for certain that sound brought the un-dead, I gave a nod to the powers-that-be for this stroke of fortune.

The door opened and the familiar stench of death and undeath rolled out to greet us. So much for that stroke of good luck.

I stepped into the gigantic entry foyer and looked around. There were stairs going up, an archway to our left and another directly ahead. Just this entry area was so massive that I found myself holding my breath as I took it all in. The vaulted ceiling was a good thirty feet up here.

The railing on the second floor had been busted. When I stepped around a series of trunks that looked to have been packed and hauled to this spot—but never taken by the former occupant—I saw a black splatter stain on the stone floor where it looked as if somebody had landed.

My eyes tracked the large and small droplets that the person—or zombie—had left in its wake as it exited through the archway directly across from the front door. Now that I was closer, I could look through the arch and see that it opened to a large living room. I could also see a dining room with a gigantic table that seated twelve off to the right. There was another archway on the other side of the dining room.

"Did these people have something against doors?" Alex whispered as she came up beside me.

"Why don't we just grab everybody and move here?" Todd called out.

I turned to see him looking through the archway that had been on the left when we entered. He had his weapon in his hands and suddenly brought it up in a protective posture.

I rushed over just as I heard the moan. I reached his side a step sooner because whatever he'd seen had caused him to take a staggering step backwards. It took my eyes a second to adjust to the shadows and gloom enough to pick out details, and as I did, I remembered the flashlight I held in my hand. Swallowing hard, I clicked the button. A shaft of light cut through the darkness, and my hand wavered slightly when it came to rest on the horrific scene.

This was a case of not having any idea how this came to pass. It made me think of how every single zombie that I'd killed or even seen had its own sad story.

"Did a serial killer live here?" Alex hissed as she peered over my shoulder and took in the scene.

This huge room would've been the one we entered had I busted one of those windows. I hadn't been able to see much since the huge vertical blinds only showed the tiniest glimpse inside. Plus, this whole disturbing scene was in the corner against the wall that had the windows.

In that corner...a child sat. To be more specific, what remained of the child sat there. His arms and legs had been chopped off, and the collection of bones near the body told me that it had been done right here. The torso had also been split open — probably by the knife that was stuck in the wall just a foot or so from the child's head.

The child's head craned over to us, and in the harsh

glow of my flashlight, it opened its mouth and moaned. Not for the first time, it unsettled me hearing such a deep and guttural noise coming from such a small creature.

The chopped up and eviscerated zombie child had a collar around his neck, and the chain attached to that collar ran to an eyebolt that was mounted on the wall. All of this made for a surreal scene that had me wondering about the residents of this place. The line "This is probably some sort of hunting lodge for rich weirdos" came to mind. But the sadness of the scene brushed that snippet away in the blink of an eye, and I took in the rest of what made this even more bizarre.

At least a dozen cats lounged about. Seeing them allowed my nose to now detect the bitter smell of ammonia that lingered under the already unpleasant stench unique to the undead. A couple were over by the zombie and, as I watched, one of them leaned over and began to worry at a tattered chunk of organ that protruded under the ruined ribcage.

"This...there can't..." Todd started to stammer and stutter.

I felt the hairs on the back of my neck stand up. All of the horror we were seeing had caused my mind to miss one important detail.

"This looks to be somewhat recent," Alex whispered as her mind obviously came to the same conclusion that I had just a few second ago.

I spun, my hand going for my pistol. Guns were a last-ditch response, but if there was a living person in this house, I wasn't going to take any chances. With my Beretta in hand, a finger coiled around the trigger, I gestured to the stairs.

I didn't wait for the other two and headed for the stairs, quickly putting my back against the wall as I began my ascent. I reached the first landing and paused. I strained to hear anything other than the sounds of the chained zombie child. I glanced back and saw that Alex was two steps below me and had her own handgun at the ready. I also noticed that Todd was still standing by the archway still staring in on that awful scene.

I opened my mouth to say something, but the moan I heard upstairs and the fact that I doubted it would do any good caused me to just return my focus where it needed to be. I took the rest of the stairs slowly, reaching the upper floor where the stench of undeath and cat urine was even stronger.

There were three archways that led into the upper level as well as one recessed doorway at the far end. I moved to the first arch and peeked in. This was a long corridor with a pair of doors on either side. All of the doors were open, so I started down the hall, my back pressed against the wall.

The first door opened to what amounted to a small video arcade. There were four pinball machines against one wall as well as five upright video games. The windows had blackout curtains, and I noticed the track lighting overhead. There were also two massive televisions mounted on one wall.

The next room was a living room. On the far side, large windows and massive glass doors opened up to a huge deck that I was willing to wager gave an amazing view of Mount Hood. There were two doors on the wall to the left and another damn archway.

We ventured in and I gave the air a sniff. I could still smell the foul mix, but it was a shade fainter than back on the main landing. We could check the area out more later if time permitted, but right now, I needed to find whatever was in this house with us.

I backed out and ducked into the other doorways in

this hall to discover a bathroom and a gym. Neither of them had any signs of movement.

Moving back to the main landing, I ventured to the next archway and peered inside. This one opened into some sort of upstairs kitchen. This was yet another location that merited looking into once we got to the bottom of the issue at hand, but across the way, another door waited. I heard the moan drift on the stillness, and I knew I would find what I was looking for through that doorway.

I checked back over my shoulder and Alex gave a curt nod. That could've meant she heard it or that she was ready; in either case, I made my way to that doorway. Each step closer ensured me I was going the correct direction to find the source as the smell grew stronger to the point that my eyes began to water, and I had to swallow hard to keep the bile rising in my throat from escaping.

I wasn't sure what I would find, but I prepared myself for it to be bad. Still, when I reached that doorway, I had to force myself to peer into the room, and it took a few mental slaps across the face to go those last couple of feet. Either Alex was feeling it as well, or she'd suddenly become uncharacteristically patient, because she didn't say a word during those several seconds that I stood without moving.

At last, I poked my head around the entry to the room and took a peek inside. A lone figure stood in the corner. It made no movement, and I almost thought that it might be a trick of light and shadow making something innocuous like a coat rack look like a person. The soft moan ended that speculation.

Only, that wasn't what had most of my attention. This was a bedroom. It had a balcony that, if my mental compass was working, looked out toward the mountain. The glass-paned double-doors had been destroyed. It seriously looked as if somebody had taken a baseball bat to them. On the covered deck were several cats. Most of them were lounging, but a few heads popped up and regarded me with predatory gleams in their eyes.

The bed was a nest of still more of the felines. I'd never seen so many cats in one place. And when my flashlight swept the room, I got chills at all the greenish orbs reflecting light back at me. I also could make out a larger lump in the bed that I couldn't identify at first. When I stepped into the room, a few of the cats stood like they were preparing to meet a challenge.

I suddenly felt like we were in the wrong place. There

was something going on here that went beyond my comprehension. Something had drawn all these cats, and now, this was *their* lair. I was the intruder…and they were not afraid.

The figure in the corner shifted and finally turned. My flashlight revealed what had been a man in perhaps his late thirties. The only visible injury was a small bite on his left forearm. He obviously saw me and started to advance. He only managed a single step before he appeared to jerk to a halt.

I scanned him with my flashlight and discovered that he'd somehow gotten his leg tangled in a mess of electrical cords. That was when I spotted a floor lamp that had been knocked over and gotten wedged behind a heavy wooden nightstand. The zombie was basically "chained" in place.

With the threat of the zombie neutralized for the most part, I edged a bit closer to the bed. A voice in my head told me not to. I drew close enough to see, and wished that I'd listened to that voice.

"What in the ever-loving fuck?" Alex said from beside me. "None of this makes any sense. What was going on here? What twisted crap did we stumble across?"

"No idea, and I doubt we would ever be able to guess

with any accuracy."

I stared at the mess in the bed that had once been another child. This one had been picked clean except for the bits that still clung to the skull. Mostly clumps of hair, but even that had been savaged by this pack of cats. I had to at least assume the cats had fed from the child. The really creepy part—besides the obvious, of course—was that it was now impossible to tell if the child had been a boy or girl.

Then the skull moved. I didn't know if it had been bumped by a cat or what, but that was enough to scare me and make me jump back. I tripped over a wad of clothing on the floor and would've landed on my ass if Alex hadn't been there to catch me. She helped me regain my balance and then stepped back out of the doorway where we'd entered.

"I think we need to grab what we can and get out of here. None of this feels right." She shot me a look and waited for me to respond.

"I think that is a good idea," I agreed as I turned and backed out of the room.

Normally I wouldn't leave a zombie at my heels, but I simply did not want to venture any further into that room.

This was wrong on so many levels that it gave me a dirty feeling all the way to my core. I felt like I'd seen something that would leave an ugly scar on my very soul.

I made the decision to skip over looking around upstairs. I had to seriously consider if I even wanted to search the lower level. After all, there were a couple of other houses nearby that we could scavenge. Maybe it would just be best to leave this one.

By the time I was halfway down the stairs, I was even contemplating setting the place on fire. I was mulling that thought when I realized I didn't see Todd where he'd been standing when Alex and I had gone upstairs.

"Where's the idiot?" Alex asked as she reached the landing where I had stopped as I asked myself the same question.

Our answer came in the form of a scream.

11

"Dammit, Todd!"

I broke into a run, making a beeline for that room with the zombie child chained to the wall. Todd had ventured in and, from the looks of things, resumed his attack on the cats. There were several feline bodies chopped up into mounds of blood-soaked fur that looked black in the gloom. When my flashlight passed over the bodies, the scarlet jumped out in an almost 3-D effect.

The young man was in the corner just a few feet from what was left of that pathetic zombie child that had been serving as the main course for who knows how many cats that had made this once opulent home into their personal den. Arrayed out around Todd, several cats were either pacing back and forth, or crouched as if preparing to launch themselves at the idiot.

289

"Dammit, Todd!" I snapped. "What the hell have you done?"

"I just wanted them to leave the kid alone!" Todd wailed. "They keep eating him."

I glanced around the room and took in the carnage. I wasn't sure I bought his story. Many of the carcasses were in the middle of the room, nowhere near the zombie child.

"Why couldn't you have just stayed with us?" Alex spat as she stepped into the archway beside me and took in the scene. I don't think she was quite prepared for what she saw because her anger deflated before she finished her reprimand. "What the hell is wrong with you?"

I agreed with that sentiment. I think I remember reading something about how one trait often seen in serial killers was the torture and abuse of animals. Of course, maybe I'd read it on the internet...so how accurate would that have been?

"You need to get out of there," I said, doing my best to keep my voice calm. We would deal with the overall problem once we got back to the others. I wanted to talk to his sister and see if she might have answers...or even a clue about her brother.

"Don't you think I tried?" Todd shot back.

He took a step towards us and several of the cats moved as if making an effort to block him. I thought that seemed a little odd, but then, this was the zombie apocalypse. These cats had been on their own for a few months. Had that been all the time it took for them to revert to a more undomesticated nature?

"You are just going to have to make a run for it," I said.

"They won't let me," Todd whined.

"They're cats!" Alex snarled, finding her voice again. "Obviously you got into the room. Just make a run for it."

"I did." His voice hitched and held a nasally quality that suggested he was on the verge of tears. "One of them jumped on me and scratched my face." He pointed to his cheek.

I shone my flashlight on him and thought I could see a set of scratches, but he was all the way across the room and I was still wearing my goggles. The thing was, with the behavior being exhibited by the cats, I wasn't about to wade into that room. As far as I was concerned, he'd gotten himself into this problem. He could get himself out of it.

Todd glanced around, and I guess he was trying to

pick the best route for escape. Finally, he made a move to his left. Sure enough, several of the cats drifted that direction as if to block him.

In a flash, he took one more over-exaggerated step to his left and then bolted to the right. He got maybe three steps before the first cat launched itself at him. It caught his leg and dug into the coarse denim material with all four paws. Todd yelped again as the feline looked to bite into his calf with its many pointy and sharp teeth.

He swatted down with the blade in his hand, but another had already launched and was scrabbling to get itself anchored to his pack. Again Todd yowled as this one bit his ear.

Without thinking, I had taken a few steps back, as had Alex. I quickly told myself that it was to give him room to exit through the archway, but deep down, I was certain that I was scared and acting out of self-preservation.

Todd was only a few yards from the arch, and I saw at least five cats clinging to him. It reminded me of this nature show where I'd seen these lionesses trying to bring down a giraffe.

Finally, he burst into the foyer. I was already moving for the front door, all thoughts of looting this place gone.

"Dammit, Todd!"

Alex shot past me as I opened it, and I barely got out before Todd staggered and stumbled out, tripping off the single step and landing hard on the river rock walkway that led to the entrance.

Unfortunately for one of the cats, he landed with all his weight and I heard a cringe-inducing snap of multiple bones along with another shrieking mewl that drowned out Todd's own blubbering and frantic cries. As if some unheard signal sounded, or maybe it was because of the screeching from one of their own, the cats that had been riding the Todd Express all disembarked, pulling themselves free and dashing away. No surprise, they all darted back inside the house through the still-open front door.

Todd continued to thrash around on the ground, swatting at himself. I was almost certain he was going to chop into his own flesh with the machete that he obviously had forgotten that he held. It was that reason I maintained a good distance from him until he gradually realized that the cats were gone.

He rolled over, pushed himself to his feet, and spied the body of the cat he'd fallen on. Its broken form was still twitching and making an awful sound that was part whine and part meow? He kicked the creature and then stomped

293

on it.

"Todd!" I barked, closing the distance between us and grabbing him by the shoulders to yank him away from the now lifeless body.

He spun to face me, and I staggered back several steps, my weapon coming around and between us before I even realized that I'd done it. A chill swept over me, and I knew that if I could see the flesh of my arms, they would be pebbled from the severe goose bumps.

"What the..." Alex started, but when Todd's head craned around in her direction, the words faded and she brandished her own machete.

"What?" Todd yelped, his eyes going wide at our displays of frightened surprise.

"Did you get close to that zombie child?" I asked, my voice sounding strangled as I swallowed the lump in my throat.

"No!" he exclaimed, instantly shoving up the sleeves to his jacket, revealing arms free of any sign of injury.

"Your eyes," I whispered, giving a slight nod of my head.

"What about them?" he asked cautiously.

"The tracers," Alex answered.

Todd looked confused for a moment before the light came on and he appeared to understand. He began patting at his body frantically, his expression crumbling from the madness that possessed him just moments before to one of absolute fear.

"N-n-no!" he stammered. "I haven't been bitten. I swear to God."

Now that I was over the initial shock of the black tracers that were stark against the whites of his eyes, I gave Todd my own visual exam and found that I didn't see anything either. Well, except for...

"The cats," I breathed. As if that reminded me we'd left the front door open to what was basically a lair for who knew how many of the animals. I spun to look back at the house.

Two cats sat in the still-open front door. One, an orange tabby, the other a mostly white one with a black splotch of fur on its right side, stared back at me like...well, like a cat. They made no attempt to move, and the orange one took that moment to splay its legs wide and begin tongue-bathing its nether regions.

"What about the cats?" Alex stepped over to me and gave me a nudge when I guess I just stood there for a moment saying nothing as this new possibility sank in.

"Okay, I am only guessing here, let's make that clear," I started. "The cats are feeding on the undead. We know for a fact that they are nibbling on the children, we all saw that. Add in what we saw inside." I made gesture with my arm to indicate the house. "It might be possible that cats are not only immune to whatever this is that is causing the zombie thing, but they might also be carrying the virus or pathogen."

Okay, I don't actually know the difference—if there is one—between a virus or a pathogen, but I think I was making my point.

"So…" Alex started, letting that word draw out as she considered my words. "You think that those little kitty scratches infected the kid?"

Todd let out a groan, and I had to admit, there had been absolutely no tact in Alex's statement. She was speaking as if the young man wasn't standing just a few feet away.

He spun around, and then took off towards the house. At first, I thought that he was going to rush back in and start hacking up more cats. He veered slightly and came to a stop in front of one of the gigantic windows. He leaned close, his hands going to his face, prying his own eyelids open as wide as possible. A second later, he let loose a wail of despair and dropped to his knees. His sobs carried easily in the quiet.

Alex leaned close and whispered, "You want me to take him down now?"

"What?" I spun on the woman and saw that her normally bright, sparkling eyes were flat and empty. My God, she was already preparing herself for killing the boy. "No! Of course not."

"You do understand—" she began, but I cut her off.

"I understand plenty." My voice came out harsh, but she didn't even bat an eye. "And I also understand that we are going to take him back to his sister."

"Why?" Alex countered. "You think you want her last memory of her brother to be seeing him like this? Let me tell you something, Evan. We'd be doing her a huge favor. She never has to know what he looks like as the infection spreads, she never has to see him turn, and she never has to put a bullet in his skull."

It wasn't that everything she was saying didn't make perfect sense, but she was so matter-of-fact about the issue of ending Todd Burns' life that it gave me still more chills

297

to match the set that seeing those black tracers had already provided. This had gone badly so fast that I was having a little trouble catching up.

I looked back over at Todd to see he was still kneeling in the flower bed in front of the window where he'd confirmed for himself what Alex and I already knew. In the relative silence of this dead world, I could hear his soft sobs.

I turned to see that Alex was still observing Todd. She'd drawn a handgun and her finger kept darting into the trigger area.

"You are just going to shoot him in the head?" I tried to whisper, but my tightening throat made it difficult.

"Would you rather I use my machete? That seems a bit harsh."

She was missing my point. I shook my head and tried to swallow. I didn't really want Todd to overhear this conversation.

"I don't want you to kill him at all," I managed to say.

"So you want him to suffer?"

I opened my mouth, but then snapped it shut. I mean, she had a point. Of course I didn't want him to suffer. However, having been a person who thought he was infected, I felt I had a touch more sympathy for the young man's situation than Alex might.

"Perhaps this is a decision that we leave to him," I said with as much calm as I could muster.

I realized that, despite my issues with his behavior, the hours and minutes of this young man's life were now very limited. His fate was sealed, and it was now a matter of when versus if.

"Do I get a say in this?" a soft voice interrupted the stare down between me and Alex.

I turned to see that Todd had gotten to his feet. His knees were black from the garden soil and his face was a slurry of mud, tears, and a few ruby pinpricks of blood that caught the light just right. His eyes were laced with those black tracers and his face already had a waxy hue to it that made it look like he was going to fall over at any moment.

"Jesus," I gushed, "I'm sorry. I mean, yeah...sure."

"I don't want my sister to see me like this," he whispered. "But..." His voice hitched and a sob tore from him as his shoulders shook. "I'm afraid. I don't want to die. I don't want to be killed. It'll hurt...and..." His face flushed and he dropped his gaze to the ground, his feet shifting weight from one to the other.

It struck me then just how real this experience had become for the young man. He'd had no real idea until this moment. Maybe it was the 'video game' mindset. Perhaps this hadn't felt entirely real to him until now.

I thought back to my younger days and remembered that feeling that I would live practically forever. In my youth, a year seemed like an eternity. Certainly not like the last five years...until the undead screwed everything up. Those had gone by in a blink. I never seemed to have enough time to do half the stuff I'd wanted.

Funny, but now, time slowed to a crawl again. Maybe it was the lack of constant input. Maybe it was the endless sense of fear everybody lived in. Hell, it might even be the hours of tedious boredom.

"I really don't want to die," Todd whimpered. "It'll hurt."

I looked at him again, and I made myself believe that I could see the sickness coursing through him. He just stared back at me with those creepy eyes that had regular tears leaking from them. That set me back a step as I considered why that fact stood out so much. I decided that I guess I figured his tears to be black like the tracers.

"So what should we do?" I asked. "You don't want your sister to see you like this. You don't want to be put down." He started to speak, but I raised my hands to stop him. "And I understand that. I doubt I'd willingly offer myself over to a relative stranger to be killed."

Murdered? I thought. *Isn't that the truth of it?* Calling it a mercy killing or whatever was solely to make ourselves feel better about the situation. I glanced at Alex and amended that thought to merely cover my own feelings on the matter. She appeared to want to get on with the killing.

"Maybe..." Todd paused and glanced from me to Alex before continuing. "Maybe you could wait until I fell asleep?"

"That would have us out here and away from the group until tomorrow," I said. "The group is expecting us to return today. If we stay gone, they might get worried and come looking. That leads to the possibilities of any of them running a greater chance of being bitten."

"I'll stay with him," Alex said after a long pause that grew exponentially more uncomfortable with each beat of my heart."

Todd looked over at her and his expression instantly became suspicious. His eyes flicked from her weapon to her face that held no expression. "Could Evan be the one to stay?" he finally asked.

Alex shot me a look that I couldn't read. I thought it might be skepticism or some form of doubt. Whatever it was, she shoved it back down and her expression returned to a blank and neutral one.

"I can do that," I said.

"What about supplies? Are we calling this a bust?" Alex asked.

I was considering the options when Todd spoke up. "I think we should still see what we can find. After all...can't catch this infection twice. If there is a situation, I guess I am better to use if things look risky."

That statement flew in the face of all the young man's actions the past few hours, but I wasn't going to argue. I also was not about to reveal to him my own situation.

I caught something out of the corner of my eye and glanced in Alex's direction to see her face flushing just a bit as she spun away from us. "Then I guess we should get moving," she said as she started back up the driveway from this nightmarish house.

I motioned for Todd to follow and the three of us headed back to the main road. When we reached it, I looked up and down as far as my eyes could see in each direction. I'd been seeking out the nearest zombies; what I hadn't been prepared for was the gray-primer painted panel van that was prowling towards us from the opposite direction that McIver Park was located.

"Everybody back," I hissed.

Without any questions, something that surprised me if I was being honest, my two companions dove back the way we'd come without a single question or comment. There were plenty of trees to take cover behind, and each of us found one in a hurry.

I peered from behind mine from my position lying flat on my stomach. I could feel the cold dampness of the grass as it soaked into my clothes, promising me that I would be miserable later. After a brief mental debate, I decided that worrying about drawing the attention of the undead placed a distant second to wanting to survive an encounter with possible raiders.

I briefly considered the possibility that just maybe these people were like me and my group. After making sure I accepted the possibility, I vowed not to attack unless I felt that I had good reason.

As the sound of the approaching vehicle grew louder,

so did the beating of my heart as its thudding in my ears started to sound like the intro to a Metallica song. When it came into view, I could barely make out a driver. The person had a wide-brimmed hat on that cast enough shadow to make it impossible to see a face.

I could hear something tinny in the background and realized that there was music being played inside that van. They didn't have their windows rolled all the way up, so the noise was drifting out, but whether it was due to their having the volume low or some other reason, I could only determine that it was indeed music being played.

The van finally reached the entry to the driveway and rolled to a stop. I watched, holding my breath as if that might be enough to magically convince them to just keep moving on. When they did, I let out a long breath and collapsed face down in the damp grass for just a moment.

I listened as the sound of the engine and the tinny music became faint and slowly faded. The relief only lasted as long as it took for me to realize that now they would be rolling towards the entrance to McIver!

I got to my feet and saw Alex doing the same. Todd, for whatever reason, was still sprawled on the wet grass. I started toward him, my hand going to the hilt of a machete on my hip. Just as I reached him, he began to stir. That caused my grip to tighten.

When he looked up at me, I breathed a sigh of relief that I almost regretted. The boy was still alive.

"We have to go watch and see where that van goes," I said, turning on my heel and walking away.

I heard him get to his feet. A moment later, he'd fallen into step beside me.

"What are we going to do if they head in towards our camp?" he asked, obvious concern in his tone.

"Follow them." I didn't think I was being flippant, but I did feel that my tone came out a little harsher than I would have liked. But seriously, what did he think we would do?

By the time we were back to the street, the van was almost to the turn-in that would lead to the park. As it approached, it rolled to a stop. For the second time in just a few minutes, I was holding my breath as I waited to see what the driver would do.

When the turn signal came on, I almost laughed just due to the absurdity of it. Seriously, who would take the time to do such a thing? The days of traffic law enforcement were long gone.

The van made the turn, and I stood there watching as it began to roll slowly along the long entrance road that would bring it to the main area of the campground. I was about to give the word when Alex took off at a jog.

I followed on her heels. As we reached the road, I glanced back and saw that Todd could only manage a very slow walk. A small part of me wanted to pull up and wait for him, but the reality was that he was literally a dead man walking. Chewie, Michael, and the others were still alive, and I needed to get to them in case this was an attack.

There was still the possibility that they might get to the big park area and simply move on since we'd already done a good job of stripping the place of anything useful as we began work on our own stronghold. The problem was that we had to jog in for almost a mile before we would know if we would then be running another mile or so to reach our area.

As I reached the first curve in the road, I glanced back one more time. I didn't see any sign of Todd. It couldn't be helped. I had to see to those who were still alive. Not that he was dead yet, but he was as good as dead.

"Welcome to our harsh new reality," I panted as I

jogged and did my best to keep up with Alex's pace which was a shade faster than I was comfortable with.

Running and I had never been friends. I briefly considered adding some kind of running workout to my daily routine. I hadn't gone that far when that thought was wadded up and tossed in the mental trash can.

As the opening ahead grew, I could not see any sign of the van. This was jacking up my already rapid heartbeat as I found the distance between me and Alex starting to decrease.

At first I thought that just maybe she was tiring. When she brought the rifle from her shoulder into her hands and jacked a round into the chamber, I realized she was simply getting ready for a fight and didn't want to rush headlong into an ambush.

I did the same, but really did not want to have to resort to firing a gun. That would undoubtedly bring the undead this direction.

We reached the fork. I knew that my people were to the right, but there was a huge and open field to the left and I could see the taillights of the van through some of the branches that bordered it.

Then I heard something that made my heart jump into

my throat: Chewie's deep bark.

A moment later, she came into view bounding across the open field. That was one of the things about a Newfie...they love everybody for the most part. These were just new friends she hadn't met yet as far as my big, lovable dog was concerned.

A voice called out, and while I couldn't make out the words, it sounded a lot like Michael. What I didn't understand was why he and the dog were this far from our camp.

"Evan?" a voice to my right called in a whispered hiss.

I turned to see Tracy climbing a fence that bordered the burnt remains of what looked to have once been a pretty nice house. Now it was a blackened husk which was why we hadn't bothered with it on this supply run.

"What the hell are Michael and Chewie doing out here?" I snapped, only giving her a glare as I started for the parked van and still unknown number of occupants.

"Marshawn was watching them," Tracy grunted as she threw her leg over the fence and landed on the ground, hurrying to catch up

That only made me quicken my pace since I saw no sign of him. The sound of the van opening up registered as the music being played inside wafted on the dampness of what was the start of a band of rain sweeping in.

As I drew near, I could now hear the sounds of adults having a conversation. As I emerged from under the still mostly bare canopy of branches, I spotted Marshawn standing about ten feet or so from the van. Chewie had moved to his side and was sitting. Her head tilted from one side to the other as she looked to be following what was being said.

"...really don't want trouble. We just need someplace to recover and regroup," a man's voice said.

Even without seeing him, I could hear fatigue. This guy was dead on his feet—in a manner of speaking. There was a breathy tremor to his voice that had me wondering if perhaps he was infected.

I was still jogging when Chewie spotted me and broke away from Marshawn to come at me in her loping run. Something felt odd and it took me a second to realize that I was smiling as I watched her come to me with her jowls flapping. Anybody that doesn't think a dog smiles simply doesn't pay attention. I could see the curve of her mouth as she bounded up, what was left of her tail swishing back and forth. Her injuries didn't seem to be bothering her in the least and I had to wonder if the worst of her damage had been the dehydration. My only concern was for the stitches, but when she reached me and my hands ran over her, they came back damp only from the rain gathering on her thick double coat.

"Evan!" I heard Tracy calling from behind me.

I didn't want to talk to her at the moment. As far as I was concerned, she was on my shit list. Why would she think it a good idea to come out here and scavenge? Why would Marshawn not only be okay with it, but apparently come along? The whole point of them staying behind was for them to just get a bit of rest and recovery time.

Okay, I was perhaps a shade hypocritical, but I quickly pushed those thoughts aside. Also, my focus needed to be on the here and now.

I saw the driver's side door of the van open and I brought my pistol up. I advanced like a bad impersonation of some cop show detective approaching an armed and dangerous suspect. I had my weapon clutched in a two-handed grip, my head tilted to the side and trying to use my good eye to sight in on my potential target.

The back door to the van swung open in that moment and I froze as two figures emerged with powerful looking hunting rifles in their hands. The weapons were impressive, and an inappropriate thought flashed through my head, *You can't hunt wabbits with an elephant gun, Doc!*

"Easy, fella," a deep voice warned.

I noticed that neither of the people who'd exited the back of the van made an attempt to raise their weapons at my own cautious, if not a shade aggressive, approach. I eased my arm down, but my finger remained wrapped around the trigger.

I heard more than saw Alex come up beside me. When I glanced over at her, I discovered that she was cradling her shotgun in her arms. I returned all my attention to the van and watched with a mix of amusement and a shade of concern as it disgorged its occupants like a clown car. By the time the last person emerged, I counted a dozen men and women.

A man stepped forward and made a calming gesture with his hands as he edged away from his group and stepped out so that he was practically right between me and Marshawn.

"Afternoon, folks," the man said as he glanced back and forth between me and Marshawn who now had Michael at his side. "We weren't looking for any trouble.

311

Honest to God, we wouldn't have even stopped if not for seeing the boy and the dog. Figured we had to roll the dice. Ain't seen any kids running around chasing dogs in a while, if you know what I mean. At least…not in a good way."

"I think I can relate." I stepped forward. Alex made a move to stick beside me, but I put out a hand to stop her before taking a few more steps toward the man.

"I guess it might sound stupid, but our thinking was along the lines of…" His voice trailed, and I could see his cheeks flush a bit in genuine embarrassment.

"If they got kids and dogs, maybe they won't be awful?" I finished what I thought his sentiment might be.

"Yeah," the man said with a nod and a nervous laugh. "Stupid. Right?"

"Not really," Alex spoke up from behind me. "Actually, it was perhaps the one thing that saved their lives when I met them."

I looked back at her and she returned the gaze, adding what might've been a wink. I was so confused. Was she implying that she could've killed our group when we first encountered her as we ran from Don and his people, or was she referring to the time she might've been the sniper that saved my butt from some zombies back when we were dealing with Brandon Cook? Either way, I needed to make it a point to perhaps get to know her better. She might be overly brazen, but she had certainly factored into my situation more than perhaps I was giving credit.

"Name's Drew Carter, by the way," the man said as an introduction. He approached me, hand extended for a handshake.

"Evan Berry." I shook his hand and then introduced the rest of my group currently present.

Drew rattled off a bunch of names as well, but I had forgotten the first one by the time he'd reached the last person. I was awful with remembering names. I just figured I would learn them as we went if these people decided to stick around. That thought hit me with something that I hadn't been thinking about...at least not until just this moment.

"Are you folks looking for someplace to settle down? Or are you planning on staying mobile?" I asked.

"Well..." Drew's face flushed once more, and I had a feeling that he was probably not used to being a spokesman. He struck me suddenly as being very shy on the verge of timid. That made me wonder why he was acting as the speaker for this group. "We are trying to find some-place we can stay in for longer than a few days. I did some work on a few of the high-end residences along this road. Houses seem to attract more trouble than they're worth. I used to fish here, and on Memorial Day…" He paused and I saw a wistful expression pass across his face, "This place was often my family's go-to spot for camping until the kids got older and we could hit the more remote loca-tions."

"I need to talk to my people, but I think this could be good for all of us."

During our brief encounter and the introductions, I'd been able to scan the rest of the faces of his group. There were almost as many women as men. And while I'd met plenty of women who were not very pleasant, I had to at least try and hold onto a shred of my hope in humanity. If this group was co-ed, then I had to hope that they would be a good choice in allies.

I made my way over to Marshawn. I could hear Tracy and Alex fall in as we all gathered together in a group.

"Should we talk to Darya and Maggie?" I asked once everybody gathered in close. I glanced down and noticed that Michael didn't appear to be paying attention which didn't strike me as unusual at all.

"Umm...where's Todd?" Marshawn asked, ignoring my question.

In all the activity, he'd already slipped from my thoughts. In my mind, I guess I saw him as already dead. What did that say about me and what I was becoming?

"He got infected," Alex answered.

I noticed that she hadn't made any effort to explain how. I guess she was leaving that for me.

"Jesus," the man breathed.

I wasn't sure if his reaction was due to her matter-of-fact tone about the loss of one of our people, or if it was in sympathy to Maggie...and, of course, Todd. Looking at the sadness in his eyes, I was going to go with the latter.

I felt Michael squeeze my hand and I squeezed his back. "So, what do we do? Do we bring these people in? Do we wait and have this conversation with Maggie and Darya?" I pressed the issue as I shot a glance over at the other group that were now watching us with open curiosity.

"I think they will go with whatever," Marshawn said. "Maggie will probably be more focused on just having lost her brother."

"Yeah...about that," I started. Michael was squeezing my hand tighter now.

I glanced down and noticed he was staring past Tracy. I could tell he wasn't just avoiding eye contact. He was looking at something. Just as I tried to get a look myself, Chewie stood up and took two very deliberate steps that placed her almost directly in front of the boy.

"What the hell, Evan?" Tracy had looked over her shoulder, did a double-take, and then spun back to face me. "You didn't put him down?"

Coming up the road was Todd. It was clear from his slow, awkward steps that he was no longer one of the living. He was passing under a tight cluster of branches, so he was heavily shrouded in shadows, but I already knew.

The group gathered around the van all craned their necks to see what it was that had our interest. Right away, a couple of them started over to intercept the approaching zombie.

"Stop!" I shouted. My voice might've sounded a bit harsh, but I'd had to really force that word out through the pinhole that my throat had become. "He was one of ours. I got him."

Pulling my machete, I approached the zombie that had

once been Todd Burns. His eyes locked on me and his mouth opened in a moan as his hands came up, reaching for me.

His eyes were filmed over, but his face, despite its deathly pallor, still showed that he'd been crying. That made it all the more gut-wrenching as I stopped and allowed him to close the last few yards before I grabbed his shoulder to pull him forward while I plunged my knife into his eye socket.

DEAD: Suffer the Children

12

Anger and Flashbacks

"You sonovabitch!" Maggie shrieked, hurling herself at me, almost managing to break free from Alex's hold on her.

"I really am sorry," I said sincerely as I took a reflexive step back when the girl tried to take another swing at me.

"You let him die. You insisted that he come when you knew he wasn't ready. I should've been the one out there. I could've taken care of myself."

"Your brother did it to himself!" Alex snapped as she jerked the younger girl around, holding her firmly by the upper arms and giving her a fierce shake. "He wouldn't listen…he did what he wanted and not what he was being told to do."

"He was just a kid!" Maggie insisted.

"What? A year younger than you?" Alex retorted. "I got news for ya… you're both just kids. If he couldn't follow simple directions, how long do you really think he would've lasted? He shot Marshawn, remember? And from what I heard when you ripped him a new one, he wasn't supposed to do that. He was going to get all of us killed. The fact that the only person who died was him is lucky on our part."

"Fuck you!" Maggie spat, throwing her head forward as if to head-butt Alex.

"He chopped a cat in half just because!" I said, doing my best not to totally lose my temper at this point.

That had been another thing I'd noticed in the zombie fiction that had been so popular until it became real. There seemed to be a mandatory rule that a kid had to be constantly causing trouble. Not listening. Thinking they knew better. You know…basically being a teenager. Only, in this environment, it was literally life-and death when they acted out. He'd certainly been doing his best to live up to that stereotype and it cost him his life. Now, it seemed that his sister was going to try and not only defend his actions, but blame me specifically for his death.

"Did we come at a bad time?" Drew asked quietly.

I glanced over and saw a variety of expressions on the faces of the people who were supposed to be our new additions. They ranged from embarrassed to apathetic. This was certainly not much of a welcome mat; nor was it any way to convince these people that they were joining with the right group.

"The way I see it, you have two choices," I said, facing Maggie after I gave a quick shake of my head to Drew. "You can calm down and understand that we didn't do anything to intentionally endanger your brother, or you can go."

I hated how those words felt as they fell from my mouth. I knew damn good and well I sounded a bit like a dick. I remembered back to that time Carl had basically said that having Selina and Michael were nothing more than a liability. I'd had some pretty nasty thoughts about him. The problem was, there were times when I'd realized that there was truth in his words. Not that I would even consider abandoning Michael at this point, but at least I was starting to understand his sentiment.

"Who do you think you are to tell me that I would have to leave." Maggie strained against Alex's grip as she spat verbal venom my direction. "My brother and I were

321

here first."

"Then go back into the woods where you were hiding when we arrived," Alex said in a whisper as she leaned forward, her mouth almost brushing Maggie's ear. "See how long you survive."

This was getting out of hand. I needed to stop things before it cost another person their life. Besides, I believed very strongly that we would need every single person we could scrounge up if we were going to stand a chance. It might seem neat to be some sort of loner with nobody to be responsible for, but in this new world, there was safety in numbers…pure and simple.

"Can I say something?" Drew stepped forward and a few of his people glanced at him with concerned expressions etched clearly on their faces.

I gave him a nod after looking around at my own people and seeing no reaction at all. I didn't see how he could make things worse.

"How are we not talking more about the fact that it seems this kid was infected by a cat?" Drew looked around at us all, his face an open expression of confusion and wonder. "You did say that was his only injury, right?"

"Yeah." I nodded to Alex, indicating she could let go

of Maggie.

The girl jerked her arms free and then took a step my direction. "I want to see him."

"I'll take her," Marshawn offered.

The two walked out of our camp and I turned back to Drew. "We can't actually be certain that he was infected by a cat's scratch."

"Duh-nuh-duhnt-duhnt-duh-nuh…" One man began doing a poor impersonation of a guitar with his mouth, but I knew what song he was trying to convey and I thought it was in bad taste at the moment considering the circumstances.

"Can it, Marty," Drew snapped.

I glanced at the man who'd just been scolded. He looked to be maybe in his forties or fifties. He had a green stocking cap with an ugly orange stripe around the base, but greasy locks of gray hair jutted from beneath. The man's face had the deep crevices of a lifetime smoker and his eyes, while blue in color, had a dull appearance. I guessed him to be just a shade under six feet, and maybe a hundred and sixty pounds.

"*Cat Scratch Fever*, man…get it?" the man said with a scowl that revealed teeth that were almost brown.

"Yeah, clever, but *now* is not the time," Drew said with a tone that made me believe he'd had to hold conversations like this with the man on numerous occasions.

I saw more than a couple of eye rolls from others in the group. I also noticed that the man was standing just apart from everybody else. It was subtle, but now that I was really looking, it seemed apparent.

"Look, I know that whole scene looked bad," I started, trying to get things back on track in regard to these people joining up with us, "but in all fairness, she did just lose her brother."

"No, I get it." Drew made a wave with one hand as if to dismiss the whole thing. "But can I ask what I might be missing. Did I hear that her brother shot that one fella?"

"When we first arrived," I said. "Fortunately, the bullet passed straight through. Marshawn is healing up fine."

"Wow," Drew gasped. "You guys are sure taking that in stride. I don't think I would've been as cool with it. And passed straight through? Am I missing something? Seriously…the dude was shot. The fact that the bullet went all the way through him doesn't seem like a good enough reason to just be…okay with it."

"It's complicated. The situation and all when we—" I

found myself starting to explain.

"Hey, whatever, man," Drew said, again waving me off. "It ain't like shit is normal these days. You don't owe us a damn thing."

I found myself liking this guy. While others might've seen his attitude as ambivalent, I saw it as...accommodating. He wasn't jumping on random bits of information and casting judgement.

"I still say we need to keep an eye on her," Alex muttered. "If she stays, she might just be biding her time until she finds an opportunity to do something terrible."

I had to admit, I'd been having those exact same thoughts. After all, how many times had I seen that exact situation play out in a show?

"She just lost her brother, for crying out loud." Darya stomped into the middle of the group, hands on hips, and anger casting death rays from her eyes.

"Yeah...find me somebody who hasn't lost a friend or family member." Alex spun on the woman. "Does that mean we need to start watching you? After all, didn't you just lose your kid? And if memory serves me, weren't you trying to blame Evan, too?"

"Can we not do this now?" I stepped between the

women.

"Wow, sounds like our camp every night," Drew said with a chuckle in his voice.

"I was just gonna say the same thing," a woman quipped. She turned to the others in the group, her gaze seeming to pass right over the man who'd made the "Cat Scratch Fever" reference. "See how stupid we sound?"

She stood there for a moment and then spun to face me. Her face was beet red. She opened and shut her mouth a few times before she could manage to stammer, "I-I-I didn't mean anything by that. I was just meaning—"

"I get it," I said with a smile that I hope she read as sincere. "But back to the main issue, we would like to welcome you to our little encampment if you'll stay. I honestly believe that this location is a good choice. Also, from what we saw, coming through the town of Estacada, which is just up the road and down the hill, they are holding out pretty decently in all this. They could be a buffer for things coming from that direction."

"I think we'd like that." Drew looked around at his people as if to get a consensus vote of approval.

I watched as one person after the next gave a short, curt nod. And just that fast, we'd bolstered our numbers to near twenty. That meant more people to divide the watch duty with, more people to hunt, fish, and build.

It also meant more people to be responsible for. Supplies were already stretched thin. We needed to make a serious run. Perhaps that van would come in handy.

I looked around at the camp and realized that Alex was nowhere to be seen. If she'd have gone after Maggie for whatever reason, she would've had to walk past us all. That meant she had to have headed into the woods in the direction of the river.

"I'll be right back," I said to the group as I headed in the only direction I believed that she could've gone without me noticing.

Sure enough, I hadn't gone far when I spotted her sitting on a rock by the bank of the Clackamas River. She was staring out at the water and made no acknowledgment of my arrival when I reached her.

I stood there for a while as I waited for her to say something. I was uncertain as to what had set her off like this. Again, I didn't know her well, but this behavior seemed out of character.

"I had to kill my own mom," Alex finally spoke, breaking the silence that existed except for the almost hypnotic and soothing noises of the flowing water.

I didn't think she was wanting any input at this point, so I kept my mouth shut and waited. She slid off the giant stone, picked up a flat rock, and threw it side-arm so that it skipped a few times across the water's surface before vanishing into the depths that looked black under the overcast sky.

I waited for her to reveal to me whatever it was that was weighing so heavily upon her. In my fairly limited experience, I'd discovered that speaking is the last thing a woman wants from a guy if she is going to share something.

"We'd been totally on our own for about three days by now…"

***

"…the last group to go looking for supplies had never come back. I had no idea if they were killed, or just decided to bail on my mom and me."

Alex wiped at her eyes with the back of her hand and knelt beside the river. She dipped her gloved hand in it and then began tracing patterns on the surface of a large flat stone as she continued.

"By now, my mom was so sick. She could hardly sit up she was so weak. I had to do everything for her, and her hand looked horrible...and smelled worse. I'd gone from house to house in the neighborhood to try and find leftover antibiotics, but nothing seemed to work.

"I tried all kinds of creams and sprays. I scrubbed at the wound, but she wasn't getting any better. I knew there was nothing else I could do besides make a run at that medical center.

"When I got there, I knew somebody had been here because of all the dead zombies. Inside, it was even more obvious. What really made my day was that somebody had already busted into the pharmacy. That saved me a lot of time and trouble.

"I headed back after finding several bottles of penicillin just sitting on a counter. It looked like somebody had grabbed them, then forgot them.

"As soon as I had what I came for, I took off. It was when I was headed home that I heard all the commotion. I saw you as it turns out, trying to get away from a few zombies or something. I had a clean shot on the leader and just did what I hoped somebody would do for me if I was in a tough situation." Alex glanced up at me and gave a weak smile. "I was almost hoping that you were one of the folks that had gone for supplies, and that you were maybe coming back with the others. I know...silly, but I had a tough time believing that those people had just up and bailed."

"You were a huge help that day. If not for you, I might've ended up having no choice but to just run and hope that the herd coming up the hill didn't decide to swarm our location. I didn't have the time to deal with the zombies because of that bastard, Brandon Cook," I explained.

"Anyways, I got over the fence and hurried to the house I'd been hiding in with my mom. Until she'd gotten so bad that she couldn't walk, we were moving to a new spot every night just so that nobody would know where we were in case somebody was watching the place.

"We'd heard a few break-ins, and since I was all alone and had to sleep some time, I just felt it was the best way to go. Plus, there were still quite a few zombies wandering around inside the walls. I didn't want them to trap us in any one spot."

"Why didn't you and the others you were with just

330

empty the place out?" I asked what I thought was a smart question.

"That was because of some of the people who'd been in our original group. This one idiot convinced everybody else that they would help keep up the appearance that nobody was staying here. He said that there weren't so many that we couldn't take them down if we had to," Alex explained.

"That's a stupid leap of logic," I sniffed.

"Yeah, and I wanted to take them down, but with my mom sick and needing me, plus the fact that I was by myself, I couldn't do it. Not all alone." Alex stood and moved into a lone ray of sun that had found its way through a broken patch of the overhanging clouds.

"I got to the house and gave my mom the penicillin that I'd found. Within minutes, she started getting violently ill. She turned all red, and started puking her guts out. I had to figure that she was allergic. I had found some ipecac in this same house's medicine cabinet. I figured it was because they had four kids judging by the picture hanging in the living room. I ran and grabbed it, making my mom drink some just to be certain that she heaved up all the penicillin.

"For the next couple of days, I gave her lots of fluids. I found a case of Ramen noodles and used the flavor packets in water to make a broth she could drink. I thought she was getting better. She was still too sick to move, which is why I went next door to raid the pantry. I had a big suitcase with wheels to transport the food.

"I was loading up when I heard the crash. At first, I wasn't sure where it came from. I only knew it was close. When I heard another, I realized it was coming from the house my mom and I were staying in.

"I dropped everything and ran. When I got there, I realized that the window beside the front door had been busted. It didn't seem possible for a zombie to get through such a relatively small slot, but I could see blackish streaks that looked like rotten blood on the edges around the busted-in window.

"I got inside and could smell them. I knew the zombies where in the house, and I ran up the stairs to my mom. I needed to know that she was okay before I searched and destroyed whatever had slipped inside.

"When I reached the top stair, I could see the door to the bedroom my mom and I stayed in was open. I hurried to it and the smell that hit me was almost enough to make me vomit. I shoved at the door and it only opened part-way. Something was on the other side...but worse than that, one of those little children...the ones you seem so intent on saving or not just killing on sight? Yeah, one of those had my mom's leg in its hand like it was holding a damned drumstick."

Again, she paused. This time it was because I could hear how her voice choked up as she tried to get through the story. I hadn't seen Stephanie actually get bitten. She'd been attacked before I got there. And even then, I hadn't been able to kill that zombie. I'd been in such shock. I'd left it for Carl to finish as I took off to the hospital when I still believed there could be something done for her.

"I rushed in, and that thing was still just staring at me when I pulled my knife. That was when it dropped my mom's leg and came at me. Its mouth was open, and bits of partially chewed meat fell from it as rivulets of blood ran down its chin." Alex sniffed and spun to stare me in the face. "And then the one that had been hiding behind the door attacked me. Its cold hands grabbed my arm before I could finish off the one that bit my mom."

We stood there in silence for a moment. I was at a loss. Even more, I didn't want to point out that this was further proof the child versions were different. Granted, perhaps even more dangerous, but her story was giving me even more evidence that the child version of the zombie is different from the adult counterpart.

"The one that attacked from behind grabbed my knife hand. I turned, it was a little girl. She might've been ten...maybe. As she tried to bite my arm, the one that had been attacking my mom moved in from where it now stood at my back. I just managed to jerk my arm free and plunge the blade into the eye of the one that had been holding my arm when I felt the pain on the back of my leg." Alex took a deep breath before she continued. "I heard the rip in my pants and the searing agony. It was terrible. Never in my life had I felt anything like it. That child tore a chunk out of the back of my leg. I felt the wetness as the blood ran down my calf. I still remember all those feelings. Sometimes...I swear I feel that pain come back. I wake up and am certain that I will open my eyes to see one of those monsters trying to finish what that one child started."

When Alex's eyes returned to me, she stopped whatever it was that she was about to say. Her cheeks flushed, and her eyes squinted in apparent anger.

"What? You think you're the only one who didn't turn after being attacked?" she spat.

That's when I realized that my mouth was wide open. She was taking my amazement as something personal?

"No, I just...it's that..." Hell, I didn't know what to say. I guess she'd just caught me off guard. That was it. Just like that girl Katy I'd met who had a nasty bite taken out of her face. She'd been the one to prove to me that immunity was a possibility. Katy had given me hope.

"I'm not some kinda freak," she insisted.

For the first time, I heard a degree of fragility from Alex. She'd been coming across as such a badass up until this point. I realized now that she might not be exactly as advertised.

"I wasn't trying to make you feel that way," I explained. "I was just so blown away. You have to admit...immunity is pretty rare. You are one of about a handful of people I've met who are immune." Then I realized what she'd probably had to go through to get to this point. "How long did it take you to figure out you were okay?"

If she'd been blushing before, it was nothing compared to what I saw now. She looked away for a moment and then turned back to me. "Just a little while. One of the members of our group that disappeared on us had been bitten on the arm like two weeks before they took off. She didn't turn. So, when my eyes didn't show the tracers within a few hours, I had to at least assume there was a good chance I wasn't infected. Unfortunately...my mom wasn't as lucky."

I'd all but forgotten about that part. Her mom had been attacked and bitten. She was definitely having the entire zombie apocalypse experience. Other than not having to deal with hunger, her mom had not had one moment that hadn't been awful. Losing one daughter right before her eyes; one daughter having to kill the other; getting sick from an infection that would've been easily handled by a doctor just weeks before. Add in being allergic to penicillin, and I felt awful for Alex's mom.

"By the time I had killed those two zombies and hurried to my mom's side...her eyes were already showing the tracers. Thankfully, I think she was so sick and just out of it that she didn't know what was happening. I didn't want her to turn...and I thought that she'd suffered enough. I put a pillow over her head, pushed the pistol into it until I felt it reach the resistance of her forehead...and pulled the trigger.

"I sat there beside her for a minute until I heard a moan from downstairs. Part of me was ready to die. I hadn't yet considered I might be immune. The reminder of that pain from the bite on my leg told me to get up and handle the situation. I went down and discovered a pair of regular zombies had wandered in through the door that I'd left open.

"It was easy to end them. After that, I went upstairs and sat down beside my mom's corpse. The stench in the room eventually drove me to leave. I knew burying her was out of the question, so I wrapped her in the linens on the bed and then headed downstairs."

Alex found a relatively dry spot on a log and sat down. I waited a moment and then decided to join her. It was a large log, so I didn't need to sit on top of her and crowd her space. I felt like maybe she still had more to say, so I just stared out at the dark swirling water of the river.

I could smell the clean scent that always followed a bit of rain. It was strangely soothing, and I have no idea how long we sat there before Alex resumed her story.

"I think I fell asleep," she started.

At first I was unsure if she was back to sharing, or if

she might be telling me about the here-and-now.

"My head jerked up and I felt terrible. I was certain this would be the start of it. Only, I wasn't about to allow myself to turn into one of those things. I got up and wandered into the bathroom. I don't know why, but I guess part of me needed to see it for myself.

"When I looked into the mirror, I saw...nothing." She paused and then gave a soft chuckle. "I mean, I saw something, obviously. Just, there was nothing wrong in my eyes. Just the normal set I've always had looking back at me."

"Did you keep checking every few hours?" I asked after another pause.

"Yeah. And even when I'd finally convinced myself that I was not going to turn, I still found myself checking." She looked sideways at me through the tear that had fallen down her face. "I still check every once in a while. Like I am waiting for it to show up...because I still can't believe it."

I couldn't recall the last time that I'd checked. After I came to accept my condition, I guess I just figured that was it. Also, I was certain that anybody I was travelling with would say something if my eyes were suddenly laced with black tracers.

"Listen, I don't know if I should say this," Alex said, snapping me back to the moment. "If you keep Maggie here, you are going to need to keep a very close eye on her. She is seriously blaming you for her brother's death. We have enough going on without having to deal with that."

"Yeah," I agreed. "But I can't just toss her out on her own. Until she does something, I have to give her the benefit of the doubt."

"Well, I'll be watching your back."

I found that sentiment very encouraging. While I had no doubts that Alex and I would butt heads again, I did feel as maybe we'd turned a corner.

We walked back to discover that Drew and his people were unloading their supplies from the van. I heard a lot of comments that went along the lines of never wanting to see (or smell) the inside of that vehicle again.

When it was all said and done, they had a couple of tents, and everybody would at least be able to be out of the worst of the elements. It was by no means perfect, but it was a start. Our community had basically tripled in size.

Eventually, Maggie returned. She wouldn't look at me, but she rolled up her sleeves right away and stepped in to help as we continued to get our area set up. I wanted to have not only a deep ditch that surrounded us, but also some barricades. Once we had some rudimentary defenses in place, we could start building some form of community housing that would offer us better protection than simple tents. One of the things I insisted upon when we had our first group meeting to discuss the plans for our cabins involved ensuring that each one had an underground bunker of sorts.

"Besides being a great place to keep and store food, it will be a fallback location if we are ever overrun. We can run some form of ventilation that will offer adequate air flow if you end up trapped inside for any significant period," I explained.

"Give this a lot of thought back in the day?" Drew snickered.

"Not this exact scenario," I admitted. "But I was always thinking about what I would need to do in the event of some terrible global disaster or even an invasion."

"By what? Aliens?" Drew scoffed.

"Nah…the Chinese."

The man looked me over and I could tell he was unsure if I was being truthful or pulling his leg. I didn't know him well; and while I like him well enough, I saw no harm in making him and his people think I might be just a shade on the crazy side.

He looked to be considering my statement when another voice spoke out. "Are we going to adopt a plan for people who are bitten? What about mandatory quarantine when folks return from supply runs?"

This was one of Drew's people. He was a chunky guy that looked like he'd probably lost a considerable amount of weight since the whole zombie thing. And if he'd lost weight up to this point, he must've tipped the scales well over the three hundred-plus mark before. His clothes could probably fit a second smaller person in them. I had no idea why he hadn't bothered to swap out yet. But then, he was still hefty. Perhaps he hadn't found anything in his new (and still at least triple-XL) size.

"I think we're still small enough to be able to rely on maybe just a simple exam," I answered. Honestly, that thought hadn't even occurred to me.

"And how long before we ain't?" the man challenged. "I don't feel like going through what happened at one of those damned FEMA shelters."

"Okay, then maybe we pair them up with somebody

341

for twenty-four hours that wasn't outside the perimeter," I suggested. "We can't really afford to have people idle for extended periods while they sit in quarantine to ensure they aren't infected."

That received a collection of nods and grunts of approval. As we went through the meeting, I could feel a sense of cohesion starting to build. For whatever reason, I was starting to feel a glimmer of hope.

13

Children and Strangers

Three entire days passed with nothing worth talking about. It was all about working on our new home. A couple of Drew's people said they remembered the location of one of those big box hardware stores. They wanted to take the van and see about locating an actual big rig to load up. It was discussed and then vetoed.

As much as many of us saw the use of such a trip, not one of us could justify the risk at this point. We agreed that it would be a great idea once our numbers reached something close to fifty or so. That would allow for an actual team to make the run instead of two people.

Instead, we started raiding the houses in the area. Many of them had sheds and lots of farm equipment for us to scoop up. The second trip out to a house just two down from the one that my last ill-fated run had been to yielded the post-apocalyptic equivalent of hitting the lottery. A small one maybe, but still a jackpot.

The team of three returned to say that the house had obviously been in the process of building a massive barn. Not only was there a plethora of supplies, but there was also a huge truck with yet another earth-mover on a trailer and a good amount of fuel.

We managed to get it all back with very little zombie interference. To help our cause, once we had everything offloaded, we took the big rig and drove back up to South Springwater Road and kept it in first gear with the engine revving high and loud as we rolled about a mile up from our location to a feed store.

That was our second jackpot. Apparently the feed store also had several pallets of dog food stacked in their store.

"Makes sense, lots of the farmers here with livestock keep herding dogs," Tracy said as we loaded several large bags into the van to bring back for Chewie.

Up until that point, after we'd run out, she was surviving off scraps. That had done her insides no favors at all much to the dismay of anybody she decided to flop down beside at night when we sat around the campfire.

Even Michael got up a few times and walked upwind from her. It was actually sad to watch. It didn't help that Chewie was far from silent in her emissions. That sound became the signal for anybody near her to get up and hurry away. She would look around with the saddest eyes and then just drop her head to the ground and make all sorts of whining sounds until the air cleared to the point where Michael would return and rub her ears or scratch her belly.

I should've known better than to get comfortable.

***

I was standing on the first platform of our very first watch tower. It was a simple bit of construction and stood about thirty feet high. We had one platform at the halfway point that was more for just adding to the stability, and then a small one at the top that could hold two people in close quarters.

The plan was to build eight of these towers. Telephone poles worked great for the frame and we'd had no problems coming up with what we needed since they were evenly spaced down the length of Springwater Road. We'd had to utilize our flatbed big rig again, and then repeat the evolution of driving back up to the main road and away from the entrance to McIver.

The first indication that there was a problem came when several coyotes burst from the woods and sped past our camp. One of them paused, looking back over its shoulder. It tongue was lolling, and even from where I was standing, I could see its sides heaving like a bellows. It didn't stay long and quickly vanished into the wall of green after crossing the narrow road that ran parallel to the trench and subsequent dirt berm we'd created in this location

I turned back to see what might've spooked the coyote. I expected to see a few zombies. When the first one appeared, I felt the hair on my arms and back of my neck stand up. My skin pebbled and my stomach received an unwelcome dose of acidic juices, sending a bubble of bile up to the back of my throat.

The little boy stepped out of the dense scrub and brambles. He might've been ten years old in life. I saw dark splotches on his arms that were probably very old bite marks. Coming out of the same dense section of undergrowth and sprawling blackberry bushes were cats.

It was like watching a scene from that old horror movie, *Ben*, only with cats. There were dozens of them. They came out to the road and then stopped. Several of the felines looked like they were searching. Their heads swung back and forth very slowly. After a moment, several of them dropped to a crouch and began to slink across the road.

Directly towards our camp!

"No way in hell," I gasped.

As soon as the cats began to move, the little boy adjusted and began to follow. Less than two heartbeats later, more of the diminutive walking dead emerged and fell in with the procession.

From where I stood, I could look out through the trees. I saw a considerable amount of movement. And then more bad news: a herd of regular zombies were forcing their way through the woods on the heels of the cats and zombie children.

It was as if this was a coordinated attack. But that was impossible, right? To think otherwise was too terrifying. Yet, the proof of it was right before my eyes.

My mind drifted to that ambush near that church. A

zombie child banging on a car had launched the adults. That noise had been enough to draw them in a specific direction, then, once they spotted me, they oriented on their target…yours truly. Now, it appeared as if this pack of zombie children were leading a herd directly for our camp. Only, I was almost certain that *they* were following the cats.

"Crap," I hissed as I realized there was no way to alert the others that did not involve screaming at the top of my lungs.

"We got a herd incoming!" I shouted.

There really was no other option. My shouting had an instant effect on the zombies…and the cats. However, it differed depending on the variety. The mob of adults that I could now see scattered throughout the woods began to stop their advance. I shouted my warning again and saw them orient on me and begin to resume their trudging now pointed in my direction. For the most part, the cats scattered and vanished into the woods.

It was the children, specifically, the one I'd seen leading the group, that dropped the temperature of my blood a few more degrees. He turned, standing in the middle of the little road and appeared to be searching the area. At last, he located me.

I studied him as he regarded me. The realization of what I was seeing sent tendrils of dread through my body. I recognized him as one of the children from back at that house. His ripped-up baseball jersey was the clincher.

I watched him as he just stood there. And then I realized something. I glanced over at the rifle leaning against the railing. It was standard issue for anybody working outside the protective trench that surrounded our encampment. You could take any of the hand-to-hand weapons you wanted, but everybody who went out carried a pistol at their hip and a rifle.

The rifle was mostly so that you could bag any game that might come along. So far, we'd only managed a few ducks, but those had been the first fresh meat any of us had eaten in a long time. I think for me it had to date back to the day Marshawn and his people had left steaks and beer behind after we'd initially parted ways.

I grabbed the rifle and brought it to my shoulder. My scope found the zombie boy's face, and I felt a shiver of excitement ripple through me with enough force to make the crosshairs ·bounce and cause me to readjust for my shot.

Just as with anytime I'd encountered a zombie child and displayed a weapon, this one reverted to just another zom. The mysterious focus that had been driving him to this point evaporated. He was headed my way now. Whatever his grand plan might've been was gone; replaced by that core drive the undead have for simply going towards the most recent stimulus.

I wasn't about to waste this opportunity. I squeezed the trigger. The hole in his face was impressive, but I could tell by the amount of dark gore that exploded from the back that his skull had basically disintegrated.

Maybe I thought that since he seemed to be the leader the rest of the zombies would just rout and wander back to wherever they came from—although I had a good idea where the children had been staying. It took about five seconds for me to see the stupidity in that idea.

The only positive thing, and this was really stretching the definition, was in the fact that now all the zombies, child and adult, were coming for me. The good news was that I was up on the tower platform. So far, I hadn't seen any zombies that could climb a ladder…much less the unstable and free hanging rope ladder we were currently using to get up here.

"Evan?" Marshawn, Drew, and a few others came jogging up the road. Marshawn called for me, and that caused several of both brands of undead to turn back once more at this most recent stimulus.

"What the hell did you do, Evan?" Drew yelped as he backed up at the sight of so many zombies this close to our stronghold.

I was too busy to answer as I sighted in on the next child zombie I could find. After what I'd just seen, I was now officially on the bandwagon to eliminate them on sight. While I was now very certain that they were different than a regular zombie, I'd also just witnessed one of them leading a concentrated attack effort.

I had no idea what limited strategy or plan a zombie child might concoct, but I was officially off the list of being curious. It was sorta like that scene from the movie, *Gremlins*. There was this part where Corey Feldman first sees Gizmo, some water is spilled, and the poor little thing screeches as little puffballs launch from his back. Billy asks Pete what he thinks of things and the kid has his eyes pressed to a View Master as he says something like, "Neat...seriously." His tone makes it clear he does not actually hold that sentiment.

I was certain that the child versions were different, but in perhaps a very lethal way that just reduced humanity's chances of surviving the apocalypse by a huge amount. There was nothing "cool" or "neat" about them. And while I still felt a desperate need to figure them out, now was not the time. Right now, the most important thing to do was to execute every last one of them.

"You okay up there, Evan?" Drew shouted as he, Marshawn, and the others started to back away towards our compound-in-the-making.

"I'll be okay as long as these bastards can't climb," I shouted back.

Bringing my rifle back up to my shoulder, I swept until I found my next target. This one was a little boy with no obvious or visible sign as to how he'd turned. I'd seen a few people like that, and it always creeped me out. For whatever reason, it is much easier to shoot a zombie with its guts hanging out than just a person with a creepy skin tone and gross eye problems.

After a deep breath to clear my head, I squeezed the trigger again. From my vantage point, it almost looked like the entire top of the kid's head came off.

By the time I brought my weapon down, my comrades

were no longer in sight. However, I did hear the deep bark of my Chewie. That meant the zombies were probably reaching the barriers we'd worked so hard to establish.

Technically, this would be their first real chance to show that we'd done things right. Everybody would probably be too swept up in the moment to really see what worked best, but we would absolutely know what *didn't* work. I had my fingers crossed that our weaknesses were few...and none of them fatal.

I dropped a few more zombies of both types, and stepped back to reload. That is when I heard the low rumble from almost directly behind me.

I spun to see a large black cat with white paws regarding me from his perch on the rail that enclosed the platform on the tower. It was very deliberately licking its paws and regarding me with the apathetic disinterest that only cats can master so expertly.

"Hey, there...cat." I very cautiously set my rifle down and unclipped the holster that held my pistol.

I was one of those people who believed that my pistol was very much the last resort weapon. It was for that reason that I'd taken to carrying a very simple .22 caliber handgun.

As I considered the animal that had made no move to indicate he was in the least bit concerned as he continued to lick his paws in deliberate, languid stokes of his tongue, I knew this was going to end with another dark stain on my conscience.

For some reason, I suddenly felt bad for how I'd scolded Todd about his then apparently senseless attacks on poor defenseless cats. Had he seen and felt what I was experiencing right this moment? Had the hair on the back of his neck stood up? Had his bladder constricted to the point that he worried he might wet his pants?

Very slowly, I brought the pistol up. I didn't worry about where I hit the cat, from this range, a shot to the body should be good enough.

I'm not an advocate of harming domestic animals. I have no problem with hunting and fishing. However, killing or torturing an animal is a practice that I always believed should face the same penalties as an offense against a person. I'd even gotten into a bar fight over it once way back when. Now? Well, my feelings hadn't changed as much as shifted.

My finger tightened around the trigger, and I had to take a deep breath to calm my nerves. Through it all, the cat simply continued to stare at me with no concern. It was oblivious to the razor's edge its life existed upon.

When I pulled the trigger, there was a dull 'pop' from the weapon and the bullet slammed into the cat's shoulder. The impact had been just enough to knock it from the rail it had been perched upon and it fell to the ground below. I made no attempt to look. I felt a sick feeling in my stomach.

If somebody walked up to me at that moment and asked why I'd done such a thing…I wouldn't have any answer that made sense. It was based solely on a feeling in my gut. I shoved the pistol into the holster and snatched up my rifle again.

I spotted a small pack of adult zombies and brought my scope to bear on them. I dropped three in short order, but the awful feeling was still there.

I dropped two more…and then I heard *the scream*. My heart thudded as the realization that somebody in our camp had just fallen slammed into me. I was already on overload, and that new revelation caused my knees to wobble just a bit.

I steadied myself and resumed finding targets. Twice more, I reloaded. And while I hadn't hit with one hundred percent accuracy, I'd dropped quite a few zombies of both types.

As my magazine emptied again, I reached for my pouch and realized that this was the last reload for my rifle. As I removed the empty mag and replaced it with the final one, I looked out over the area at all the downed bodies.

A small surge of bile raced to the back of my throat with a bitter burn that was starting to seem permanent. As I forced it back and took in the scene, I suddenly felt less bad about having shot a cat. Everywhere I looked, I saw swishing tails as what had to be perhaps a hundred felines in all shapes, sizes, and colors as they prowled through the area. Many were sitting beside a corpse. Some were in the act of tugging at a strip of flesh, others chewing and swallowing their most recent bite.

I noticed that they would scatter if an adult zombie stumbled their direction. But they were like the tide as they would all rush back in the moment it was clear and begin feasting anew.

There was a symbiotic relationship that seemed to exist between the child version of the undead and these cats. I wasn't sure if it was universal, or simply something unique to this group. Perhaps it was akin to a remora and a shark. I'd seen them snack on some of the children, but not to the extent they were feeding on the corpses strewn about.

A sudden flurry of gunfire came from the direction of the camp, snapping me out of my ruminations. I desperately wanted to climb down and rush to the battle taking place.

Looking down, there were several zombies gathered at the base of my tower. It would be very unlikely that I might be able to get down, take out enough to clear a path, and run to the battle raging at our camp.

It was then that a new thought crept up from the dark corners of my mind and planted its flag in the middle of my conscious thought. If all my comrades were killed in this attack...I would most likely die up here on this platform.

I instantly dismissed that notion as I told myself that, if worse came to worse, I would at least make an attempt to escape this spot. And I would keep my .22 handy just in case. If I went down and knew that death was certain, I would simply eat a bullet.

A realization struck me. *What the hell was I thinking?*

Okay, while it is most likely that a .22 round to the temple would put me down, there certainly was the chance it could fail.

There was an explosion of leaves as a figure burst through some of the thick ferns and shrubs in the direction of the camp. A figure was backpedaling and stumbled, falling on his or her behind. Right on this person's heels came several zombies — a mix of children and adults.

I brought my rifle up and sighted on the safest target. The zombie toppled as I put a round in its head. The person was too busy fighting off a pair of the undead to notice. The sounds from below pulled my attention to the base of my tower as the undead gathered there were starting to turn and move towards this newest possible meal.

I knew it was never going to be clear, so I waited just long enough for it to thin. As soon as space permitted, I slid down the ladder just as I'd done on so many construction jobs.

I had a boss that used to get highly pissed off when I would do that. If he caught me, he always pitched a fit.

"Ladders have rungs for a reason, Mister Berry." He always tried to intimidate me with his size, but it hadn't ever worked out the way he wanted.

I hit the ground and pulled my machete as I slung the rifle over my shoulder. Shoving the nearest zombie forward, I hacked at the next closest and felt that familiar sting in my hands as blade met skull.

"They breached our little berm and then a bunch fell into the trench," Alex gasped as she moved my direction. "Enough fell in that a few dozen were able to make it across the trench on the backs of the ones that fell."

I could not imagine the number of zombies that it would take to fill a trench that was perhaps ten feet deep and at least that far across. There had to be more than just what I'd seen. Obviously, they hadn't filled the entire trench that circled our camp, but enough had fallen in a concentrated area to cause a problem. We would have to address that…if we survived.

A trio of the children emerged to my left from behind a massive boulder. One of them couldn't be older than two or three years old and was even more unsteady on its feet as it toddled my direction. He was stark naked, and his body was covered with scratches in addition to a few spots that looked like perhaps he'd been nibbled on by the cats.

I didn't even think as I kicked out with one booted foot and punted him backwards and into the rock. My next move was to cleave the skull of one child and kick the feet out from the other. Before the little one could regain its feet, I moved just enough so that I was able to stomp my heel into the middle of its face. I heard and felt the crunch as its skull gave. I chopped at the third as I stomped a second time to the crunch and squish as the toddler's head gave way completely.

An adult zombie swiped at me just as I turned to help Alex. I hadn't seen this one, and its hand connected with my face hard enough that it made a meaty slapping sound. My eyes actually blurred for a moment, and I felt a hot stinging on my cheek and jaw.

I gripped my machete, but it had gotten too close and I couldn't bring the weapon up effectively. I stabbed out and actually heard the skin rip. A wave of stink rolled out as the paper-thin layer of skin on this woman's belly gave way, her insides vomiting forth from the gash I'd just created.

It was bad enough that I gagged and then sprayed a stream of watery vomit in the zombie woman's face. That caused my stomach to do a barrel roll. Apparently nothing was nailed down internally and all the remaining contents from my earlier meal made a hasty exit. I vomited again, this time with eye-watering force.

All that did was add another level of stench and pu-
trescence to an already foul scene. I stumbled back, my
arm swinging wildly as I tripped over one of the downed
children I'd just ended.

Of course, despite the force with which I'd expelled
the contents of my stomach, there was a good amount of it
down my front now. That wasn't helping me regain control of my bodily functions. The woman flopped onto me,
and that was when my bladder totally let go.

I shoved at her as she tried to grab me while her teeth
clicked together just inches from my throat. A dollop of
some of my liquid laughter splatted down on my face as I
jerked from side to side while I struggled to avoid a bite
that would end me. Being immune was not going to matter if this zombie managed to clamp her teeth on my neck
and rip open my jugular.

It wasn't supposed to happen like this. I'd managed to
get through so much to make it to this point. And sure,
that might seem overly egocentric, but I wasn't ready to
die yet. I certainly didn't want to die like this.

I was sickeningly aware of a million sensations that
were hitting me all at once. Pain, regret, fear, and so many

others. Physically, I can't ever recall feeling so foul. I had vomit all over me, I'd wet my pants, and I could feel the insides of this zombie soaking my stomach through my layers of clothing and jacket.

There was an awful sound, and then my face was splattered with a slurry of vile, thick, syrupy goo that might've been blood once upon a time. The only thing I could dredge up to be thankful for at the moment were the goggles I wore. They'd become such a part of being out-side the perimeter that, half the time, I would forget to remove them when I was in camp.

Something grabbed my shoulder, and I knew this was it. I would die here. I braced for the feel of teeth to rip into me, and then felt my body hauled across the ground.

"Come on, Evan, on your feet," Alex hissed.

I scrambled onto my stomach and made it to my knees. Looking around, I had to pull my goggles down in order to see. There was a nasty gash in the top of the head of the zombie that had been on top of me. Putrefied brain matter spilled from the wound.

"What the—" I started, but Alex cut me off.

"Look, for whatever reason, I came out here to see if you were still alive. You are. Now we need to get back and help the others." Without another word, she turned and started back towards our compound. As she did, she veered whenever necessary to drop any zombie that she would pass.

As we made our way through the woods, I lost count of how many corpses littered the ground. Since she'd been the only one to come this way, I had to attribute them all to Alex. It was an impressive tally.

I also began to notice that, at least by appearances, the dead zombie children had been hacked up versus just a single stab to the head through the eye or temple. There was no denying Alex had a reason to be angry, but this was behavior bordering on psychotic. At least in my opinion. I would have to keep an eye on her...provided we survived the next several minutes.

The closer we got to the main camp, the more I could hear — sounds that filled me with a sense of dread that nearly overwhelmed to feeling of urgency that compelled me to continue.

There were shouts, screams, and cries for help. Mixed in that were the moans of the undead, the creepy baby cries, and Chewie's growling bark. If there is a soundtrack for Hell...this was it.

I reached the berm and could see a handful of zombie children trying to scramble up the steep embankment. There was also a single adult version with them. This was a visible study of the truth to their differences. The children had all gone to their hands and knees. The adult was trying to walk upright and, just as we arrived, toppled over backwards and fell hard, tumbling down and colliding with one of the many large rocks we'd unearthed during the digging of the trench. I was certain I'd heard bones break.

Alex didn't even slow as she reached the base of the steeply inclined dirt hill. She caught the first zombie child and yanked it back by the hair. A small axe seemed to appear in her hand, and she chopped down hard, burying it in the top of the little girl's skull. There was a splash of chunky darkness as the body was cast aside. Alex was already grabbing the second child by the time I started up the berm.

Her second killing was almost more horrific to witness as she caught the zombie child by the heel. While the child versions are no faster than their adult counterparts, I swear this one tried to hurry and escape. I am certain that it looked over its shoulder, but because it looked over the left and Alex had the axe in her right, perhaps it didn't see the weapon. It never switched into what I was now considering "standard zombie mode" as it continued its attempted escape.

Jerking the child to her, Alex hacked at the back of the child's head. Twice, her blows struck between the shoulder blades with a teeth-jarring crack. The third strike hit at the base of the skull, breaking it open somewhat. It was the fourth that completely shattered the skull into at least two large pieces.

I made quick work of the adult and then joined in finishing off the remaining zombie children. As I did, I had to shut out the sounds of Chewie's frantic barking. I could tell she was very upset.

When I reached the top of the berm and looked down into the trench we'd been so proud of, I felt my stomach roll. It was a writhing sea of arms and legs straight out of a nightmare. As I watched, a face broke free from the mass and I swear it locked eyes with me. I know in my rational mind that these creatures have never shown any sort of emotion on their faces, but I couldn't help but project. I am convinced that I saw a hopeless state of despair.

Of course, there was no way I could reach the thing.

Besides, by the time I'd taken three steps down the berm, it was gone. I glanced at Alex who was standing about halfway down and considering the scene before us.

Just past the trench was the start of our fence. It was supposed to be a secondary defense after the hill and the huge, deep ditch we'd dug. I could see the strands of barbed wire had been snapped like nothing. There were chunks and bits still clinging to the wire, but it had been totally useless.

I had to force down my own sense of despair. The defense I'd been so proud of had utterly failed. And now, just beyond those snapped strands of barbed wire and the thick bushes that obscured being able to see the camp, my people were fighting for their lives.

"You ready?" Alex glanced back at me.

I looked at her and noticed that her face was drained of all color. Her lips almost looked purple they stood out so starkly.

"For?" I moved closer to her, wondering what had brought her fear to the forefront.

She turned away from me, and I saw her body tense. Surely she couldn't be about to do what I thought she looked to be preparing for. My gaze slid to the trench and

I could see movement in both directions. So many of the zombies hadn't made it and were now wandering freely in the makeshift moat.

Before I could really get my mind wrapped around what I *thought* Alex might be planning, she took off in a few bounding steps, reached the bottom of the berm, and launched herself into the air. She landed on the other side with plenty to spare.

Okay, it was only ten feet. Even with just a few steps, the jump wouldn't be that big of a deal. Only…with the undead filling our moat, it wasn't a jump you wanted to botch. This was playing the childhood game "the floor is lava" with completely real stakes.

I couldn't spend too much time thinking. Alex had already taken off at a sprint for the camp. I watched her vanish through the branches, leaving me to do what needed to be done.

I took a deep breath, instantly regretting it as the foul stench of the undead flooded my mouth and nose. The oily sensation was enough to make me gag, but I shoved that aside as I took off at a sprint.

My eyes were fixed on the other side of the trench. As I reached that last step before I would go over the edge, I pushed off with everything I had. My body went airborne and I had the briefest sensation of flight...until I landed. My feet tangled and I ended up skidding on my stomach.

Other than some skinned knees and the palms of my hands, I appeared to be fine. I grabbed the machete I'd been holding from where it had skidded to a stop after I lost my grip.

Somewhere, in the back of my mind, I heard my mother telling me that I was going to poke my eye out running with an unsheathed weapon. I told that voice that, if this was the worst possibility waiting for me by the end of the day, I'd be okay.

I hurried off in the direction Alex had vanished. The sounds of battle were growing louder. When I emerged on the other side of the dense foliage that our camp hunkered down in the middle of, that sound amplified as if somebody had just turned the volume knob to eleven.

While I still hadn't become instant-name-recall familiar with all of Drew's people, I at least knew them by face. The first cluster of people my eyes lit upon were absolute strangers. Five faces I'd never seen before.

The thing that saved the closest one of these strangers came in the form of the three undead that turned my direction from my immediate left. I chopped with a sidearm swing, my blade almost making it through cleanly. I yanked my hand back in what was now instinctive response and pulled the weapon free.

I spun to the second zombie, prepared to come down with an overhand attack to keep my profile narrow to the third zombie while also allowing myself to drop my shoulder when it reached me. That move was one I used often in these situations. A zombie's inability to adjust causes it to walk right into my dropped shoulder and take the brunt of my attack. Usually I catch it in the chest and send it flying backward. That made for an easy kill.

The first part of my move went off without a hitch. In fact, it was all good until I instinctively threw myself in the direction of the third zombie in order to knock it down. I met empty air and again found myself falling hard.

I rolled, my eyes looking every direction as I sought the zombie I knew to be close. One of the strangers had moved in and spiked it in the top of the head. The woman had a knit cap pulled low and a scarf around the lower half of her face, but I could absolutely tell it was a woman by the curves. She reached out with a gloved hand.

"Sorry, didn't realize you knew it was right there on

you." She pulled me to my feet and stepped back. "Nice combo move by the way."

And then she bounded off to cut down a pair of zombie children moving in behind one of the living. It was a pitched battle with more zombies than I'd ever faced. As I chopped, I found myself having to switch hands simply due to fatigue. One after another, the undead fell. On several occasions, I found myself shoulder-to-shoulder with an absolute stranger.

It was impossible to do more than give a nod of acknowledgement. When I found Marshawn, I felt a wave of relief. He'd taken Michael up a ladder to what was the start of our planned catwalk construct. It was supposed to eventually crisscross the entire camp. It would allow the patrolling sentry to have an unobstructed view of things. That idea sprung up before we'd gotten very far with the trench. One night, I'd been on patrol and rounded the corner of a tent when I collided with a walker.

Besides scaring me, it made me realize that the undead don't always moan or cry. Also, they move slow enough that it is possible for them to actually sneak up on a person.

Seeing that Marshawn and the boy were safe was a

huge relief. As for Chewie, she was posted up right below them. Anything that came close would find itself being bowled over. Maybe they'd worked it out over a few practice runs, but the whole thing looked surprisingly well-oiled. Marshawn never missed when the big Newfie would plow into an approaching zombie. I had the chance to observe one instance where he actually spun away from his current cluster of targets to end Chewie's latest victim. Maybe Michael was involved, but it was impossible to give it much more than passing attention.

I turned to cut off a pair of undead moving towards a young woman who was trying to free her machete from the skull of a zombie. A quick assessment told me that she didn't have any other weapons. My jog changed to a sprint and I took down the first one by severing its head which tumbled to the ground and came to a stop on its ear a few feet away. I didn't need to look to know it wasn't completely finished, but at least it was no longer a mobile threat.

The second one was a simple matter of me grabbing it by the shoulder. I spun it to face me and then drove the tip of my blade into its eye. The scream that came at that exact moment caused my hand to lose its grip just enough for me to drop my blade. It happened so perfectly that it took me a few heartbeats to realize the zombie hadn't been the one to scream.

I turned as I collected my weapon and spotted the source of the scream. It was Alex. She was on her knees with her machete buried deep in the face of the zombie sprawled on the ground. The problem existed in the two zombie children that looked to have caught her by surprise from behind.

During the melee, her wide-brimmed hat had obviously fallen or been knocked off. To complicate the issue, her hair wasn't in a hair tie any longer. It was streaming around her face and fluttering behind her. One of the children had a fistful and was tugging her backwards by her hair.

The second child looked to be utilizing that distraction to her advantage as she moved in from the front. It had managed to get ahold of Alex's jacket sleeve. The woman was jerking back and forth in an attempt to escape. As I started for her, I saw her yank so hard that the child with a fistful of hair fell back with a clump of her reddish-brown locks.

I heard her scream again, this time it was one that was

372

more pain-based than fear. She was now thrashing about, kicking out and trying to shake the one off her arm. All that did was cause her hair to fly about, making it easy for the child to grab another handful of it in one fist.

The child moved in again, and I could see its mouth opening. Alex was trying to shake her head back and forth, but it was useless. Her weapon was also stuck, and she was too panicked to think rationally and grab one of the blades dangling from her belt.

I arrived just in time to knock the child back. Alex yelped, and I saw another handful of her hair fluttering in the zombie child's fist. I stomped on the child's arm and drove my own blade into its face.

I saw one more, and it was in "basic zombie mode" as it trudged to me with its arms wide and hands grabbing at the air in a twisted caricature that looked like it wanted a hug.

I'd just finished off the zombie child of perhaps seven or eight and then I looked around. It was then that I realized everybody else seemed to be either catching their breath, or wiping off a weapon. Scanning my own surroundings, there were no more threats.

We'd done it. Our little group had survived its first

full-frontal attack. The undead had come in huge numbers—led by a child, I reminded myself—and we'd managed to defeat them with what looked to be minimal casualties.

I turned to Alex and saw that she was curled up into a ball, her arms wrapped around her knees which she held tight to her chest. She was sobbing and whispering something over and over. I approached her very slowly, not sure what her reaction might be. At last, I was close enough to hear.

"I'm not ready…I'm not ready…I'm not ready…"

14

Company

I knelt beside Alex. Honestly, I was at a loss. Up until this moment, she'd always come across as such a bad ass. I figured we needed her more than she did us. To see her like this was...confusing.

"You okay?" I warred with the idea of putting a hand on her shoulder, but decided against it.

"Do I look okay?" Her face tilted up to mine and I could see the redness around her eyes, the tracks made by tears that cut through the dust on her face. Her nose was running just a bit and the clear fluid from the left nostril was about to touch her upper lip.

These were the sorts of things you seldom saw on the pretty faces of the Hollywood version of a zombie apocalypse. When Alex simply wiped at her face with the back of her hand, basically leaving a smear across her face that could only partially be attributed to tears, I had to appreciate the reality of the moment even more.

"It's all fake," she whispered. It was so soft, that at first, I didn't think I'd heard her correctly or if she'd even spoken. Then she continued after a harsh sniffle. "I've shot in plenty of ranges. Wasted plenty of rounds on targets, even clay pigeons. But I didn't so much as nab a deer. First time I got one in my sights, my hands shook so bad that I almost dropped my rifle."

I wasn't sure what this had to do with anything. Perhaps I wasn't seeing the big picture. I mean, in the short time we've travelled together, I've seen Alex fight and take down plenty of the undead.

"When those things busted into the room with my mom and me, I froze." She took a deep, hitching breath before resuming. "It was my mom that pushed me out of the way. That's why she cut her hand, because I was just standing there like an idiot and would've probably gotten bit myself if she hadn't acted. When the infection set in, I was afraid to go out on my own. I only did it when she started getting delirious. Her fever was so bad that I could feel the heat pouring off her. That was what finally drove me to make that run to the hospital."

We sat in silence for a spell. I looked around and saw that the rest of the people, both those I knew, and those I didn't, were already making a dent in cleaning out the corpses scattered on the ground. I needed to be a part of that evolution so that folks didn't start thinking that I felt myself above the crappy details around camp.

"I actually shit my pants," she mumbled. "The first time I rounded a corner in that damn medical center and came face-to-face with one of those things. I've never been so scared."

I was embarrassed for her, but I understood completely. This was nothing like the books, movies, television shows, or video games. We lived in a constant state of fear that wore down on the soul.

"Hey!" I brightened. "You still saved my butt that day. You picked off those zombies when I was trying to get up that hill."

"I was drunk," Alex replied.

I looked at her with a raised eyebrow. I wasn't sure what that had to do with anything. Her shooting had been expert, and she'd saved my ass that day. I could still see that camo-wearing figure on the hill give me a salute before vanishing into the woods.

"I'd gotten blasted and decided to just go out and end it all. I had this stupid idea that I would go out in a hail of bullets as I took out as many zombies as possible. They'd stolen everything I loved, so I was going to kill until there were no more rounds left in the rifle, then I would switch to pistol and go until I had only one more round. I was going to eat a bullet as my last act."

I took that all in. It didn't make me see her any differently. All it did was make me see her as human. She had the same fears and frailties as the rest of us.

"We should get up and help," she said, clapping her hands together and then wiping at her eyes one more time.

"Okay," I agreed.

I stood and reached down to offer a hand. She glanced at it for a second and I believed that she was going to refuse. Instead, she took my gloved hand with hers and pulled herself to her feet.

I headed over to where Marshawn was helping Michael climb down from the beginnings of our catwalk. He was wincing, so I knew that his bullet wound was bothering him. He insisted that he was not in need of painkillers.

"We only have so much of these babies," he'd said one

day. "I think we should save them for something a bit more serious. This injury sucks, but it was a clean one and it is healing. The pain is bad, but manageable."

"Umm..." I glanced over my shoulder at the bustling camp, "...not that I'm complaining about their help, but who exactly are these people?"

Marshawn looked past me like he was seeing them for the first time. His eyes didn't widen or narrow, they just swept over everything before returning to me.

"Yeah...they showed up just a moment before the zombies. If not for the fact that they came in from the opposite direction and then jumped right in to help fight them off, I might've believed they were shady. Maybe even that they brought the herd with them." Marshawn leaned in close before he whispered, "But we should still watch them. I have a vibe...like something ain't right."

Imagine that, I thought, *something not right in a zombie apocalypse.* What I said was, "Do we have a designated spokesman or leader?"

"I guess that would be me," a man said as he strolled up making almost no noise at all.

I spun, and if I hadn't known better, I would swear that the guy was sneaking up on us in order to maybe eavesdrop. The man was tall and thin. If you just glimpsed him and didn't focus, he might be able to pass for Christian Bale. His eyes were like two pieces of coal, almost black as they stared right through you, burning a hole wherever they stayed for too long.

He had a nasty scratch that ran down his left cheek that looked suspiciously like somebody had raked him with their nails. His smile was cold, and despite having heard it probably a million times, I'd never understood that "smile that doesn't reach the eyes" comment until this very minute. I now understood Marshawn's trepidation. This guy gave me the creeps.

"Name's Griffin Alistair Marshall. Most folks call me Griff...or hey you." He laughed, and it sounded wrong. As if perhaps his body wasn't sure how to process the noise it was making, or maybe the muscles simply weren't used to that sort of action.

"Evan Berry." I extended my hand to shake his and glanced down when he made no effort to reciprocate. My hand was covered in gore. I wiped it on my pants, but figured it would be best to just let things be on the handshake front. I did notice that Marshawn remained silent during this exchange.

"Looks like you folks have been putting down roots," Griffin said as he looked around like he might be noticing our little camp for the very first time. "We don't want to intrude, and if we ain't welcome, we'll be moving on." The man paused and looked past us in the direction of the river. "Just ask that maybe we be allowed to fill our water containers?"

I felt a tinge of guilt shade the edges of my soul. While this guy might look like the serial killer next door, he seemed genuinely nice. Sure, I get that most folks said that about Ted Bundy, and if this guy was travelling alone, I might send him on his way.

"I have to put it to the group, but I think we have plenty of room," I replied. "Either way, the river is free. Fill up."

"Much appreciated," the man said with a nod that was almost a bow.

When his head came back up, I was almost certain I'd seen that he'd been looking over at Alex. I berated myself for letting my mind get the best of me.

My shame was increased when I looked over to the people that made up his group. Of the eight people, three of them were women. One of the males was a boy no older than fifteen...if that.

They all looked exhausted. It could've been from the battle we all had just fought against the horde, but this fatigue looked like it went to the core of their souls. A few of them wore blank expressions that could simply be a shut down after all the killing. There were more dead zombie children than I think I'd ever seen. I doubted that anybody could've gotten through this fight without having to take down at least one. If it was weighing on them even a fraction of what I felt, then they had every reason to have those blank expressions.

"I'll let my people know," Griffin said as he excused himself and headed over to his group.

I watched as he reached them, a part of me still sharing in Marshawn's gut feeling. I needed to see how his people interacted with him. Did they flinch or all start staring at the ground? My eyes were specifically focused on the women.

He reached them and there was nothing that stood out. At least until the young boy started talking. He was being very animated with his arm gestures. I noticed a couple of the other members in the group step back. Now expressions were looking anxious.

The kid started becoming more agitated, and a few of the group went so far as to reach for him. It looked like they were trying to calm him down. He jerked away each time, and once, he shoved one of the members of his group away with enough force to knock the person over.

The moment that happened, Griffin jerked the kid toward him by the shoulders and put his face right in the kid's. I couldn't hear anything, but I saw the kid sort of go limp. His face went pale enough that I was able to see that change from where I stood.

I thought it was over, but then the kid jerked away suddenly. Now it was his turn to lean into the face of Griffin Alistair Marshall. He said something with enough venom that I caught the low rumble.

In a flash, Griffin brought his fist up into the kid's chin. I had no problem hearing the crack of the blow. It obviously landed right on the button, because the kid dropped like a sack of potatoes.

Griffin stood, brushed himself off as if he'd gotten dusty during the little confrontation, and turned back to me. He glanced over his shoulder, obviously giving the word to collect the kid, before returning to where I still stood with Marshawn.

"What you must be thinking," he said with a laugh that sounded very fake. "It seems that one of our people lost a loved one in the fight."

That would explain the scream, I thought.

"He insists that one of *your* people just stood by and watched it happen."

Now I was more than a little curious. That seemed like a pretty serious accusation.

"That man there...if I'm being totally forthcoming." Griffin's arm extended, and he pointed at Marshawn.

"Say what?" the big man growled, taking a menacing step forward.

I turned and put an arm up to stop Marshawn's advance. It was like using rice paper to stop a charging bull. He barged past and stepped right into Griffin's space, despite being at least six inches shorter, it ended up being the taller man looking up at the shorter when Marshawn bowled the man down.

"Whoa!" Griffin barked from the ground.

I glanced up to see that his people hadn't moved to come to their supposed leader's rescue. They only appeared to cluster tighter together.

"That's enough!" I snapped, moving around Marshawn to install myself between the two.

After I was certain that things weren't going to escalate, I extended a hand to help the man off the ground. I was absolutely re-thinking my position of having this group join ours.

"I didn't say I believed him," Griffin began, his voice sounding frighteningly calm considering the situation. "I was only relating what was said. I made it very clear that accusations like that can't be tossed out so carelessly. There was a lot going on in the heat of the battle. I doubt anybody would simply sit idly by and let another person be mauled by those monsters. That was probably just his grief talking."

As I listened to this man speak, I got a dirty, oily feeling like I was talking to a televangelical used car salesman. Yes, he was saying all the right things, but I was constantly drawn back to his eyes where I saw that coldness that never seemed to thaw in the slightest.

"Maybe we need to take a step back and consider things a little more," I said. Only, it was more of a blurt, and I know my face reddened when everybody turned my direction.

I'm not a shy person by nature. I've never really had

that much of a problem speaking my mind, but at the moment, I felt totally off balance. There was something here. I couldn't put a finger on it, but I was drowning in the creepy vibe this guy was putting off in waves.

"I totally understand, Evan," Griffin said, turning to me with what I am sure he thought was an expression of understanding. All I saw was the jackal circling the downed wildebeest...waiting for its chance to pounce on the weakened creature and feast. "And I will get my people gathered up in the meantime. Maybe you should meet with them and see what you think. And I will abide by any decision you make. If ejecting Mister Romanowski is what will make this work, we will respect your decision."

My mouth dropped open as I was about to protest. I wasn't advocating throwing anybody out on their own. Before I could utter a word, though, the tall, lanky man was already striding away.

"They gotta go, man," Marshawn whispered as he stepped up beside me.

A very big part of me agreed. The problem that I had was that we needed to add to our numbers. This group would almost double our population in one fell swoop.

There was no way that I, or anybody else for that matter, could expect to like every single person we met. Our chances at survival were better if we added able bodies to our numbers. It was simple math. More hands make easy work...or however that saying went.

"They seemed nice enough to me," Tracy said.

I turned to see her, Darya, Alex, Drew, and a handful of others gathered up and standing just a few feet away. Chewie was sprawled at their feet, and I could hear her soft snores as her side rose and fell. Michael's head peeked around Tracy's legs and as soon as he spotted my dog, he pushed through and went to sit beside her.

"I think we need to get everybody together," I said after I realized that all eyes were on me and waiting for something. "I am not going to be the one to decide who joins us and who doesn't."

"Actually," Drew stepped forward, "I think this is exactly the sort of thing we need a leader to decide."

All eyes, including my own, turned in the direction of this soft-spoken man. I hadn't learned too much about Drew's past before the zombies, but I had discovered he'd been a personal trainer. I tried to reconcile that image of a man so calm and laid back as a trainer. All the ones I'd ever encountered were either total muscle heads, high-strung pep rally types, or the sleazy salesman sort that really only cared until you signed the contract that they knew you'd only use for the first month.

"I think this is more of a group decision," I countered.

"Sure, and the group can have their say, but the ultimate choice needs to be yours, Evan."

"And why is that exactly?" I cocked an eyebrow at the man and gave a rolling gesture with one hand, inviting him to elaborate.

"The bottom line is that there needs to be somebody making the tough choices. We, as a group, need to understand that we won't always agree, but that we want what is ultimately best for us. If we try to pretend that this is some big picture-perfect democracy, then we are going to fall apart."

"Are you saying we need a dictatorship?" I scoffed, hardly able to believe what I was hearing.

"Nope, not at all. But if you adopt this idea that everybody can just do his or her thing, pretty soon, you'll have people opting out of important functions. They'll want to come along for the ride and live off the sweat and blood of everybody else without doing any of the work or taking any of the risks."

This was quickly getting outside of my comfort range. Maybe I wasn't the right choice for this leader they sought. What I was hearing sounded much too dictator-y for me. I've always been more of a live and let live kind of guy. It wasn't that all I could do was follow, I just didn't ever feel the need to be the one telling others what to do.

"Everybody cool off for a minute." Marshawn stepped forward, raising his hands to silence the group. "Give me and Evan a minute."

He didn't wait for the others as he took me by the arm and led me over to a copse of ferns and trees. As soon as he deemed that we were out of earshot—at least that was my assumption based on what was happening—he turned to face me.

"Listen, man, I get it. You don't wanna be the one making waves or looking like the hard ass, but here is the honest-to-God truth…" He paused and took a deep breath. "You have a level head. You don't act on a whim. You have had so many things happen that would've sent me over the edge. This new group is one example. I just don't like the guy, but you are actually entertaining the idea of letting his group join. You could've dumped Neil any time you wanted and I doubt that anybody would've batted an eye."

I wasn't sure he was making a very good case for me being a leader. After all, Neil had betrayed us to Don Evans despite how things ended, and I was having the same bad feelings in my gut that he apparently had in regard to this new batch of survivors.

"People like you, man," Marshawn said simply. "You got something that just makes people open up...trust. We will all have your back. And there's gonna be some bad shit ahead, but it's okay. We can get through it...but not if we don't have somebody at the helm."

"Why not you?" I asked, genuinely curious.

Marshawn was an imposing figure. I certainly wouldn't want to tangle with him. Also, he was medically trained. That was a very important skill. We certainly needed that more than we needed a high school music teacher — one that never even made it through his first day on the job.

"I'm a hot head."

I had to bite back a laugh. He'd been anything but since I'd known him. Granted, that hadn't been very long, but still...

"Just take my word for it," he said when my skepticism obviously bled through to my face.

"What if your gut is right and these people are bad news?" I asked.

"I don't think it's all of them." Marshawn glanced over his shoulder in the direction Griffin and his people had gone. "I just don't like the guy in charge."

"This sucks," I said to myself more than to Marshawn.

"We'll get through this," Marshawn comforted. "We just need to keep an eye on each other's backs."

"So do we let them join?"

That question hung in the air for several seconds. I was starting to believe that Marshawn was going to leave it all in my hands. When he spoke, I breathed an inward sigh of relief.

"I think it is the best choice. Maybe we pair up his people with one of ours for all work details. Leave Griffin to me. I'll be his shadow." The big man cocked his head at me for a moment and then shook it sadly. "Wow, I gave you a perfect set up and...nothing."

"Jokes? Now? Sorry, man." I shrugged. "Just not feeling in a joking mood."

We both headed back to the main group. Everybody seemed to be in animated conversation when we walked up. As soon as we arrived, all mouths shut and eyes turned to us with varied expressions that ranged from concern to apprehension to confusion.

"So, are we adding this group to ours or what?" Drew asked, stepping forward.

"I believe it is for the best," I announced.

Again, the reaction was mixed. I noticed that more appeared to be for it than opposed or concerned.

"However, until we get a better read, I am going to insist that everybody be paired with one of the newbies." This announcement was met with a murmur that rippled through my little group.

"So…we are letting them in, but we don't really trust them?" somebody called out.

"I think that will be the way of things for at least the foreseeable future." That was greeted with a lot of nods. Everybody was starting to see things more clearly. This was a new reality.

As this conversation went on, I couldn't help but notice Maggie and Darya huddled close together, set just a bit apart from the rest of the group. Was I going to need to have them shadowed as well?

"We got more incoming!" a voice shouted in the direction of where Griffin and his people had withdrawn.

Our conversations ended abruptly as everybody went for weapons on instinct. As a group, we advanced, prepared for whatever awaited.

DEAD: Suffer the Children

15

Last Straws

I slid down the against the trunk of the tree where I'd just dropped the last zombie. A part of me wanted to laugh at that thought. It would be kinda nice if that was really the last of the undead. I shoved those wishful thoughts away to consider this most recent skirmish.

The problem with this newest group of undead had been apparent. Many of them were freshly turned. Not that I would consider myself an authority, but I'd started noticing that older turns were a bit dried out. I hesitate to say mummified, but they were certainly more like beef jerky than a slab of steak fresh from the butcher's block.

"So, where do you think this bunch came from?" a voice said, snapping me out of my moment of relaxation as I caught my breath.

I'd never realized that killing zombies was so tiring. Again, the Hollywood icon was proving to be much more problematic in ways not considered. After all, I don't imagine it would've looked cool to have some handsome hunk or stunning starlet bend over and rest their hands on their knees as they sucked in great gulps of air. All the nasty, sweaty people around me wouldn't even make it as background extras. We were soaked in sweat and rotten blood. Many of us had bits and chunks of rancid flesh and brain clinging to our clothes.

I looked up to see Griffin, of all people, standing there with a massive blade that had all manner of vile fluids dripping from it. He also had a good deal splattered all over his clothing. If nothing else, it told me that he'd rolled up his sleeves, so to speak, and joined in on the battle with everybody else.

"Only lost the one," he said, taking an uninvited seat beside me. "Always a shame to lose somebody, but I guess it solves one problem."

I shot a look over at the man, my eyebrow raised. I hoped he saw it as a gesture for him to elaborate. Honestly, I was too tired to ask a question that I wasn't certain I wanted the answer.

"Oh, yeah. I guess you were on the other side of the camp from most of my people."

Griffin made that statement almost sound like an accusation. Again...too tired to get into it. I waited for him to continue, which he did after only a brief pause to drink from his canteen.

"Adrian went down under a few and none of us could reach him in time." My blank look was enough to cause him to elaborate. "The young man who was so worked up at losing his family member. The one who went off half-cocked and blamed one of your people for the death?"

As he spoke, a few things began to percolate in my brain. The first was an unfortunate sense of relief that the person who'd made such a ridiculous statement about Marshawn being a casualty. That thought was followed by a torrent of others not nearly as comforting. For one, things just don't work out that conveniently in my experience. The other was the more disturbing. It was this thought that raised concerns to a flashing yellow light in my brain.

I hadn't heard *the scream*.

That might seem mundane if you've never heard it before. It is very significant. It is the sound of unimaginable agony. That is the sound a person makes as they are being ripped apart and eaten alive. Nobody alive this deep into the zombie apocalypse could possibly be in existence and not have heard that sound. I have yet to witness somebody fall to the undead that does not make that sound...that pure scream unlike any other.

"Poor bastard went under a handful of the things. One of them had his throat in its teeth as it damn near seemed to ride him to the ground." Griffin pulled a dirty rag from his back pocket and wiped off the worst of the gore from his blade as he spoke. "Can't say I'm glad to lose one of ours, but if anybody had to fall...maybe it's for the best." He gave a half-hearted shrug.

For somebody professing to be at least marginally upset about the death of one of his people, he sure didn't sound very upset. I had to wonder if anybody else witnessed the fall of this Adrian person.

"Do you guys want to have any sort of service or anything?" I offered. Despite my inner warning bells, I felt I should at least offer the right thing. "We have a policy about burning the bodies, but we can certainly get everybody together and observe your loss."

"Does that mean we will be allowed to stay?" Griffin

said with a degree of enthusiasm that held no signs of his former display of remorse.

I glanced at him and then leaned back against the tree. I was really too tired for any of this at the moment. "We will give it a trial run. There will be some conditions, but we can deal with that a little later. Why don't you get your people together and break the news? As soon as we get the camp cleared, we can build the bonfire in the softball field, have a service for your guy, and then burn all the bodies."

"That sounds like a Jim Dandy idea to me," Griffin exclaimed as he hopped to his feet. "I'm sure my people will be thrilled to hear the good news. I don't think any of us looked forward to going back out there. You just don't know the terrible things you will run into. And the zombies seem to be the least of the problems."

I watched him as he strolled off. He was actually whistling as he did. It took me a few seconds to recognize the song *Flagpole Sitta*. Seriously...who whistles a song like that?

I gave myself a few more seconds of peace and relaxation before forcing myself to my feet. I made my way to where I saw Marshawn and a few of the others gathered around the edge of the trench. That seemed like as good of a place as any to start.

"What are we doing?" I asked as I strolled up.

"We need to deal with this problem ASAP." Marshawn gestured to the trench where dozens — perhaps hundreds — of the undead wandered aimlessly. The only ones not staggering around, bumping into each other, were the ones that noticed our presence and had moved to cluster at that spot.

"Hopefully we have a few minutes," I sighed. "Send a couple of people over to the groundskeeper's shack. They most likely have a weed killer sprayer. Grab it and see if we have some gas left in any of the cans. I'm pretty sure we still have a few gallons left."

"Good idea," Marshawn agreed. He tapped a couple of people on the shoulder and took off.

I stared down into the pit of undeath. A few children had ended up in the mix. I was not the least bit surprised to see them gathered up in a small group by themselves. What did bother me was how they were obviously watching me. It was as if they were studying me and my every move.

Twice, I was almost certain I saw a couple of them imitate my arm gestures as I directed people around the area.

I'd spread the word that, instead of building a bonfire and wasting resources, I wanted the bodies tossed in the trench. I knew I shouldn't have to specify, but I made it clear that they needed to spread the corpses out. I didn't want to inadvertently build a ramp for the zombies still active to use and climb out. From the mixed looks I received, it was easy to tell who was insulted that I'd felt the need...as well as who hadn't even considered the option.

When Marshawn returned, I told him to hold up. I grabbed the nearest person and sent them to tell Griffin and his people the plan. I explained that we would be holding a brief memorial to the fallen Adrian and then torch the undead along with his corpse.

It was well over thirty minutes before Griffin's people arrived. They were carrying the body of their fallen friend. As I watched them approach, I realized they had wrapped the body in a sheet. It didn't mean anything at first.

As a few people said very brief words that almost sounded generic and rehearsed, I felt that niggling sensation in the pit of my stomach again. It wasn't until they finished—much too fast if I was being honest with myself—that they hoisted the corpse and actually gave it a "1...2...3!" toss into the pit.

There was a part of me just starting to connect a few dots. The problem was that I couldn't be sure this picture was one of my own making.

I hadn't really studied the sheet-wrapped body. Had there been an obvious wound in the area of the throat? Or had it been just a simple head wound? The blood on the sheet looked surprisingly reddish-brown. Only, it wasn't as if I could demand they pull the body back up and un-wrap it.

I was torn, and trying to figure things out when Grif-fin produced a bottle of something, popped the top, and slung it so that the contents splattered the sheet shroud. There was something not right here.

The problem I had was now there was no way I could have that body retrieved. I certainly couldn't demand it be unwrapped so that I could confirm the man had actually been bitten on the throat.

I looked up as Griffin tossed a wooden match into the trench. The tiny flame hung on as it flipped end over end until coming to rest on the filthy sheet. In an instant, the flame grew, spread to a few of the wet spots created by whatever had been in that bottle, and then erupted in a 'whoomp' just like the backyard barbecues of my childhood.

When Griffin glanced over at me, he appeared to be studying my face. Did he think I was on to him? Hell, was there anything to be on to? Or, was I just making myself crazy with paranoia?

The feeling in my gut continued to grow as the fire began to spread. Now many of the still-mobile undead were catching on fire. They in turn were spreading the flames like they spread the zombie infection. But this time...there was no immunity.

As the fire grew, the stench increased with the additions of roasting, rancid meet, hair, and whatever else was in that pit. I gagged a few times before I realized that I hadn't joined the rest of the others who had retreated to escape the funk.

Neither had Griffin.

Each time I glanced his direction, I swear he was watching me out of the corner of his eye. I kept staring at the now blackened sheet as it began to flake apart and blow away on the breeze. I could see bits and pieces of the body it had contained, but I currently had no idea what I was even looking for.

Did I expect to get a good enough look at the man's

throat to know for sure if he'd been attacked the way Griffin had described? It proved to be a moot point. Once enough of the sheet had burned away, I discovered that the man was lying face down. It would be impossible to tell.

As soon as I'd made that discovery, I'd looked up to discover that Griffin had retreated from the lip of the trench. *This was all too much of a coincidence*, the voice of reason screamed in my head.

Again I was struck by how this would play out if my friends and I had been sitting in the theater watching it unfold on the big screen. That was it. I made up my mind that, despite what I'd said earlier, Griffin would have to go. I could offer sanctuary to any of his people that wished to stay, but I could no longer sit back and let him live in our compound.

Marshawn had told me that our people would back me. I knew he already had a hard spot for the guy, so I doubted he would be a tough sell. It would come down to Alex, Drew, and a few others.

I headed into our camp. I wasn't sure where I'd find Griffin, but I was hoping to corner him alone. I had a feeling this would turn into some sort of scene. What I didn't want was for it to blow up and become a fight. Killing the living was very low on my list of priorities.

As I came out of the numerous tall ferns that were scattered everywhere in these woods and arrived at our main camp, I glanced around. It was hard not to feel a bit of pride in what we'd already accomplished. Of course, my defenses hadn't been quite as effective as I'd hoped, but even this was only a minor setback.

There were now seven tents up in our space. We would have to consider either expanding this location — which had seemed so large when we'd started just a short while ago — or create a second camp. Had I been willing to let Griffin and his crew remain, we would be cramped to say the very least.

I spied the man and almost smiled at my good luck. He was by himself, and I could see all of his people gathered several feet away. From the looks of it, they were having a bit of a conference.

For some reason, I adjusted my path and headed their direction. As I approached, a couple of them spied me and even from as far away as I was, I heard them shushing each other.

After some hasty and whispered talking, one of them

detached from the group and turned to face me. She seemed to collect herself, take a deep breath, and then approach me. I briefly wondered if my presence merited so much preparation. How did people see me?

"Mister Berry, is it?" the woman asked as she reached me several feet from the group that were watching us, but trying their best to not look like it. "Look, I don't know what you want, but maybe you should talk to Griffin. He made it very clear to us that he will take care of things. None of us want to be the one who says or does the wrong thing."

"Wrong thing?" I asked. Her face paled and I swore I saw tears start to well up in the cusps of her eyes. "I don't understand."

"We don't want to go back out there. It's just too..." The woman paused as her voice began to crack.

"Who said anything about making you go back out there?" I asked with as much compassion as I could pump into my tone.

Now, more than ever, I was certain that there was something brewing under the surface of this scene. Griffin wasn't what he seemed, and these people were somehow under the illusion that he held their fate in his hands.

I was about to say something when the sound of a vehicle approaching began to echo off the cavern created by all the overhanging tree limbs. I turned in the direction I knew the access road to be.

This didn't make any sense. I'd chosen this location solely based on the idea that I was certain it was remote. Yet, Maggie and Todd had witnessed their group attacked by raiders. Drew's people had arrived, then Griffin and his followers...or were they prisoners? Now this? Perhaps I should rethink things.

I turned back to let this woman know that we would continue this conversation, but she was already gone. She'd returned to her group. Also, I glanced over to see Griffin emerge from his tent. It wasn't lost on me that he was carrying a rifle.

"Nice out of the way place you picked, Evan," Marshawn quipped as he came up beside me. "Did you leave a trail of freaking bread crumbs or something?"

I shot him a withering glare and then scrambled up the ladder to our unfinished catwalk. From up there, I would be able to see what was approaching.

It took a moment. And during that brief spell, I couldn't help but keep glancing over in Griffin's direction.

407

He seemed just as riveted as everybody else. The way he kept gripping and then re-gripping his weapon led me to believe that he was just as in the dark as the rest of us about the approaching mystery vehicle.

That…or he was anxious for their arrival.

Marshawn climbed up beside me and brought the hunting rifle he was carrying up to his shoulder so he could look through the scope.

"I want you to be ready to nail Griffin if I say," I whispered, despite the fact that there was no way that the person of interest could hear me from this far away.

"When you say nail—" Marshawn began.

"I mean blow him away," I cut the man off.

"Ummm…okay."

The two of us returned our attention to the ribbon of asphalt that wound down into the park. The park I'd been so certain was the best chance for us to build a stronghold in peace. We'd faced less opposition in the original house I'd stayed at with Chewie, Michael, Carl, Betty and Selina.

Had I been so set on this choice that I hadn't considered the popularity of it might be an issue? My mind was trying to argue both sides, but I shook it away and returned my attention to the approaching vehicle.

At last, a flash of metal winked through a break in the greenery. A red pickup truck came speeding onto the main campground road that wound past many of the park's sites. The way the driver handled the vehicle as it took the corners led me to believe that the driver was more than a little familiar with this place.

As it veered left down the narrow road that would bring it to the boat ramp area, I caught a better glimpse of the vehicle and its occupants. There were at least five people in the back. I couldn't be certain how many were in the cab, but I thought I could make out two distinct shadows. I would round up to four to be safe. That would be a total of nine if my guess was accurate, and possibly less. I doubted there would be more...but I would just have to be ready for anything in the seven to twelve range and adjust accordingly.

There was one thing for sure, the driver was in a hurry. That was another reason I was convinced that he or she was very familiar with this place. A couple of the sweeping curves were taken at a speed that elicited shouts from those in the cargo area.

"Where do they think they're gonna go?" Marshawn asked as they rounded another curve that had them coming straight for us now.

When they rounded the next one, they would see our perimeter. The berm cut across the road about twenty yards from where they would arrive in our general area. They would either stop, or else they would have a bad day.

The fact that the zombies were still cooking off wouldn't do them any favors. In fact, I was willing to bet that, if we'd started that fire just a few minutes earlier, these people might not have shown up due to the smoke now rising through the canopy of trees. They didn't look like they were raiding. They *did* look like they were running from something…or someone.

Sure enough, the truck rounded that curve and came to a stop. At least the driver had the sense to slow instead of slamming on the brakes. Now I could see into the cab with no problem. There were only two. I was happy that the number had skewed low.

"Umm…we got movement," Marshawn hissed.

I glanced over to see Griffin edging towards the woods. It could be something as simple as him wanting to flank these people. Whatever the deal, I didn't trust him.

"Stand fast, Griffin," I barked.

The man glanced at me. For a moment, I thought he might actually take off. A part of me wanted him to run. It would be the final thing to confirm my suspicions. My distrust would be validated.

Instead, he stopped and turned back to face me. I did notice that he had a scowl on his face for a moment. It was also not lost on me how fast he wiped it away and replaced it with that congenial smile that was as fake as any I'd ever encountered.

"Your camp...your rules," he called back.

Not sure it was *my* camp, but whatever. I climbed down from the perch.

"Keep him in your sights," I called up quietly to Marshawn when my feet touched the ground.

"If he even scratches wrong, I'll blow him away," the big man promised.

I wasn't sure I wanted him that trigger happy, but it would have to do. I hurried to where the truck continued to sit idling.

When I reached the trench, I had to stifle a gag from the stink. I also had to get a running start and jump across. I landed only slightly more gracefully than my last attempt.

"You know," Alex called as she walked over to a cluster of trees to my left. "You could always drop the bridge instead of jumping."

We'd built two of the little wooden bridges when we first made the trench. They were operated off of some clunky block-and-tackle kits we'd found in the groundskeeper's shed. I didn't want to admit that I'd sort of forgotten about them in all the excitement.

Without a word in response, I scrambled up the berm until I reached the top. I waved a hand, making sure to keep in a low crouch so as not to reveal anything that would make an easy target.

"Can anybody help us?" came the call from somebody in the truck. "One of our people is hurt...bad. Not bitten!" That last part was added hastily.

"Hurt how?" I called back, still not ready to show myself to these people.

"Shot with an arrow." There was a pause. "We just need a place to hunker down for a day or two until we can take care of our friend. We have our own food, so you don't have to worry."

"How did you know we were here?" I challenged.

"We didn't," came the immediate response. "Honestly, we just thought this was out of the way enough that we could catch our breath. We didn't have any plans of staying. Just needed someplace where we could cut that arrow out of our friend."

"Cut it out?" I asked, a little confused.

"Bastards used barbed arrows on our people." I could hear the anger and frustration in this man's voice. "Look, we don't even need to spend the night. Just let us tend to our friend and we will roll out of here."

I decided to take a chance and stand up. As I rose up over the lip of the big dirt mound, I saw that the man I'd been speaking with was standing outside of his vehicle, but hadn't come out from behind the driver's side door of his pickup.

We made eye contact, and I could see that the man was sizing me up and probably at least as nervous about this encounter as I was. I doubted I could put his worries to rest with anything that I said. Unless…

"Listen, we have a nurse here. Maybe you can bring your friend in and have our guy look at him." I felt kinda bad about volunteering Marshawn's services like that, but I was not picking up a dangerous vibe from these folks. Maybe they either had a better plan about where to set up, or would like to join us. Both options were currently on the table.

"Wow, thanks, man!" the individual gushed.

He stuck his head inside the cab of the truck and said something to the occupants. After that, he rushed around to the rear of the vehicle. I watched as everybody began to move around. It took some work, and I thought I heard a few moans. It was impossible to tell if they were coming from the bed of the truck or back up the road and in the woods.

At last, they had a person that they put on a makeshift stretcher. As they were getting ready, I motioned for two nearby members of our group to get the drawbridge lowered and into place.

The group from the pickup reached where I stood waiting and paused.

I motioned for them to go across. As they passed, I got a look at the person on the stretcher. It was a woman and the arrow was jutting from her side. That made me cringe. If it was barbed, I wondered if it had perhaps pierced something vital. If that was the case, there was almost nothing we could do for the person. It wasn't that I didn't appreciate Marshawn's talent, but I wasn't foolish enough to think he could perform surgery. Hell, even a qualified doctor would struggle in this environment.

"We really appreciate this," the spokesman for the group said as he stopped in front of me.

He'd hung back to bring up the rear. And now that we were face-to-face, I could get a better look at him. He was close to my height, but definitely older. I guessed him to be in his late thirties or maybe even early forties. He had blond hair and blue eyes that squinted just a bit. His build was slight, smaller than me by a good twenty pounds at least.

He stuck out his hand to shake and I peeled off my glove to reciprocate the gesture. When we shook, his hands had a roughness to them that told me they were used to hard work.

"Andrew Greene," the man said by way of introduction. "I really do appreciate this. I know you guys didn't have to let us in…much less offer any sort of help."

"Evan Berry, and…yeah…about that…" I wasn't sure how to word things.

"Relax, I get it," Andrew said, casting a glance over his shoulder to see his people as they encountered a good number of ours, including Marshawn who was already examining the person on the stretcher. "I'm not a doctor, but I know her odds are slim. A gut shot with a barbed arrow? Hell, who knows what that punched a hole in. If she doesn't bleed out, what are the chances she makes it through recovery without getting some kind of infection." It was more statement than question. He glanced around the woods. "Not exactly a sterile, surgical environment."

I nodded as I felt a surge of relief sweep through which instantly made me feel just a bit guilty. "Do all your people understand that?"

I hated asking that question almost as much as I disliked the guilt I was already stuffing down. I didn't want to come across as an ass. And if there was a possibility that this group was going to join us, I sorta wanted things to start on the right foot. Still, I had to know what to expect.

"Let's just say that everybody has already said their goodbyes…just in case."

I didn't know what degree of relief was the appropriate amount. I was pretty sure my levels bordered on inappropriate. The thing is, I already have two members of my group pissed at me and one who might be a wolf in sheep's clothing.

"So, you say you guys got attacked?" I said as I began

walking into the heart of our little camp with Andrew.

"Yeah. We pulled off Interstate 205 to search for supplies. I used to drive UPS in the area, and I knew of this mobile home park. Figured that we could at least check it out to see if the risk was worth the possible reward," Andrew explained. "We'd just pulled in and got out to check one of the outer units when this freaking school bus roared past the entrance to the park."

I felt a lump form in my throat. It couldn't be... No, I dismissed quickly before Andrew could resume his narrative. After all, that other little band of punks back in Damascus had been driving around in a school bus as well. They were large, sturdy, and probably not a bad form of transportation if you had more than just a few people.

"We all heard the brakes squeal and knew that the person driving or one of the passengers had spotted us. We'd been in two trucks at that time, and everybody ran back to them. We have a variety of weapons, but our ammo supply is about tapped."

I needed to hear what this guy had to say before I came at him with a million questions. The first thing I needed to know is just how much he saw of his attackers.

417

"When the bus came flying backwards, we were just climbing into the trucks." Andrew paused and took a deep breath. "They had a fucking machine gun mounted on the top of the bus."

Scratch that. I didn't need to know any more to be certain.

"They cut down four of my people and destroyed the other truck." Andrew glanced at me, and I could tell he was considering how much more to tell me.

I decided to save him the trouble. I related my own encounters with Don Evans. It took a while, and as I told my tale, more of Andrew Greene's people had gathered around…along with several of Griffin's.

As I told my story, I felt so many emotions. All of them began to cluster together to form another: Resolve.

"And that is why I don't have any other choice." That last part was more just me thinking aloud.

Marshawn picked that moment to emerge from the tent where he'd been trying to save a person's life. His grim expression told me the outcome before he gave a slight shake of his head.

I'd done the one thing I knew I couldn't. I'd let the bad guy live. Okay, so maybe that wasn't an entirely accurate or realistic stance to take.

I knew what needed to be done, though. Otherwise, more people would die unnecessarily. More atrocities would be committed out of a pure and evil hatred.

I stood up and looked around. Sure, Griffin needed to be dealt with, but I didn't have any solid proof that he was evil. I'd yet to see him do anything that I could classify as wrong. Suspicious? Sure. But blatantly wrong? No.

With Don Evans, that was an entirely different tune. In this moment, I had no doubts as to what I should do.

"I have to kill Don Evans."

DEAD: Suffer the Children

Zombie

The Cat Mansion

"Your mom and dad said for us to get everything packed that we will take," Ethan McDermott said to the two boys who made no acknowledgement of his presence.

He stood there for a moment as the two boys continued to hoot and yell at the pinball machine. It was as if they hadn't heard him, but since he'd practically yelled those words from less than ten feet away, he doubted that was the case.

"Trent, Ian! Did you hear what I said?"

"We heard you, Uncle Ethan," Trent, the older of the two said over his shoulder as he smacked the side of the pinball machine, causing the 'TILT' lights to flash.

"Yeah, Uncle Ethan…we heards you," little Ian parroted, almost nailing the snotty ambivalence and disdain exhibited by his older brother.

"Then move your asses!" Ethan snapped after several seconds passed and Trent went so far as to launch another pinball into play.

Glancing up at the televisions mounted in the game room that normally ran sports and music videos, he saw varying scenes of the unimaginable horror that was sweeping the world. The two boys both made loud pro-testing groans before reluctantly leaving the machine.

At nine, Trent was what Ethan considered the epitome of a spoiled rotten rich kid. He was often coming home from the private school he attended with a note from the faculty explaining that his behavior and bullying was a problem.

That fault rested solely on the shoulders of the boy's mother, Ethan told himself. He made a sweeping gesture with his arms to usher the two boys through the door. The young-est, Ian, looked up at him as he passed and stuck out his tongue. It took all his restraint not to bop the seven-year-old brat under the chin to teach him a lesson.

"Go to your rooms and grab your backpacks," Ethan said between clenched teeth.

As the day had gone from bad to worse, he'd had to

fight every urge to just walk out and never look back. He'd never really been that close to his sister, and he thought the husband was a pompous jerk that needed to have his ass kicked one good time to remind him that all his money didn't make him invincible.

"When are Mom and Dad gonna get home?" little Ian whined as he trudged down the hall and into his bedroom that was probably twice the size of Ethan's apartment in one of Portland's less than desirable neighborhoods.

"When they walk in the door," Ethan snapped.

He pulled out the pint of bottom shelf whiskey from his coat pocket and took a pull from the bottle. As he stuffed it back into his coat, Trent exited his room.

"Mom says you aren't supposed to drink in front of us," the boy said with a sneer. "I'm telling."

"I don't give a fuck."

That made the young man's mouth open in a silent 'O' that invited a backhand if Ethan was just a few steps closer. The boy looked as if he was about to say something, and then obviously thought better of it.

At least he ain't a complete idiot, Ethan mused.

"Now, get downstairs. We need to be ready the moment that your folks get here." Ethan turned on his heel and headed down without looking to see if the boys followed.

When he reached the main floor, his eyes rolled. The number of bags, footlockers, and giant suitcases were ridiculous. If his sister and her husband thought that the people at the FEMA shelter were going to allow them in with that much crap...well, he looked forward to that confrontation. He turned to head for the kitchen. He knew where a quality bottle of whiskey was stashed.

Just as he reached the hall closet that her sister used to hide her liquor the same as their mother had when they were younger, a loud bang sounded at the front door. He turned, but the two boys darted past.

A thought occurred just as the boys reached the front door: *Who the hell would be banging on that door? Certainly not his sister or her worthless husband.*

"Mommy! Daddy!" Ian squealed as Trent turned the lock and threw the door open.

It most certainly was not their parents. The man that stood in the doorway was short and verging on obese. With his insides dangling from a nasty rip in his protruding gut, it was even more pronounced.

Being across the foyer, Ethan was just getting a whiff

of the horrible monster, but the boys were already both staggering back as vomit spewed from their mouths in dual geysers of bile.

Ian stepped wrong and fell back as Trent turned and ran a few steps before dropping to his knees as he continued to heave the remaining contents of his stomach in a wet splash onto the tiled foyer. Ethan had seen enough on the news to know what was now stumbling into the house. The only problem was that he was not carrying a weapon.

Turning, he sprinted to the kitchen. The first thing he spotted was a medium-sized cast iron skillet that he'd used earlier to make their dinner of fried potatoes, onions, and smoked sausage. Of course, the boys had complained and insisted that was no kind of dinner their mom ever had made for them. He hadn't missed the "had" in that statement. The house had a full staff of servants. If he was a betting man, he was willing to guess that this man was one of the groundskeepers.

As he rushed back into the room, he saw that there would be no way he could reach Ian before the monster staggering towards the small boy. One voice in his head began to insist that it wasn't his problem. He didn't even like his nephews. But there was a piece of him that drove him forward and demanded he protect the child.

As the gutted gardener flopped down and grabbed Ian by one arm, Ethan threw himself at it with all he had. He slammed into the lump of dead flesh just as its mouth closed on the young boy's forearm.

There was a shriek as the collision occurred. It was horrible and unlike anything that Ethan had ever heard in his life. Coming to a stop, he pushed away from the foul-smelling corpse and took a firm grip of the pan's handle.

He'd heard enough to know that these things only went down one way. With everything he had, Ethan brought the pan down on the head of the creature that was struggling to get to its hands and knees.

The sound was like a muted church bell as the flat bottom of the cast iron weapon connected solidly with the top of the skull. Ethan yelped and dropped his weapon as a stinging pain buzzed through both his hands.

As for the zombie, it'd fallen back to the ground, but was struggling to return to its feet. Ethan considered retrieving the skillet, but his hands sent a veto to his brain.

The sound of feet scurrying up the stairs caused Ethan to glance over his shoulder. Trent vanished from view down the hall that led to his bedroom leaving him and Ian alone with the zombie.

Correction...zombies.

Two more staggered in through the open front door. Knowing he was not prepared for a fight, Ethan scooped up the wailing Ian and ran for the stairs. He glanced over his shoulder to see the zombies bumping into each other in a slow-motion pinballing that had them careening off the stacked luggage as they reoriented on him and made their way to the stairs. The little boy seemed to gain ten pounds with every stair climbed.

As soon as he reached the landing, Ethan tried to set the little boy down, but the child clung to him with all he was worth. It took a considerable effort to pry Ian's hands from around his neck. When he was free, the child began to scream in absolute terror as his eyes found the trio of undead making their slow ascent of the stairs.

Grabbing the boy by the hand, Ethan scurried down the hall that Trent had disappeared into. He could see the boy's door was shut and had to skid to a halt and open it. He flung it open and spied a pair of feet just as they vanished under the bed.

He basically flung the younger boy into the room and then yanked the door shut. Turning, he ran back to the arcade. Set just off it was a cleaning closet. As he ran, he cursed his sister for not having any proper weapons in the house. He reached the arcade, his eyes darting over his shoulder to ensure one of the undead wasn't on his heels.

Opening the closet, he grabbed the first thing he thought might be a suitable weapon: a broom. He rushed back up the hall and arrived at the landing just as the first zombie reached the top of the stairs.

He shot a quick glance at the front door and allowed himself to breathe a sigh of relief that no other zombies had stumbled in...yet. By now, the second one had reached the top.

He took a few steps backward as he tried to decide how best to handle the situation. An idea came; it seemed a bit far-fetched, but it might work. If nothing else, he should be able to clear a path and make a run for it. His conscience could go screw itself. He needed to get the hell out of here. Bringing along those two brats would slow him down. Plus, he could still hear the little one bawling his head off. That would attract attention that he didn't want or need.

The nearest zombie closed the distance and Ethan swung as hard as he could. The head of the broom connected and sent the zombie slamming into the railing. Its lack of coordination did the rest as the zombie flipped over and plummeted to the floor below, landing with a sickening thud, crack, and splat.

He'd been more prepared for the electric buzz that shot through his hands this time, and managed to keep his grip on his weapon. Good thing, too, because the next zombie was already on him.

Bringing the broom up across his body this time, Ethan charged, catching up the zombie as he did, and sending it over the railing as well. He watched it as it fell gracelessly to the floor, landing just to one side of the first one he'd knocked over. Its head connected solid with the floor and burst, spraying chunky black brain matter like a rotten melon.

By now, the one he'd first hit in the head was reaching the top of the stairs. He stalked up to it and jammed the end of the broom into its face. The zombie toppled easily, but only fell a few stairs until it connected with the wall and came to a stop with its feet in the air.

Ethan charged in and began plunging the end of the broom handle down on the zombie's face again and again until it was a ruined mess. At some point, he punched through an eye socket and apparently ended the zombie.

Rushing down the stairs, Ethan reached the front door and looked out into the dark yard. Reaching over, he hit the main switch to bring up the exterior lighting system. What he saw made him let out his own soft cry. Standing just at the end of the walkway were three children. Their eyes were filmed over and the black tracers that the lady on television had spoken of could be seen very clearly.

He looked past at the gate and saw the dark outlines of at least a dozen more children. He had no doubt as to their condition.

Where had they come from? It took him a few minutes, but then he thought his sister had said something about one of the neighbors having a birthday party.

He was trapped. Those children were between him and the detached garage where any vehicle he might consider using was parked. Very briefly, he considered making a run for it, but then he realized that eventually his sister and her husband should be arriving soon. The same driver that had picked him up and brought him here had left to fetch them. Hadn't they said they were leaving the hospital where he was chief of staff and she was the administrator within the hour? And that call had been — he glanced at his watch — just about an hour ago. If they'd left on time, then the ride out here was about another hour.

He slammed the door, but not before he realized that the zombie children hadn't advanced. They were just standing there...watching him. That was almost more frightening, Ethan decided as a shiver coursed through him.

Turning back, he looked at the mess splattered all over the foyer. One of the fallen zombies was still struggling, trying to crawl for him. Its back was at an angle that left no doubt it was broken. It was pulling itself by its arms, but not having much luck as the legs were obviously useless.

Taking another long pull of his bottle, Ethan strolled casually up to the struggling creature. The stink was bad enough that it threatened to send the contents of his stomach spewing from his mouth. It would only add to what the boys had already done, and there was no way he would clean that up. His snotty sister could deal with it. Of course, she would fob it off on her staff.

Glancing at the corpses on the floor, he amended that to what was *left* of her staff. *After all*, Ethan thought, *what other reason would three Mexicans have for being here?*

He put an end to the last zombie and took another

431

drink. It was the end of that bottle. Well, as far as he was concerned, his sister owed him. He went back to her so-called secret hiding place and grabbed a bottle. He read the label and had to admit he'd never even heard of the stuff before. The only thing that mattered was the word "whiskey" on it.

He took a drink and shrugged. He doubted it was worth the price his sister probably paid for it, but it was decent enough.

Stepping back into the foyer, Ethan set the bottle on a table and decided that he needed to get the bodies dealt with or he was not going to be able to hold his liquor in much longer. He knew his sister had one of those big walk-in sub-zero freezers. And again, it would be her problem.

It took a bit, and he had to finally walk away, find a towel to cover his face and then return to the task, but eventually he got it done. To celebrate his completion, he took another long drink. By now, his head was floating, and the edges of his vision were a bit fuzzy.

He sat down on a chair and cocked his head. The kid had finally stopped bawling. He'd been so focused on moving the bodies that he hadn't realized it. That brought another idea to him.

He walked to the front door, each step taken on unsteady tiptoe as if he thought he might make a sound that would jinx the hoped-for result. Cautiously, he opened the front door.

"Fuck," he hissed, slamming it shut.

In the short glimpse he'd taken, he saw the three children from earlier. They had gotten closer but were now five. He knew he'd seen more on the driveway, but he'd only managed a very brief peek.

A new idea came, and Ethan dashed through the house. He threw open the back door and skidded to a stop. He'd found the rest of the children. They stood scattered around the yard. Again, they didn't advance, but they were there, and that was enough.

He staggered back through the kitchen and pulled his phone from his pocket. Hitting his sister's number, he listened as the recording came on stating that "all circuits were busy."

He was stuck.

Walking into the living room, he plopped down on one of the couches and nursed the bottle until he dozed off. He dreamt of his nephews leading the mob of undead children from the front and back yard as they hunted him. Just as Ian was about to bite into his arm, he woke with a start.

He swatted at himself at first, still unsure if it had been real or a dream. When he regained his composure; he looked around and realized that the first traces of sunlight were coming through the windows.

It took him a few minutes to comprehend that morning was dawning and there had been no sign of his sister or her husband. Getting to his feet, he wiped at his eyes as he crept to the window. Looking outside, he felt the chill of reality twist at his gut.

The children were still outside. He pulled the blinds and backed away. This was impossible. And where was his sister and her useless husband?

Ethan paced the room several minutes until it dawned on him that he had heard nothing from the boys since the previous night. He'd seen enough on the television to get an idea as to what most likely happened. Ian had been bitten. That meant he maybe had three days before he turned, but there were some reports of it happening within minutes.

Eventually, he crept up the stairs. He reached the door

and pressed his ear to hear. Silence. A familiar stench tickled at his nose, but he had to be sure it wasn't just the lingering stench of the zombies from last night.

"Ian?" he called in a voice that was barely louder than a whisper.

At first, there was nothing, then something moved. It was like the kid was dragging his feet across the floor. A second later, the slap of a hand against the door sounded.

Ethan jumped back. The slap was followed by another...and another...and another. That sound followed him as he backed away and then ran down the stairs.

***

The next days were a blur of drunken misery as Ethan made his way through every bottle his sister had stashed. Then the power went out.

He'd never realized how remote the location of his sister's house was until then. The first night was shrouded in a darkness that had him huddling in a corner a shivering mess.

As the days and nights passed, Ethan alternated between angry, hysterical, and delirious. The booze amplified each of those emotions to unmanageable levels, and forgetting to eat half the time only made it worse.

At some point, he began to notice that the slapping on the door had continued. At first, he convinced himself that it was his imagination. At last, he made his way up the stairs to check. Sure enough, that slapping was real...as real as the zombie children that continued to stand outside.

One afternoon, as Ethan stared out into the front yard, peeking through a break in the curtains, something caught his eye. A cat.

He pulled one of the chairs around so he could continue to watch. If he was going to be stuck here until somebody came to rescue him, then at least he could enjoy some entertainment. That cat was walking right up to those kids. Sooner or later, they would notice and probably pounce on the stupid thing.

When it came up beside one of the children, a little boy in a baseball jersey, and sat down, Ethan actually rubbed his hands together in anticipation. But nothing happened. The kid looked down and then returned its undead gaze to the front door.

At one point, the cat leaned over and tugged a piece of

loose flesh from the little boy's leg. Still the undead child did nothing.

And the days continued to pass.

When he was down to the last of the food consisting of dry cereal that tasted like cardboard, Ethan realized that he might very well die. Nobody was coming. There would be no rescue.

Through it all, as the days passed, the children remained. Even worse, more cats began to gather. They were feeding on the children! Not in great amounts, just a nibble here and there.

And the pounding.

It chased him through his nightmares every night and taunted him through his haze as he now made his way through his sister's pride and joy…her wine cabinet. Ethan hated wine, but he hated being sober even more.

Twice more, he'd gone to the door. Both times, the children had not advanced, but they remained; even worse, there were several cats sprawled on the patio. One of them hissed at his sudden intrusion and he went to kick at it, but the animal easily dodged him. That had the unfortunate result of causing the children to advance.

Ethan had slammed the door.

One morning, he woke to what he was certain was another human being calling out. He rushed to the window to see an old man making his way up the driveway.

The kids were nowhere in sight!

Ethan ran for the front door and threw it open. His relief was short-lived as he watched the small shadows detaching from the many bushes that decorated the yard. The old man saw him as well as the threat at almost the same time.

He took off at a run, but Ethan slammed the door shut and locked it. He was down to some sort of nasty cereal that tasted awful…but it was his and there wasn't enough to share. When the screams started, he tried to drown it out by plugging his ears, but that did no good.

To make matters worse, it now sounded like both boys were pounding on the door upstairs. Long after the screaming stopped, the pounding continued. No matter where he wandered inside the huge home, he could hear…feel the pounding.

The was no hope. Fate had dealt Ethan its final cruel hand, but if was to die here…he would finish off those two brats once and for all. As he downed the final bottle of wine, the fog of inebriation fell much faster. Things clouded, and that was when the voice in the back of his head came to the front in full volume.

KILL THEM.

Grabbing a cleaver from the kitchen, Ethan went up the stairs. He wasn't providing them mercy as much as he was getting in the last lick.

***

Ethan looked into the mirror. He had to get close to see in the gloom, but they were there. The tracers that announced his infection.

He heard a soft meow followed by a series of deep purrs. Looking out into the master bedroom, he could see Trent lying basically helpless on the bed. His head sat an awkward angle from where his neck had been broken. Already, the cats were feeding. All the zombie could do was turn its head one way or the other.

Downstairs, the dismembered Ian was still chained to the wall. That hadn't been nearly as fulfilling, but when the little bastard had bitten him, the plan of killing them outright had changed. Now, the brat would spend eternity sitting in a pool of his own guts. His arms and legs set right where he could see them.

Could zombies see? Ethan didn't know.

He'd opened that front door long enough to wave one of the hacked off arms at the cats gathered on the porch. He'd lured a bunch in before slamming the door shut and locking it again.

After he's lured Trent upstairs and snapped his scrawny neck, he'd tossed the body in his parent's bed. He'd noticed a couple of the cats following them, and once the boy was tossed aside, they made slow approaches on the body. Eventually, they realized that the buffet was open…and helpless. Ethan laughed as he watched the cats feed.

***

Staggering out to the balcony, Ethan couldn't peel his tongue from the roof of his mouth. He knew he didn't have long. He was ready to end it. Only, his hands lacked the coordination to hold a blade, so slashing his wrists was out.

A flicker of thought stayed long enough for him to act on it. He would throw himself over the balcony headfirst to the paved walkway below. Surely that would end him.

He could see the railing, it was only a few steps away. He staggered forward one step and then everything went dark. He felt something slam into his body, but it hadn't been enough.

His vision cleared long enough for him to see that he'd merely stumbled and fallen. He was still on the balcony. His head tilted, allowing him to look back into the bedroom. He couldn't see that far, but he knew that Trent was still on that bed, and the cats were feasting.

A smile turned the corners of Ethan's mouth up as the last breath escaped him. His body shuddered a few times and was still.

The first twitch came from the fingers on his left hand. A cat watched, considering this potential food source. When it sat up. The cat hissed and backed away.

The creature rose to its feet and began to pursue the cat in slow, unsteady steps. Its pursuit led it to one of the nightstands where it became tangled in the collection of cords belonging to the lamp as well as the adjustable bed.

Eventually, the zombie found itself in a corner. With nothing to attract its attention, it eventually stilled.

Standing. Waiting.

MAY DECEMBER
Publications

**The growing voice in horror
and speculative fiction.**

Find us at www.maydecemberpublications.com
Or
Email us at maydecemberpublications@gmail.com

TW Brown is the author of the **Zomblog** series, his horror comedy romp, **That Ghoul Ava**, and, of course, the **DEAD** series and the **New DEAD** series. Safely tucked away in the beautiful Pacific Northwest, he moves away from his desk only at the urging of his Border Collie, Aoife, (Pronounced Eye-fa) his Frisbee catching Border Collie Tyrion, or one of his Newfoundlands, Freyja or her younger sister Loki.

He plays a little guitar on the side...just for fun...and makes up any excuse to either go trail hiking or strolling along his favorite place...Cannon Beach. His hobbies include training his Newfoundlands to be show dogs working on their championships, water rescue working on their WD titles and draft carts working on their DD titles. And we should never forget to add his two African Greys named Lisa and Paul. He answers all his emails sent to twbrown.maydecpub@gmail.com and tries to thank everybody personally when they take the time to leave a review of one of his works.

He can be found at www.authortwbrown.com. The best way to find everything he has out is to start at his Author Page. You can follow him on twitter @authortwbrown and on Facebook under Author TW Brown, and also under May December Publications.

CPSIA information can be obtained
at www.ICGtesting.com
Printed in the USA
BVHW011435170419
545798BV00018B/54/P